Patsy was born, Margaret Stone on 4th of April. Her due date should have been 17th March, St Patricks Day and Patsy was he Father's pet name for her.

Patsy was a real Dundee lass. She worked in the office of the local jute mill as a wages clerk. In those days long before computers. Her means of calculating wages and bonuses was with a slide rule.

When Patsy, a working mother with 5 children, was finally able to pursue her love of writing, her husband, Andy, proudly presented her with her first laptop.

My Granddaughter, Stacey

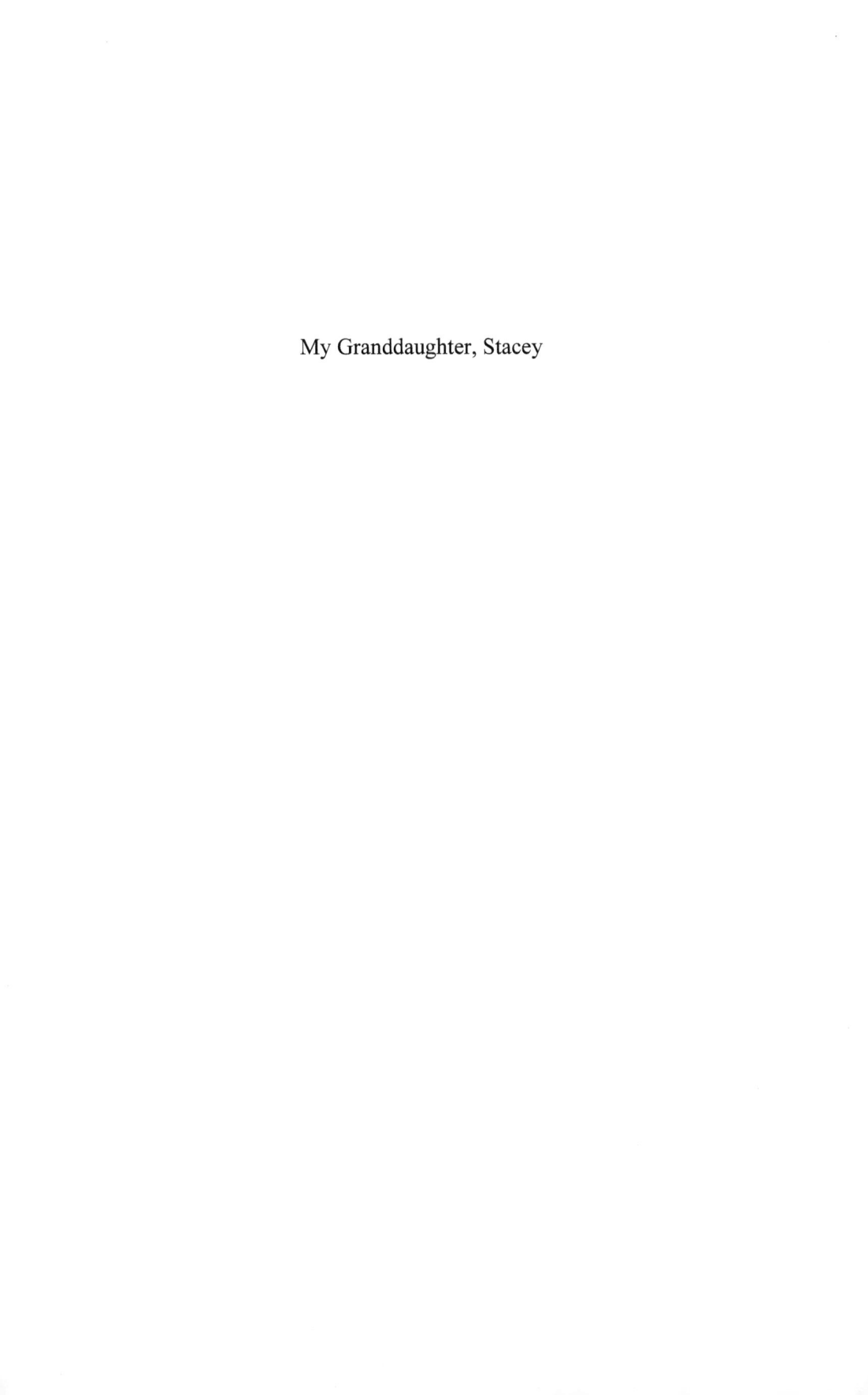

Patsy Barry

The House on Juniper Drive

AUSTIN MACAULEY PUBLISHERS™

LONDON * CAMBRIDGE * NEW YORK * SHARJAH

Copyright © Patsy Barry 2023

The right of Patsy Barry to be identified as author of this work has been asserted by the author in accordance with sections 77 and 78 of the Copyright, Designs and Patents Act 1988.

All rights reserved. No part of this publication may be reproduced, stored in a retrieval system, or transmitted in any form or by any means, electronic, mechanical, photocopying, recording, or otherwise, without the prior permission of the publishers.

Any person who commits any unauthorised act in relation to this publication may be liable to criminal prosecution and civil claims for damages.

This is a work of fiction. Names, characters, businesses, places, events, locales, and incidents are either the products of the author's imagination or used in a fictitious manner. Any resemblance to actual persons, living or dead, or actual events is purely coincidental.

A CIP catalogue record for this title is available from the British Library.

ISBN 9781528959599 (Paperback)
ISBN 9781528960328 (ePub e-book)

www.austinmacauley.com

First Published 2023
Austin Macauley Publishers Ltd®
1 Canada Square
Canary Wharf
London
E14 5AA

To my family and especially to Stacey, my Granddaughter and Pam,
a family friend.

Synopsis

The story is narrated by the central character, Judy Vernon. It is her recollection of the assortment of people, the good, the bad, the weary and the eerie, who through the years, took up residence in the house at number eleven Juniper Drive in Fairfield (A fictional place on the outskirts of the city of Dundee).

Juniper is in the most part a humorous story in the respect the narrator tells her story from childhood (expressing her views as a child would). She not only sees, but repeats everything in a childish way, which frequently causes embarrassment to her parents.

Judy's feelings upset and perturb her because she can't explain to anyone, least of all her own self, the strange and bewildering phenomenon which some refer to as second sight. The ability to witness an event before it happens wreaks havoc with her life. This psychic energy also appears to link her with the house on Juniper Drive.

Central characters:
Judy Vernon and her parents, Ralph and Gloria

Paul and Amy Royle: Paul is manager of the local bank in Fairfield and Amy is a teacher at Fairfield High. Amy has the greatest influence on Judy and becomes her role model. And then when Paul is tragically killed, Amy sells the house on Juniper Drive.

John and Daisy Keller, daughter, Paris and son, Roman: The Kellers are a gypsy like family, common and uncultured—but wealthy in the extreme. Their wealth baffles the uppity, class conscious residents of Juniper Drive. But what really infuriates them is failure to discover the source of Keller's great wealth. (This is also left to the reader's imagination.) Mayhem descends on Juniper with the arrival of the handsome, yet outrageously wild and unprincipled Keller kids.

Richard and Jean LaVell and identical twin daughters, Meredith and Maxine: Richard LaVell is a stern and rather sinister man. On the day the family moves into the house, Judy annoys LaVell when she pays them what he sees as an unwelcome visit. When he attempts to guide her out somewhat forcefully, the touch of his hand on her shoulder awakes a dormant psychic energy and she is filled with the sense of something dark and fearful. Judy's immature mind, her subconscious, unable to cope with the intense fear, locks away in her mind whatever awful thing his touch had summoned. This remains the focal point throughout the story.

When Jean LaVell does a disappearing act with her daughters, a heartbroken Richard puts the house on Juniper Drive up for lease.

Danny and Win Rafferty and their five children, Eamon, Michael, Molly, Noreen and little Daniel: The Raffertys are an Irish family who rent number eleven through an agency. Through their own goodness this family become respected and loved, but especially little Daniel who is 'backward.'

The Rafferty family add their contribution to the plot in a spectacular way and when they leave, LaVell has the house closed and shuttered with the specific order it be left that way for all time.

In the last part of the book, Judy has reached adulthood, but still retains a special, yet unexplainable tie with the house on Juniper Drive. She makes the greatest effort to locate the one man who, although he terrifies her beyond reason, is the only one she can approach with an offer to buy the long vacant and now derelict house he still owns.

In her long quest to find LaVell, Judy unearths many sins as well as the secret her life-long nemesis had been so desperate to keep. And finally, dramatically, she opens her mind to confront the horror which is locked inside.

The house on Juniper Drive finally gives up its secret.

Chapter One

Since as far back as I can remember, I loved that house: the house on Juniper Drive. Like metal to a magnet, it drew me. True, it was splendorous. It did have what people might call a wow factor. But for me, there was something deeper, something much more…spiritual. It was an awareness of what I can only describe as an uncommon bond with the house on Juniper Drive: something that began even before my birth. It was almost as if I were a significant part of the very mortar that bound it.

Oh, how it stood out. Number eleven Juniper Drive was truly regal and magnificent. It commanded a position of prominence, right at the head of the street where it overlooked and dominated the other ten houses on Juniper Drive, five on either side. When I was very young (what you might call my formative years), I used to think of these ten houses as subjects bowing before their queen. Silly really, but you see, I was hostage to a vivid imagination. An imagination that one day would turn out to be more than simply fanciful and childish. It was an acute awareness.

Juniper Drive was a street of unsurpassed elegance. On the right side were numbers one to nine and on the left two to ten. But right at the top, number eleven, a big, majestic house which was encircled from front to rear by a mosaic display of floribunda and shrubs. It really and truly was the most stunningly beautiful garden.

But I think—and this wasn't simply from a child's viewpoint—the most eye-catching feature of the house had to be the huge windows which stretched wide across the front and reached almost to the ground. Fine white lace draped elegantly and with one pull of a cord, the curtain gracefully swished and glided open across the vast tinted glass windows which allowed the world only a muted view of the inner sanctum and yet, those dusky windows seemed ever eager to open and welcome in the clean, perfumed air and all the sounds of nature.

And oh, how that great carved oak door with its polished brass number plate and letterbox pulled at my heartstrings. Not to mention the huge shiny brass door knocker with the chubby face. My whimsical nature loved the way that it smiled, broadly and cheerily as if it were inviting everyone to come and visit. Or maybe it was all just my childish perception of a place that, for whatever reason, filled my senses.

Mum still relates in a kind of terror how one day when I was only two, no more than a baby, I managed somehow to wander off. Of course, a mother's worst nightmare is to turn and find her child gone. After a frantic search, they found me. It seems I had toddled onto the lawn at number eleven. My mother, the queen of dramatics, narrates with a flourish of her perfectly manicured hands how she found me gazing spellbound at the house, talking in a way that belied my infancy. It appears I was telling the house to be good until I came to live there and look after it. I was rather an odd child. Well, each and every time that story's rehashed, she always lapses theatrically into a cold sweat and a fit of the quakes.

Fairfield is no more than a village just a stone's throw from Dundee. It's a very select, well-chosen place which was developed and specifically targeted for business and professional people who didn't want to stay within the smoky grime of an industrial town. This rural setting which was within easy reach of the city yet still keeping that, *away from it all,* country feel was the perfect alternative.

Juniper Drive is part of that small rural estate of upmarket houses built in the seventies to accommodate those with, '*A penchant for serenity and sophistication.*' That was how the new estate called Fairfield was cleverly advertised. Although the message in the slogan was clear. This was a place for people who could afford the grandeur. The price tag was the real status symbol. Needless to say, every house was snapped up by high earning professional people.

My parents bought a house on Juniper Drive and moved to Fairfield when Dad accepted the post of consultant cardiologist at the city hospital. I was born two years later, on 4 April 1980 to be precise.

I'm Judy Vernon and this story is my account of the strange, often perplexing attraction that drew me to the house on Juniper Drive. It's how I remember the assortment of people who, through my childhood and adolescence, took up residence in that house of secrets. There was every type: the likeable, the odd, the weary…and the eerie. This is also the story of my quest to find answers to the strange occurrences I experienced but couldn't understand. Singularities which, as time would tell, pointed to my own destiny.

I had very little recollection of the people who lived in the big house at number eleven until after my second birthday. I was too young to remember in any great detail the odd couple who owned the house around that time. About all I remember, what sticks out most in my mind, they never seemed to speak to anyone. Not even to each other. As far as I'm led to believe, they never ever stopped to courteously pass the time of day with a neighbour. It was more than uncivil; it was downright hostile the way this unpleasant pair strutted by and ignored every one of their neighbours as if they were inferior beings.

There was one other thing that I was very aware of, even at that young age. If I was in the garden playing, those two hurried by, head down, eyes averted as if casting a single glance in my direction might corrode their eyes. They just weren't like normal neighbours who gushed and smiled at the sight of an awestruck, open mouthed child tottering around the garden with a floppy doll clasped tightly in her arms.

She, the pixilated one, was small and sort of bent. Her eyes were beady like those of a crow and her nose was hooked like a parrot's beak. 'A poison dwarf' was the way, Mum unceremoniously referred to her. He, the husband, was a giant in comparison to the weedy little woman who didn't so much walk by his side but was forced to trot in an effort to keep up with his long-legged stride. They were as weird as each other.

According to my mother, the ex-army colonel was a purple faced lout who looked scary enough to bring her out in goosebumps. Anyway, when they sold up and left, my mother's relief was emphasised in the way she clasped her hands together and cried to the heavens, 'Praise the Lord.' And she never called them by any name other than *'them,'* as if a bolt of lightning would strike her if she spoke their name and all she ever said about *them* was that *they* were not our kind of people…whatever that meant.

I was four years old when virtual newly-weds, Paul and Amy Royle, bought number eleven and moved in shortly after. For the first few months, Amy never seemed to have time for little more than a hasty 'hello' in passing. I think Mum took it personal. She was one for deep and pleasant conversations.

Eventually, as mum's response changed from cool to distinctly icy, Amy must have decided the time had come to clarify the reason for her lack of social grace. She explained that every minute of her and Paul's spare time had been taken up with getting rid of the dingy paint and wallpaper throughout the house. Apart from the horrendous decoration, the entire house was just plain filthy. Amy said the odd couple surely didn't know what a scrubbing brush was for. What's more, the work to be done was set to dominate their every weekend for some time. It was an exhausting business but making the transformation together and with their own sweat and tears was important to them.

That was the storm breaker! Mum, the ice queen melted, and she made Amy promise to come to ours a couple of nights a week. Just for a bite of supper and a couple glasses of wine. "You have no idea how taking a break away from it helps," Mum said in that know-it-all way she had.

That was the time a bond of friendship was created and for me it was the beginning of an era. Because of Amy's natural goodness and kindness, along with this great, natural ability she had to communicate with the young, I was filled with adoration. She was the one who made the first nick in the whittling of my character.

Amy came to teach at the village school when Paul was promoted to manager of the little bank on the corner of Main Street, just up from the local shops. It was one of those typical village banks where there was always a warm and friendly atmosphere. The people who worked in the bank happily passed the time of day with customers and the bank tellers were genuinely nice people who didn't glower insidiously over silly half rimmed glasses, openly showing annoyance when a person had the gall to come in to make a transaction. When a parent and child came into the bank, there was always a lollipop for the little one. Paul made sure of that because that's the sort of person he was. Kind and thoughtful.

I had a distinct feeling that, although my dear mum liked Amy and Paul tremendously, she was just a touch envious of them because they were the new owners of the finest house on the estate. My mother's attitude could at times be snobbish and high handed.

"The mortgage must be crippling," she said in a tone that suggested Mr and Mrs Royle had bitten off more than they could chew. What she really meant, and she might just as well have come right out and said it. 'How dare they afford a better house than ours?'

But as their friendship deepened and they spoke freely of slightly more personal things, it turned out that because Paul was the bank manager, his mortgage was interest free and that was how they were able to afford number eleven. "One of the perks of the job," Amy honestly admitted.

At any rate, I sensed immediately that Amy Royle adored me as much as I adored her. Amy was to be my heroine of all time and my role model through life.

I was coming up for five and just about to enter primary school when Mum became pregnant with my little brother. I couldn't fathom out at the time because she was always rushing to the bathroom to be sick and all I could do was listen to that tortuous retching whilst my heart was filled with fear that my mother was caught in the grip of some dreaded lurgies. After one particularly bad bout of vomiting, with streaming eyes prominent in the sickly pallor of her face, my pitifully sorry for herself mother forced a wan smile.

"Oh Ralph, it has to be a boy," she told Dad as he daubed her perspiring brow. "I was never this sick with Judy."

When I heard those words of praise that I, as a girl, was blameless for her state of torment the sense of pride was intoxicating. I hadn't caused her the suffering of every morning having to unceremoniously hang onto the toilet and retch. Oh no, not me, it was a *boy* that did this to her.

Amy Royle had abounding sympathy for mum's plight when she told her of the morning sickness that went on and on, day and night. And then Amy witnessed for herself, mum's rush for the bathroom and listened to the anguished sounds.

"I'm terrified of being sick," Amy admitted, wincing at the thought. "All that heaving and retching: I'd die if I had to go through that all day every day."

Well, bottom line, being the caring person she was, Amy just had to do anything she could to ease the situation and so she kindly offered to pass by our house on her way to school and collect me then bring me back when school was over. And that was the day which would lead me to realise my ambition to see inside the house on Juniper Drive.

Although I had always looked at number eleven with a kind of reverence and wondrous adoration, I had never actually been inside. It's entirely possible of course that was part of the mystique. I had been with my mother on visits to other neighbours. I had seen the inside of practically every house on the street…but never number eleven.

I can only suppose that with all the renovating as well as carrying on her profession as a teacher, Amy's busy schedule didn't allow much time for fraternising with the ladies of our street. Morning coffee and tittle tattle. Ergo, I never had the privilege of actually walking beyond that awesome door.

Many times, I imagined the house whispered my name as I passed. I told mum, but she laughed in that mocking way adults have as she tried to explain something she herself knew nothing about. "Houses don't speak, Judy, what you hear is the whispering of the wind."

"Twaddle!" That's what I said…but only to myself.

It was on a warm afternoon as we walked the pathway to Juniper. Amy carried my satchel in one hand and lightly held my hand with the other and then she said, "Tell you what, Judy, why don't you and I sit out on the back lawn and have a picnic with a nice glass of cold milk and some chocolate bickies before you go home."

"Yes please," I gasped, happy and grateful at the offer of refreshment, but more excited to see if the inside of the house was as beautiful as the outside. It was also an opportunity to see if number eleven was as welcoming as it appeared.

When I walked beyond the front door, the first sight to greet me was the wondrous display of flowers that bedecked an elegant walnut occasional table. Small, circular and highly polished, it sat right in the centre of the spacious entrance hall and on it a vase of glorious blooms. It *was* as welcoming, as warm and as splendid as I had imagined.

I was to learn that throughout the year that table always had seasonal flowers to greet visitors to the house: in the spring, lilacs and daffodils; in summer, roses of every variety and colour that perfumed the air and at Christmas, poinsettias.

As the year nudged forward towards (as Amy put it), the season of good cheer and 1985 was drawing to a close, so too was my first year at school.

Charles, my little brother, was a handful on account of the fact he didn't sleep much and cried a lot. It wasn't all that bad having a baby brother in the house…but it wasn't all that good either. I have to admit there were times I wished Charles would go back to wherever he came from.

Amy saw my frustration. "Don't you like having a baby brother to care for?" She asked.

"Suppose so," I said half-heartedly. To enthuse might give the impression I was keen as mustard, and it would be a lie. Yet, I couldn't give Amy the notion that I was totally heartless. "It's just that…"

"What?"

"When Mum changes his nappies, he's very smelly." As proof of my suffering, I held my nose between thumb and forefinger while disdainfully giving my opinion. "No wonder she was always sick when he was in her tummy."

Amy howled with laughter and said, "Well baby boys are different from baby girls."

That was it, my cue. On the subject of baby Charles, I grabbed the chance to make certain Amy was left in no doubt about the inconvenience he caused me.

"I just don't know when I'll *ever* get a proper night's sleep." I emulated my mother's sigh when she expressed the torment of sleepless nights, while trying my best to appear tolerant.

That afternoon, Amy stepped in with a solution to all my troubles. "I suspect Judy's just a teeny bit put out with the baby and all," she told Mum. "How do you feel about letting her stay over sometimes at The Royle Residence?" (That's what she and Paul jokingly called number eleven.) "You can't be in two places at the same time, Gloria, seeing to Charles *and* getting Judy ready for school."

"Oh, Amy, I think that would do Judy a world of good, make her feel less excluded."

It was sorted! I was going to stay with Amy and Paul on a temporary basis. I rushed to fetch my toothbrush and pyjama case and practically dragged Amy up the street.

There was such a feeling of love when I walked through the front door, and it wasn't only Amy and Paul's love I sensed. It was the house itself. I could almost feel it breathe and sigh. It wasn't a frightening sensation. If anything, it was—comforting. With each passing day, my obsession with number eleven intensified.

It was coming up for the most exciting time of the year for kids, Christmas. It wasn't just the little ones in the infant class. The whole school was alive with fun and laughter at the making and hanging of Christmas decorations.

Snow had gently fallen while everyone slept, turning Juniper Drive into a winter wonderland. To add to the magic of the season, every house had hundreds of fairy lights in the trees and around the windows and doors. The entire street was aglow with the twinkling, coloured lights and it was enchanting.

I was almost six and old enough now to understand more about the meaning of Christmas and the joy of giving and sharing. Amy taught me all that. She took the time to explain in detail the things that were beyond my ken. Amy didn't talk over my head as if I were of no consequence. Oh no, not Amy, she talked *to* me and *with* me. She didn't treat me like a child who couldn't possibly understand. Amy treated me like a person. Amy Royle was a teacher alright, the best there was, but more than that she was a humanitarian.

Paul brought a Christmas tree that was so big, he had to cut the top off to get it inside and then Amy asked me if I would like to help her decorate it. My heart was bursting with adoration and pride as one by one I chose and handed Amy the pretty coloured baubles. And then I held my breath as she gently placed a beautiful silver angel right at the top.

I don't know what made me say it. Maybe it was because she looked so joyful, but I just came right out and surprised myself as much as Amy when I asked, "Are you going to have a baby?"

The question must have been so unexpected she burst into laughter and there was a strange sort of look on her face.

"What made you ask that?" She said.

"I just felt it," was my honest answer.

"Oh, you are a funny child." And then she opened her work box and took out something white and lacy that she had been knitting and her eyes were strangely moist. "I'm preparing just in case God gives me a little girl of my own," Amy told me, and she folded her arms over her tummy.

"Then you are?" And then the strangest sensation that I didn't understand coursed through me. I look back now and see that that was my first real taste of jealousy.

Chapter Two

There were only three more days to go until Christmas when a young man walked into the bank and asked to see the manager. As was the way when a meeting was requested either with the manager or any of the staff, Mrs Gill, who was the receptionist asked, "Do you have an appointment then?"

"No, I don't," he told her and for a few seconds his eyes narrowed in a kind of defiance.

Mrs Gill felt herself shiver. "Well, I'm sorry…" she started to say.

"But it's important!" His interruption was more in the way of an insolent demand than a polite request. And then, perhaps grasping the fact that being brash would get him nowhere, he was suddenly pleading. "Please, I'd be very grateful if Mr Royle could spare me just a few minutes."

He gave his name as Mason Ramsay and Mrs Gill didn't like him one bit. It was nothing she could put a finger on. Maybe it was the way he nervously shuffled his feet or drummed his fingers on the counter as he spoke. But there was something. His entire body language was wrong, and, in her opinion, he was either drunk or drugged. Still, it wasn't her place to make decisions on which customers the manager should or should not see. Mason Ramsay was asked to wait while she checked.

"There's a young man outside, Paul. I've never seen him before but he's quite desperate to have a few words with you."

When she told Paul of the unscheduled customer Mrs Gill looked uneasy, hesitantly biting back the words that stuck like crumbs in her throat. What she really wanted to say was that the customer didn't look trustworthy and warn Paul if he had come to plead for an overdraft or a loan to be prudent. But she had been disciplined at the last bank for voicing her opinion, so she erred on the side of caution.

"I don't like the look of this one, Paul. It might be better if…what I mean is…shouldn't I pass on your apologies and tell him to make an appointment?"

It was sound advice, but Paul being the considerate person he was, could never turn someone away. Especially not at this time of year if there was some way he could help. Unfortunately, he disregarded Mrs Gill's advice and instead gently rebuked her.

"Now, now, Betty," he said, "where's your Christmas spirit?"

"But, Paul…Mr Royle…"

"A couple of minutes won't hurt, so show the customer in," then he had an afterthought. "Tell you what, Betty, give it about five minutes, then buzz my office on the pretence that I have another appointment and the customer is waiting."

That simple request was to be his undoing.

"As you wish," Betty Gill said frostily.

"How can I help you?" Paul smiled kindly at the rather scruffy young man who walked into his office and a moment later the smile left his face.

"You can help me by filling this with money. Call it an early Christmas present." Ramsay sniggered and a trickle of saliva ran down his chin as he took a plastic bag from one pocket of his duffle and a pistol from the other. "Don't try to play the hero now." He wiped the saliva with the back of his hand. "Just you do as I say and we'll both go home happy." Staring wildly through glassy eyes his hand shook as he threw the bag onto the desk.

"Listen to me," Paul spoke softly and calmly, for he was now aware this young man was drugged to the eyeballs…and desperate. "You don't want to ruin your life by doing something this silly." All Paul wanted to do was reason with the boy. "Hey, look son," he said cheerfully, "it's Christmas, go home and spend it with your family. If you walk away and forget this happened, I'll do the same."

Paul's lip twitched nervously. Looking down the barrel of a gun would bring the sweat to anyone's brow, and he could feel the perspiration gathering.

"It's too late to walk away. Fill the bag or I swear I'll use this." Frantically, he began waving the gun around saying, "I've nothing to lose so fill the damned bag—**now**."

Paul hesitantly picked up the bag right at the moment the telephone on his desk rang and as he instinctively reached for the phone, there was a loud bang. And that was the last thing Paul heard.

The children in the first year of primary were singing a Christmas carol when the headmaster walked into the classroom. He kind of whispered, "You should go home Amy, Paul's had an…accident."

Her first thought was that Paul had probably slipped on an icy pavement and Amy made a silent prayer that he hadn't broken an arm or leg. That would really put the kibosh on the festive season. But there was such a look on the headmaster's face, pitying, and it sent a cold shiver through her body. Amy threw her coat over her shoulders without even taking the time to put her arms in the sleeves and ran.

It was the sight of a police car on the road outside her house that really made Amy panic. This wasn't normal practice. Why send police to inform her of a simple accident? If that's all it was surely the head would have passed on the message. It had to be a lot more serious than that. But never in her wildest dreams could Amy have surmised the nightmare that was about to shroud her and shatter her world.

At the sight of a rather frantic Amy running toward them, a weary looking policeman asked, "Mrs Royle?"

"That's me, I'm Amy Royle. Paul…my husband…he had some sort of accident."

That was when a WPC, no more than a slip of a girl, took Amy's arm and guided her towards the front door of number eleven. "Maybe we should go inside," she said.

I wasn't allowed to go anywhere near number eleven that evening, and Mum just cried and cried. I knew something was very wrong when my normally smiling mother tearfully warned me not to ask questions when I saw Amy.

I overheard snippets of hushed conversation. "Mrs Gill at the bank being treated for shock…that crazed junkie with a gun…the killer had been captured." I didn't understand what it was all about, and no one would tell me what had happened so, without exactly knowing why, I cried too.

The little church in Fairfield was filled to capacity on the day of Paul's funeral. Amy was deathly pale and looked like she hadn't slept in a week. Looking back now, I realise she must have shut down and closed her mind to what was happening for she walked around in a daze, not noticing anything or anyone. Not even me.

All she wanted was Paul, but he was never coming back. She was there in body, but not in mind, heart or soul. It was only when Paul's coffin was lowered into that deep, dark pit, only then did Amy's mind finally take it in and her screams were enough to wake all the dead in that cemetery.

By their capacity for compassion and understanding, the Royles had touched so many lives. And then that crazy, drugged up boy not only killed Paul, he all but destroyed Amy when the new life she carried died too. An entire community was left embittered by one selfish, insanely destructive act.

At assembly, the head of Fairfield High made an announcement. "Sadly, due to tragic circumstances, Mrs Royle will be taking a few weeks off and will return when she is well enough."

The sound of true distress filled that hall. All around there was the sound of heartfelt weeping for a teacher, a colleague and a friend. The headmaster's voice was croaky and all trembling with holding back tears he daren't shed.

"I am not going to lecture this morning. I simply want to advise and make all of you aware of the dangers of dabbling in drugs. I need to warn all of you of the danger too in following by example anyone who not only flouts the law but considers themselves above it."

One of the older boys called out. "You mean like Mason Ramsay, sir?"

The head stood for a moment or two scanning the sea of young faces that looked to him for reasons—answers, and with fervency born of despair he shouted out. "Can you understand what I'm trying to get through to you? Taking drugs isn't an innocent game. It is not, as some profess, a harmless pastime. It becomes an addiction that leads addicts onto a path of ruin and degradation."

He took a handkerchief from his pocket, wiped his forehead then staggered slightly. The deputy head sprang to his feet and eased the headmaster onto a chair before taking over.

"Mr Smith is a bit under the weather this morning." Well, that was obvious to all, but the deputy felt it needed to be said. "I'll reiterate the point Mr Smith was making. *There is nothing cool about taking drugs.* Mason Ramsay, the boy who took the life of Paul Royle, was a promising student with a bright future until he was seduced by the excitement and false euphoria that drugs give." And then he warned them in no uncertain manner. "If ever you are tempted, think of Ramsay and the cowardly thing he did to feed his addiction."

From somewhere in the hall a sad, faint voice asked the one question everyone wanted to know. "How is Mrs Royle, sir?"

"Mrs Royle is…as you might expect her to be under the circumstances. I thank you for your concern."

Fairfield High was filled with fury and loathing that one of their own, an ex-pupil, had blotted the character of, not just the school where he was taught, but the community as a whole.

Waiting for Amy to return to Fairfield was like an eternity and at times, I despaired of ever seeing her again. This woman who had gained a place in my heart was suddenly and inexplicably gone.

I was told and accepted that Paul had gone to heaven. My grandma had gone to heaven. Our cat had gone to heaven. Even my pet hamster had gone to heaven. But no one said anything about Amy going to heaven with Paul. So where was she? I was too young to understand that she needed time to grieve…so I fretted.

Weeks passed, winter was dwindling and there was the promise of an early spring. My fretting had become a sort of tormented pang in my heart. I did what I did every evening after school. I finished my homework, then sat at my bedroom window where I had a clear view of number eleven. Day after day, vigilantly I watched for anyone coming or going and then it happened. A car that was familiar to me drove up the street and stopped. Amy had come home.

Oh, that feeling of such sublime relief. It was like taking a deep breath of fresh air and then like a greyhound out the trap I was off and running, excitedly calling out her name, "Amy, Amy." She heard me and turned with her arms outstretched.

Seven weeks is a long time in a child's life. For me, it had been an eternity: the waiting, the not knowing. But now Amy was back, and things would be like they were before…wouldn't they?

She hadn't changed in any way and yet she was different, sort of fragile. She seemed smaller than I remembered.

Amy said, "I've missed you," and my heart soared with happiness. "Look how you've grown in those few short weeks." But her voice was hollow and there was none of that bubbling enthusiasm.

I drew back and was about to say, "You're not my Amy." But she was. The only difference being she was no longer the Amy I remembered and idolised.

I realise now that what was missing was the vital spark of life. It had gone and her smile was no longer glowing and zestful, but empty and sombre. I looked at her through tears, clasped her hand and in that instant, vividly and clearly, strange images of Paul flashed into my mind. I was suddenly engulfed in such soul-destroying sadness and heartache. Right there and then, I didn't understand what savagery had caused this sensation. Only time would give me the answers.

The key turned in the lock, but when she opened the door, Amy just stood there looking sadly at the vase of dead and decayed flowers on the hall table. This one symbol more than anything marked her great loss.

I remember saying, "Don't worry, Amy, we'll get fresh flowers."

She must have thought how simple it was to replace dead flowers, but she could never replace Paul. Right there and then, Amy fell to her knees, and wrapping her arms around me, began to sob almost silently. I don't think she had eaten in weeks because even through the heavy camel coat she wore, her body felt almost skeletal as I clung to her. For the first time, nothing I said or did could make Amy Royle smile.

Chapter Three

"It's going to be awkward, Ralph, coming face to face with Amy again after all these weeks. I know I'll have to speak to her eventually. But what will I say?"

Mum's voice carried through the open living-room door, and I could tell by her tone, she was anxious. They would see me if I stood in the hallway listening to another of their *private* discussions and I'd only be sent to my room. Stealthily, I sat my backside on the third step up the stairway where I could peek through the banisters and hear every word of this conversation clearly. I was also able to see what was going on without them seeing me. I called this my advantage point.

"Don't speculate, Gloria." Dad sounded gently chiding about her lack of confidence. "Just stay your normal self and the right words will come."

"Funny thing about awkward situations, Ralph, the harder you try to say the right thing the easier it is to slip up. Oh God. I've just had a terrible thought. What if…"

"What?"

"Judy!"

Dad groaned a long, drawn out, "Oh," and rubbed his brow thoughtfully. And then to my horror he said, "you might just have to put a big tight gag around her mouth."

I felt vexed and rightfully so. Didn't I have as much right as them to speak? And then in a voice that positively dripped assurance, Mum said, "Don't worry, Ralph. She's a bright little girl and once I explain the do and don'ts…she'll understand."

"Well for everyone's sake, I hope so," he said dubiously.

That evening, after a short, sharp lecture about holding my tongue, Mum made her decision. "Time to bite the bullet," she said courageously. "Let's go and see how Amy is."

As we walked the short distance to Amy's house, I was aware of mum's steps kind of faltering, as if this weren't really such a good idea and her courage seemed to wane. I could feel her indecision as she gripped the brass doorknocker which would announce our presence and bring Amy to greet us.

We started to step inside the hall and that's as far as we got. Amy looked small and tired out and her voice was muted under the big white handkerchief she held to her face.

"I'd love visitors. I really would only not yet; not today." Amy stood rigidly by the walnut table and kind of barred our way instead of leading us into the sitting-room. "Please don't think me ungrateful, Gloria, it's just that…"

"I know, I know," Mum said hoarsely. "When you're ready—in your own time—just call out and I'll be there."

Amy bent and planted a lingering kiss on my cheek and as she did, I had another clear vision. I saw Paul's smiling face and once again, felt that strange stabbing ache in my heart.

Fairfield High welcomed Amy Royle back with open arms when she returned to teaching. Only now, she kept herself very much to herself rather than mingle.

Number eleven Juniper Drive, that haven of love and contentment where Amy and Paul laid the foundation of their perfect marriage, was now the panoply that shielded her from the outside world and gave her seclusion. But as weeks turned to months, her need for seclusion became an obsession. That was when her sister, Grace, stepped in and *demanded* Amy's weekends be spent at their house.

Grace told her reclusive sister, "You're too young to shut yourself away." She nagged incessantly, yak, yak, yak, her argument being, "This hermit's life isn't what Paul would have wanted for you. There's still a world out there, Amy. Do you think you'll be cast into hell for daring to live in it?"

"Damn it, can't you just leave me to mourn Paul?"

"Mourning is one thing, but you're wallowing in self-pity," Grace said disapprovingly. "Paul will never be gone as long as you keep him in your heart. Aw, please, Amy, come to us. Meet new people, socialise and start living again."

There was eventually no fight left in her and Amy reneged. "Alright I will, I will," she shrilled. I guessed it was more to keep the peace than anything.

Amy made a pact with her sister to make the long drive. Perhaps not every weekend as Grace had asked. The best she could promise was most weekends, but only on the condition that Grace stopped that relentless nagging.

Then it was Friday and school was out. Intently, I watched the small suitcase being packed and Amy watched me too from the corner of her eye. The reluctance to comply with her sister's orders and keep the promise she had made showed in the way Amy put things into the case and then took them out again and again, re-folding and re-packing. She didn't want to go, and I wanted her to stay.

"Are you coming back?" I asked fearfully.

"Of course, I am, Judy." Her answer was cheerful. Perhaps a bit too cheerful for right there and then the reassuring pat of her hand on mine filled me once more with an inner sadness. I felt what she must have been feeling that the talons of a great bird were slashing and clawing at her heart.

"Where are you going?" I could feel my bottom lip trembling and fought to hold back the tears. "Is it very, very far away?"

She put her arms around me, and I recall thinking why oh, why wasn't I old enough or wise enough to understand the way grown-ups think? If I understood things better, then perhaps this feeling that my world was crumbling around me might go away.

I felt the gentle, comforting beat of her heart as she held me, still and silent until she had picked the right words to explain. Finally, she held me at arms-length. The sorrow and regret in her eyes filled me with a kind of desperation.

"Listen, Judy. Think of life as a long, long road, and along that road there are steep hills to climb. Now, because it can be so hard to climb many of these hills alone, you…you need someone special to walk with you and hold your hand. It was easy when I had Paul to hold my hand and walk beside me. Now he's gone and being alone is so very, very hard. My sister just wants to ease some of the loneliness. Does any of this make sense to you?"

It didn't, but I nodded anyway and said in what I hoped was a reassuring and worldly-wise manner, "I can hold your hand and walk with you."

"Oh, my dear little best pal." She laughed, only not her normal happy laugh. This was a melancholy sound that made me want to cry even more.

"I can! I will!" My honesty, my commitment, surely, she could see that.

"There was never any doubt in my mind, Judy. But you see, I made a promise that I have to keep. That's why I must go to stay with my sister and her family. Not for good, only over the weekend and I'll be back first thing Monday morning."

I supposed it was an explanation of sorts. Another promise for her to keep only it did nothing to make me feel better.

I watched Amy drive away in her little red car, waving until she turned out of Juniper Drive and out of sight. I remembered the perpetrator of all her heartbreak and misery, and I don't think I've ever hated anyone more than I hated Mason Ramsay.

I missed Paul too, but when I told the priest all he smilingly said was that Paul had gone to a better place. I didn't believe him. There was no place on earth better than Fairfield, so how *could* I be expected to believe such tommyrot, such utter twaddle that the hole in the ground where Paul had been put was a better place?

Anyway, a promise made was a promise kept and Amy returned on a bright Monday morning looking relaxed and totally composed. She was even smiling and seemed…the only word I could think of was how Mum described the statue of the Virgin Mary—serene.

I went with Mum after tea to visit Amy. She told Mum how Grace and Allan, her husband, had gone all out to make the weekend as wonderful as possible. She was glowing as if life had been breathed back into her and it didn't go unnoticed by my sharp-eyed mother.

"Something's happened! Tell me all about it." Mum now seemed to be filled with the same glowing excitement and I was forced to wonder if it was catching.

"Well, Grace invited five of their friend's round on Saturday for a get together."

Amy began to chatter happily about this get together and it didn't escape my attention that the only name she mentioned, the only one she kept talking about was David. It was David did this and David said that, and David brought his guitar and entertained everyone. It turned out David had been at school with Allan and as chance would have it was now the vicar in their parish.

"And did David bring his wife?"

I couldn't help noticing the flippantly suggestive way Mum put the question to Amy and it kind of puzzled me. Her face had taken on a really impish look too.

"Actually, he's a bachelor." Now Amy had that same impish look. "Although for the life of me, I can't understand why," she said with an innocent flutter of her eyelashes.

"So, he's handsome?"

"Oh, dear lord above," Amy sighed rapturously. "He's much more than handsome. David…well, David's witty, talented and clever." She blushed guiltily. "He's a lot like Paul actually."

It was as clear as the nose on your face. As young as I was even I could see it. Amy had a crush on this David person. She stroked my hair and suddenly, I was swamped by a sort of fluster that was somehow laced with contentment. It took my breath away. Looking back now, I realise that weekend which Amy wanted so badly to avoid, had turned out to be a weekend of enchantment. It was also the weekend her healing process began.

Summer was a glorious time in Fairfield. The scent of a thousand roses carried on the breeze through open windows that welcomed the perfumed air into pleasant and tasteful homes. Fairfield was now a cultured, desirable and much sought-after location for the discerning house hunter. But Juniper Drive was still the jewel in this particular crown.

As the weeks rolled by, it was with a great deal of reluctance that I finally accepted *David* was Amy's friend too and oh, how I resented it. So, maybe she did like him. But did she have to talk incessantly, irritatingly about him from Monday to Friday? I overheard her tell my mother that she thought it was so cute the way I scowled at the mention of David's name, but that I would understand and not be so jealous when I met him. Understand what? It's true I was jealous. I had a right to be. I'd practically moved into number eleven until she met *David*. Now I was no more than a visitor.

He'd cast a spell over her, that had to be it. Sitting alone at my bedroom window, I became carried away on the wings of my childish imagination and pictured David as an evil magician who took on the guise of a vicar to capture the fair Amy.

"Why are you sitting in your room when you should be out playing with the other children on such a beautiful evening, Judy?" My peaceful seclusion had been invaded once more.

The fantasising came to an abrupt end the moment I heard mum's voice. It seemed I wasn't even going to be allowed the luxury of wallowing in abject misery. "I don't want to go outside and play silly games," I huffed. "I am not a baby anymore, Mummy. I'm almost eight."

Oh, that feeling of superiority, to be seven going on eight (even though my eighth birthday was almost nine months away.)

"Oh, darling, don't be in such a hurry to grow up," I was told in that oblique, parental tone.

Those few words were enough to douse the fiery scorn that spat like red hot embers from my lips. Treating my parents with contempt didn't come naturally to me anyway. Although I did have a knack of copying grown-up's haughtiness when they wanted to convey a point without sounding spiteful or bitter. I exercised this benign, adult mannerism when informing Mum of my life's plan. "I'm going to sit here and read and read until I'm clever enough to be a teacher."

It was the second week of the school holidays and on Friday afternoon, Amy blew me a kiss and called from the car's open window, "See you Monday," as she drove down the street. Why then was her car driving back up the street when this was only Sunday? Something must be wrong.

I dropped everything and bolted up to number eleven, not stopping until I got to Amy's open front door…and ran straight into a man I'd never seen before. A stranger and he were in Amy's house. I looked up and gazed wide eyed at this Adonis. He had thick black curly hair and wore jeans and a T-shirt, and my first impression was that he must be a film star because only real live film stars were this handsome.

"Don't tell me! Let me guess," he knelt down on one knee and a dimpled smile showed his perfect white teeth. I was helpless to do anything but gape. "You must be Judy, because Amy told me Judy was the prettiest little girl in the country. So, it must be you."

This was David and now I understood!

"Judy, darling, I'm so excited," Amy hugged me and began stringing a whole story together without stopping to draw breath. "We were having this conversation over dinner last night and I happened to mention how much I needed a holiday but had no one to go with and then David said it was the same with him, he longed for two weeks in the sun, but it wasn't much fun on his own so yesterday we went to the travel agent…together." She finally stopped to breathe. "And you'll never guess…"

I was already guessing and just knew I wasn't going to like the end of this story.

"There just happened to be a late cancellation. So, tomorrow we're off to sunny Spain. I'm only here to collect some summer clothes." Amy rattled off the story like it had been rehearsed and one thing struck me as odd. She didn't look at me as she spoke. Amy always looked straight into my face when she told me something. I think I knew there and then. Amy had found the special someone to walk with her on that road through life she told me about.

Later that evening, I sat quiet as a mouse on the third step from the bottom and listened to another one of those conversations that wasn't meant for my ears. Mum was telling Dad how Amy had rushed home for holiday clothes because tomorrow she'd be in Majorca with Mr Wonderful. What a strange name I thought. He must be the only vicar in the whole world to be called the Reverend David Wonderful. It suddenly struck me that if they got married, Amy would be Mrs Wonderful and I wasn't entirely sure which I preferred: Mrs Royle or Mrs Wonderful.

I watched through the spars on our banister as Mum went into fits of laughter when she said, "Amy *insisted* they had reserved *two* bedrooms."

"Well, David is a man of the cloth," Dad answered. "Maybe he has high principles."

"High principles, my arse," Mum hiccupped with the wine glass poised halfway to her mouth. "You can believe *that* if you like. He might be a vicar and she's a widow but they're both human and lust comes in many disguises. You know what they call Majorca—the island of *love*. Somehow, I don't think decorum is going to be on the menu."

I couldn't understand what was so funny about having separate rooms. They weren't married, so didn't it stand to reason they couldn't very well share a bed like married people do? Or even a room for that matter. This was *another* one of those times when grown up logic mystified me.

It was a tanned, relaxed and utterly happy and contented Amy who returned from that holiday in Majorca. Her face was glowing, her hair was lustrous like it used to be, and she had lost that skin and bone look. It was a surprise, but a good one because I had given up hope of the Amy, I adored ever being returned to me.

But there was an even bigger surprise in store. Two weeks later, Amy came home to Fairfield after her normal weekend absence. Ecstatically, she flashed the sparkling sapphire and diamond engagement ring that graced the third finger of her left hand and announced her forthcoming marriage to David Stockton.

It was all very confusing. I just had to ask Mum. "Why is Amy marrying Mr Stockton and not Mr Wonderful?"

Mum seemed even more confused than me. "Where on earth did you get the name Mr Wonderful?" She asked. So, I was forced to confess I'd eavesdropped on her conversation the night Amy left for Spain.

My Mother got all flustered and twitchy in obvious embarrassment. It was strange, although quite funny to see her in one of those half laughing, what to do now predicaments. I was seriously warned *never* to repeat a word of what I'd heard to Amy. And I never did.

Amy was full of the joys, always wistfully fingering and gazing at her sparkling new engagement ring. That was the time too, whenever Amy was near to me, I had a glorious sensation of wallowing in euphoria. It was a feeling that I didn't really understand, so I took it to be that Amy's joy was simply rubbing off on me. Then in one brief day, the joy was cruelly and unceremoniously snatched from my heart and replaced with a crushing despondency.

It had been a year of changes and surprises. But the biggest surprise of all came when the 'FOR SALE' sign was put outside number eleven and only two days later, before I'd even had time to catch my breath, the word 'SOLD' was pasted over it. What's more, the new owners wanted a quick entry.

Amy came to say her goodbyes and take one final look around the house on Juniper Drive before the new owners took possession.

"A cash offer I couldn't refuse," she told Mum. "What's more, it was way over the asking price. What could I do, Gloria? What would you do in my position?"

My mother had a deep intake of breath and then a moment of contemplation before speaking her thoughts. "They must be filthy rich." She was more wide-eyed and astonished than I had ever seen her. "They actually just signed a cheque for that kind of money, like they were simply buying the weeks groceries?"

"I've never met the people. It was all done through our respective solicitors. My solicitor told me they didn't even look at the house because they knew which one it was, and they wanted it. They instructed their solicitor to make a ridiculously high offer to ensure they got it. Believe me, Gloria, this was as big a surprise to me as it was to anyone. I expected the house to be on the market for months not days."

Like only a fly on the wall, I listened to them talking. Was my presence so inconsequential they didn't even notice how upset *I* was by all this upheaval? I couldn't even get a word in edgeways. Every time I opened my mouth, Mum told me to 'shush' and all I wanted to know was where Amy was going to live. Much aggrieved, I moved to the third step where I could listen unseen.

My patience was rewarded. At last, the answer came when Mum asked, "What will you do now? Will you live with your sister and drive that long distance to the school every day?"

"We've...brought the wedding forward." Amy was fiddling with the sapphires and diamonds again so that she didn't have to look Mum in the face. "I'll be moving in with David until then." She blushed and stammered as if she was committing the ultimate sin.

"Oh, you're a silly moo," and Mum hugged Amy sort of protectively. "You have nothing to be ashamed of," she assured her.

"There's something else, Gloria! I can't bring myself to tell Judy."

I held my breath and waited, instinctively knowing that a door, a very important door was about to close on my life. I listened in a kind of disbelieving horror to Amy's tearful confession.

"I'm leaving Fairfield High next week to teach at a school nearer to where I'll be living. I can't be expected to travel fifty miles each way every day in all weathers."

So, there it was and the only thing I could do now was put on a brave face and see my darling Amy on her way without sorrow or regret: she more than anyone certainly deserved that much.

There are times in vivid flashback I remember that moment and wonder if Amy thought perhaps being hung drawn and quartered was the price she'd have to pay for happiness. She fell in love with a man who loved her back. It was as simple as that and there was no reason on earth why she should feel guilty about it. The fact of the matter was, her marriage to Paul had been such a happy one that she wanted more of the same. Amy was never going to forget Paul or the awful thing that happened to him. She was now merely continuing her journey on life's long road...with someone else.

"Would you like to come with me, Judy, just while I take one last look around the house?" Amy held out her hand and when she took mine, it struck me how safe it felt to hold the hand of someone you trusted. If this was how Amy felt with David, who was I to grumble?

The door creaked slightly when it opened and Amy said, "That hinge could do with a drop of oil." She walked over to the walnut table and tears fell like dew drops onto the petals as she bent to smell the roses.

"Aren't you taking your table?" I asked.

"I decided to leave it because this table was the first thing Paul and I bought for this house." She said it in that explaining way that had become so familiar to me. "It doesn't seem right somehow for me to take it away, Judy. Don't you agree?"

My head nodded slowly, but my lips made no sound.

"However, I gave the solicitor a letter to pass on to the new owners asking if they would be kind enough to always have fresh flowers here. I told them it's in memory of a wonderful man. A sort of superstition that the fresh flowers will ensure he's never forgotten."

We walked to where Amy's car was parked. She stood for a moment nervously jingling her keys and then she said, "Time I was going, but I'm not saying goodbye, Judy, I'm saying au revoir," and then in answer to my look of bewilderment she added, "that means, until we meet again."

Why did all good things have to come to an end? Mum said it was life and we all have to move on. If something good ends the chances are it might be replaced by something better.

"By all accounts the new owners are very rich." The way my mother said it was positively snobbish. We weren't poor, but it was as if rubbing shoulders with **extremely** rich people was going to make **her** the cream of society.

Fairfield was about to learn that rich didn't necessarily mean class and the peace and tranquillity of Juniper Drive was about to be shattered…the Kellers were about to arrive.

Chapter Four

Curtains twitched as the moving van rolled up the street and stopped at number eleven. Following closely behind the van was a sleek, black Jaguar car that seemed to take up most of the road when it parked…Or perhaps, selfishly abandoned would be a better description. It had indiscriminately blocked two driveways. The Kellers were here, and they were making their presence felt.

The street suddenly became a hive of activity with doorsteps and driveways being swept, gardens weeded and lots of chatting over fences. In truth, everyone wasn't industrious. They were just plain nosey.

The story had circulated—as stories do—and gathered momentum as it went. By all accounts, the new owners of number eleven were fabulously wealthy, therefore everyone was curious to see what they were actually like. It was whispered that they could possibly be stars of the stage and screen. Maybe even akin to royalty. They had by all accounts paid cash so by definition it was assumed they must be upper class. What an error in judgement that was.

Doctor Thomson from number eight came out of her house, got halfway down the path then froze. She jingled her car keys looking slightly perplexed at the way her car had been blocked in. Our friendly neighbourhood GP smiled and called out to Mr Keller, "Excuse me. I realise you must be terribly busy, but would you be kind enough to move your car just enough to let me out of my driveway?"

It was a reasonable enough request and delivered with smiling politeness too. Doctor Thomson was therefore unprepared and left reeling when her courteousness was met with calculated rudeness.

"Listen to me, lady," Keller pointed a finger at Doctor Thomson in the most threatening and loutish way. "I don't think it's asking too much for *you* to leave it five minutes. Like you say, I'm busy. So, the answer is *no*. My car stays where it is until *I'm* ready to move it."

The way he growlingly refused to move the offending vehicle left everyone open-mouthed, but none more than Dr Thomson. She looked ready to explode. Such behaviour had never been heard of in Fairfield.

"I appreciate your dilemma: now please appreciate mine." Her jaw was set, and it was obvious she was struggling to hold onto a modicum of respectability rather than, under such circumstances, let loose the rage that was building up inside her. The rage won. "I'm a doctor and I've just had a call to attend a medical emergency. Now, get your fat lazy arse into that driving seat and move that frigging car or I'll be forced to call the police." Dr Thomson glowered disgustedly at her new and exceedingly selfish neighbour.

As one of the removal men passed, Keller motioned with his head in the direction of Dr Thomson and sniggered, "One thing I hate is a fucking bossy bitch."

"I heard that," Ruth Thomson screamed, "and I have witnesses."

"Yeah, you look the nosy type. Whad ya do, ride around on your broomstick listening into private conversations?"

That was when pottering in the gardens and over the hedge gossiping ceased as eyes and ears incredulously watched and listened to the farce which was taking place right on their doorstep.

"Well," Ruth Thomson sneered, "looking at that monster of a car, I guess it's true what they say about men and their motors. A big car compensates for what they don't have in their trousers."

Keller let out a great belly laugh, winked slyly and answered sarcastically, "Just goes to show what little you know…for a *doctor*."

"You obviously think you hold some kind of licence to break the law with impunity from prosecution. I hope one day you're in painful need of a doctor and he can't come because some selfish *bastard* has parked across his drive." Her composure hadn't only really and truly slipped it had nosedived into snarling fighting talk. What's more, Doctor Ruth Thomson had never been heard to utter any swearword stronger than 'damn' and she had just used a really bad swearword.

Keller lounged against the magnificent Jaguar with his arms folded, sniggering, and not in a joking way either. He looked positively malevolent.

"Oh, I don't think that'll ever happen, lady," he sneered arrogantly. "You see, I pay my doctor more for one visit than you probably earn in a week. When I snap my fingers nothing, but nothing, stands in his way."

Keller's whole demeanour shouted 'bully' and I heard Mum mutter to nobody in particular, "I wonder if he'd be so tough if some big Irish navvy asked him to move his bloody car."

At that moment, a tanned, pretty woman hurried to intervene. "Please, John," she said with a kind of dignity that didn't match her common look, "be a darling and move the car. After all, the whole street doesn't belong to us."

This was Daisy Keller and her quiet authority held power. Without as much as a grunt, Keller all but jumped to attention and moved the car, allowing Dr Thomson to exit the street.

Piece by piece their possessions were carried from the van into the house and every time an item of furniture was taken from the van, as if she were sending out a message to everyone, Mrs Keller called to the removal men, "Be careful with that please, it cost a small fortune."

Of course, no one in the street denied their furnishings were expensive, but in mum's opinion, they were garish in the extreme. "Quiet, quite vulgar," was how she put it.

Personally, I was in awe of the ostentation. But hey, what did I know? I was a child and had still to learn the difference between tasteful and tasteless.

Their somewhat rowdy and spectacular entry into the street was taken by everyone to be testimony to the kind of people they were, and the residents of Juniper closed ranks. If aggression were what they wanted, aggression was what they'd get.

The name Keller was now a source of scornful gossip. With my own ever flapping ears, I heard the maligning slurs that Mr Keller was one to be wary of. He did seem a bit of an ogre. But as far as I was concerned, Mrs Keller had an earthy quality and that appealed to me. She wasn't all la-di-da and it was patently obvious she hadn't been born with a silver spoon in her mouth either.

When I walked past number eleven (which I did quite often), Mrs Keller was sure to call out, "Hold on a minute, sweetie," then she would hand me a bar of chocolate and with twinkling eyes that always seemed to be smiling say, "Sweets for the sweet."

I didn't care what anyone said about her. I liked Daisy Keller. She was my kind of people.

There was a lot going on within the walls of number eleven with workmen coming and going. Then only two weeks after they moved in, the entire street received gold embossed invitations to attend a housewarming party at the residence of Mr and Mrs Keller, 11 Juniper Drive. Not one single person turned down the invitation.

The wolves were baying at the moon, waiting for Saturday to come round so they could get inside the big house, take a good look round and have a juicy bone to chew on for the next month at least.

A state of the arts music system carried soft music throughout the house. Tasteful music at that surprisingly enough: Bach, Rachmaninov, Tchaikovsky, yes and even Matt Monroe. The way she hummed along in a dreamy, rapturous way, I suspected Matt Monroe was Daisy Keller's favourite.

Mrs Keller mingled with the guests, introducing herself as Marguerite, but in the same breath explaining, "Well, that's my given name, but I prefer plain old Daisy."

The ladies all stood around sipping their wine and tittering genteelly without much in the way of facial expression, whereas Daisy Keller obviously didn't give a damn about laughter lines. She crinkled her eyes and laughed out loud.

John Keller stood like lord of the manor, surrounded by all the male residents of the street, including my father. All of them were there solely with the duplicitous intention of finding out what business Keller was in.

Dad was the first to ask outright. "What exactly is your line of work, John?"

"This and that," Keller said warily. "What's your line of work?" He played sort of catch as catch can by answering each question with a question.

"I'm a consultant cardiologist." Dad didn't brag and puff out his chest about what he did for a living. If anything, he was more inclined to be blasé about his profession.

"Well, whadda ya know, a doc, eh. I'll know whose doorbell to ring if the old ticker gives me problems, then."

Keller laughed and joked but still didn't give any indication where he had acquired his wealth. He had to notice how frustrating it was when he answered the questions with a long spiel…without really giving much away. What you might call talking a lot and saying nothing. Maybe this was Kellers' defence against people who saw themselves as upper class and looked on it as their right to tactlessly question why people so short of social graces like the Kellers were so affluent and financially endowed. The evening had turned into a game of cat and mouse.

The good neighbours were gathered under this roof, each and every one with a purpose in mind. The females, my own dear mother included, were desperate to poke their upper crust noses into every room, but especially the bathroom. By all accounts, the team of highly-paid craftsmen who entered number eleven were there to turn the conventional bathroom into a masterpiece of Italian marble complete with a sunken Jacuzzi and gold fittings in the exotic shape of bare breasted mermaids. Daisy herself put the finishing touches. Lots of soft fluffy towels in pastel shades and everyone monogrammed with gold lettering.

"How tacky," Harriet Granger sniggered with raised eyebrows. However, she was devoured by jealousy nevertheless *and* it showed.

Daisy had happily told the little group, "Be my guest, have a snoop round our happy little home," and that's exactly what they were doing…snooping.

The little group meandered into the master bedroom.

"Oh, now this *is* over the top. She really has taken ostentation to the limit." If Ruth Thomson hadn't known whose bedroom this was, she might have been, as I was, in awe. The deep piled carpet was a delicately pale lilac to match the inlaid flower design on every piece of the exquisite cream furniture and the huge four-poster bed was draped in luxurious cream lace.

Right through the house, they mocked and maligned behind Daisy's back until they'd finished their snooping.

Emily Robb, who lived at number nine said, "That bathroom must have cost a pretty penny." Slyly she waited for Daisy to do as any one of them would do…brag.

All Daisy Keller said was, "Oh, it did, but then again what price comfort," and offered no information on the exact cost.

I sat on the window seat quietly sipping a delicious milk shake Mrs Keller had made especially for me. I watched and listened as the so-called refined ladies waited until Daisy was almost out of earshot, then continued maligning her lack of expertise in interior design as well as her hospitality. I wanted to shout out that real ladies didn't behave in such a mean and petty fashion. Daisy Keller may be coarse and common by their standards, but she was still more of a lady than anyone here. She wouldn't go into a person's home, eat the food and drink the wine then call the hostess nasty names behind her back, not like them.

When Daisy went into the kitchen, I followed her. "Thank you for the milk shake, Mrs Keller," I said politely and held out the delicately carved glass.

She looked upset and I guessed that the snobbery was getting to her. If I heard some of the snide remarks, then obviously so did Daisy.

She smiled and bent down to kiss my cheek, cooing in that soft voice. "Thank you, sweetie, would you like another?"

Her grey silk dress rustled, and I caught the soft, sweet aroma of violets. How that delicate, gentle perfume suited her.

"No, thank you, Mrs Keller." I burped involuntarily and it made her laugh…really laugh for the first time that night. And then I said what I'd been taught to politely say when offered too many refreshments. "I've had an ample sufficiency." Well, I already felt like I was going to burst so here's to what another would do.

Meanwhile, in the lounge, the men were still insistently probing, without much success too I might add, as to the business venture, investment, windfall or whatever it was that had put Keller into the super-rich bracket.

"You still haven't told us what business you're in." Dad just wouldn't give up. It must have been like a thorn in his flesh wondering why these people who looked like they'd be more at home in a gypsy caravan could afford this place.

Without warning Keller's voice suddenly boomed above the hubbub, "Iron and steel." Was he at last ready to tell? In an instant, the room was quiet as everyone waited with bated breath and then he roared, "The wife does the ironing and I do the stealing, ha, ha, ha," and he laughed so hard his shoulders shook.

But the laugh was on the gentlemen of Juniper. Keller had obviously discovered this was the best and only way to put a stop to unwanted probing into his affairs.

They didn't find out that night, nor would they ever find out where Keller made his money. The origin of his wealth would forever remain a mystery.

"Have you any family, Daisy? This is such a big house for just the two of you."

It was mum's turn to probe, and she did probe so eloquently. Mrs Keller would end up divulging all her family secrets without even knowing she'd done it.

"We have a boy and a girl, but they've been staying with their grandparents at our villa in Spain until we got settled in here." Her eyes became all dewy and moist at the mention of her children.

Mum had tears in her eyes too, but I think it was the mention of that villa in Spain that did it. I've always had a sneaking suspicion Daisy only mentioned it to twist the knife a little before continuing.

"Paris is seventeen. We called her Paris because that's where John and me," Daisy put a forefinger to her lips, "or should that be John and I?" She made a dismissive gesture with a hand positively laden with diamond rings, "Anyway, we spent our honeymoon in Paris, never left the penthouse suite for a week and…she was the result. Then there's little Roman who's fifteen, he…"

"Let me guess," Mum interrupted before Daisy gave graphic details of their son's conception, "you were in Rome?"

"Our second honeymoon would you believe. *Well,*" she nudged Mum with her elbow and winked, "you know what honeymoons are like. I needed a second one to get over the first. But never in a month of Sunday's could I have guessed there'd be three of us on the return flight. I came back pregnant again and that was when I told John, no more honeymoons. Let's just stick to holidays. So, we bought the Spanish villa." Daisy guffawed loudly while the other ladies continued to titter in that falsely genteel fashion.

"When will we have the pleasure of meeting your children?" The smile on mum's face was so forced it looked painful.

With the gentlest of sighs that was like a soft breeze, Daisy said, "They come home tomorrow," and you could almost see the fluttering of her heart at the prospect of holding her children again.

"So have they been attending school in Spain?"

"Well, to let you understand," Daisy sort of grimaced uncomfortably. She seemed a touch reticent as if this were a subject, she wasn't content to talk about. Nevertheless, she drew back her slight shoulders and said, "my children are what you might call…free spirits. We decided private tutoring at home might be best for them. So, we hired a private tutor. Mr Gregory is a retired headmaster who came highly recommended."

By this time, they were all thinking along the same lines. There was more to this than meets the eye. My mother probed deeper. "And will Mr Gregory…"

"Good grief," Daisy cut her off mid-sentence, "your glass is almost empty," and she practically snatched the glass from mum's hand then made a rush for the sanctuary of her kitchen.

I stood at the kitchen door silently watching Daisy. The blush, that nervous twiddling with her earring, her entire body language positively screamed that Daisy was uneasy about something. I had the distinct feeling Paris and Roman were a bit more than simply free spirits.

Whatever it was, everyone expected the Keller children to be like, no one was prepared for the actuality. Hell was coming to Juniper.

Chapter Five

Life in Fairfield was quite sedentary and that was the way most people liked it. After all, wasn't that the appeal of owning a house there? Whereas the more socially animated might consider living in this rather oldie worldly village tediously serene, it was happily acceptable to residents who enjoyed the benefit of serenity. This was a peaceful spot, unaffected by the grind of industry and the rough and tumble of city life…until now.

The Keller kids' homecoming was more like the start of World War Three and the residents of, not only Juniper Drive, but Fairfield as a whole got the rudest of wake-up calls that bright and sunny Sunday morning.

The dignified calm associated with this classiest of rural retreats was broken by the sound of a car horn blasting out 'Colonel Bogey' from the start of the drive right up to the entrance of number eleven.

It must have felt like sacrilege to the mechanic who had to install such an obscene thing into that beautiful Mercedes. But the biggest heartache must have been for the person who had to spray over the original creamy white and turn such a magnificent machine into a shocking pink monstrosity. Dad took one look and winced as if someone had just drawn their nails down a blackboard.

As soon as the Keller's front door opened, "Come in, come in it's nice to see you," blasted forth at about a hundred decibels from the music system which only last night had played such beautiful melodies. Now, whereas John and Daisy Keller might consider it quaint and welcoming to greet their family this way, others weren't so enraptured. At that point, every door and window in Juniper Drive slammed shut in an effort to blot out the unholy racket.

Mr and Mrs Keller senior more or less dived from the front seats and not too elegantly either. The rear door opened and a pair of long, shapely and highly tanned legs protruded. The girl, who I took to be Paris Keller, slithered in a deliberately seductive way from the back passenger seat. Roman got out the other side, stretched, then cast an impassive glance down the street. I watched in awe at these diversely out of character people who had descended on our refined community.

John senior, with his curly black hair tied back in a ponytail and one gold earring gracing his right lobe, looked the epitome of pure-bred Romany. Verity Keller's pink shell suit and blonde hair piled high on her head certainly brought a very big splash of colour to the street. It was evident and ever so painfully obvious that pink was Verity's favourite colour and the brighter the better.

I noticed one very strange thing that day. The birdsong ceased somewhat abruptly, and I would forever wonder if it was the blaring of Cornel Bogey from the car horn, the shocking pink Mercedes, or the fearsome sight of Verity and John senior that frightened them away. Then again, in all possibility, it could have been news of the Keller kid's homecoming that had chased them to pastures new.

Daisy's squeal of delight as she hugged her in-laws reverberated right down the length of Juniper. "We knew the kids were coming home today but we didn't expect you back from Spain so soon. Why the hell didn't you let us know?"

"It's just a flying visit, honey bun." Verity fluttered her jet black, heavily laden with mascara eyelashes as she gestured every word with manicured hands which were even more ring laden than Daisy's.

"So, what brought you back?"

"There was some urgent business John had to take care of. We'll be jetting back to the villa in a couple of days. Just thought, aw to hell with it, might as well kill two birds with one stone. We could hand deliver these two then spend time browsing the new homestead." She cast an unimpressed glance down the street. "Mm, not bad if you're into cemeteries, a bit quiet for my liking. Not even a pub in sight. I suppose this is what's called a classy neighbourhood."

"Remember I told you about the house that caught our eye when we drove through here about a year ago? Well, this is it. Come and see." Daisy excitedly grabbed Verity's hand and almost dragged her inside. "C'mon kids, I'll show you your rooms."

It was Paris I couldn't take my eyes off. She wore teeny, little hot pants and the skimpiest little halter neck top. I'd never seen so much naked flesh before and by the look on Mr Granger at number ten's face, neither had he.

George and Harriet Granger were newlyweds and the youngest residents on Juniper. Mum called George a living doll on account he was so handsome. Anyway, George had been busy trimming the hedge when the pink Mercedes drew up and now the clippers were poised over the hedge, but nothing was happening. Why? Because George was too busy drooling at Paris Keller who was now sauntering slowly towards him, wiggling her bottom in the most exaggerated way while her breasts bounced in time with her steps.

I have no idea what Paris said when she bent provocatively across the hedge so that her very short shorts rode up, exposing her bare buttocks. The only words I caught were what sounded like…bedroom and baby oil? Well, George's mouth fell open at whatever Paris had suggested. The next thing I knew, Harriet, wielding a lethal looking trowel positively flew at Paris shouting that she should crawl back to the brothel she fell out of.

It was a bit scary for someone going on eight to witness two young women raring to scratch each other's eyes out. It was when Keller and Daisy ran from the house screaming, "What the hell are you doing to our little girl?" I took off before the feathers and fur started flying.

"What's a brothel?" It was a simple enough question. All I wanted was to find out what Harriet meant, and I couldn't see the harm in asking my mother to explain.

"Where on earth did you hear that?" Gloria Vernon, my moralistic mum was utterly apoplectic. "You've been to the Keller's again," she spluttered, "did you hear them talking about a…a…"

I realised then that I had said a word that little girls shouldn't be heard to say. Who would be the one to blame for talking of such things in front of me? Who was the likeliest person to be accused of putting the word into my mouth?

"It wasn't Mrs Keller," I cried, jumping to Daisy's defence,

"Then who said it?"

"It was Harriet Granger! She just told Paris Keller to crawl into one." I was a true innocent. "Honest, Mum, they're going to fight because Paris said something about baby oil in George's bedroom."

That was it! Mum almost fell over her own feet rushing to get to the thick of the action, only to discover the skirmish was over and she'd missed the main course—but dessert was still to come.

Some people are born to make peace and others are born to make war. Paris Keller was only happy when a battle raged, and she was at the forefront. She was a natural born troublemaker who revelled in animosity that was of her making.

It took Paris all of ten minutes to think up her next move. "I'd like to go for a walk and make the acquaintance of some of the neighbours if that's fine by you, Mummy?" She could play the part of chaste and innocent to perfection, and all for Daisy's benefit.

Of course, when Paris Keller said she wanted to make an acquaintance what she really meant was she was on the prowl for trouble. Paris wasn't one who needed a big stick to stir trouble. Her tongue was enough.

"Alright, sweetie, but don't get into any more bother. The natives aren't all that friendly, as you may have noticed." It was hard to believe anyone could be so genuinely naïve as Daisy Keller.

Paris smiled sweetly and her dimpled cheeks made her look so angelic it was almost impossible to see the devil inside. "Don't worry, I won't let anyone bully me," says she. Huh, as if anyone would dare.

It was true I had a vivid imagination, but Paris Keller being bullied and browbeaten. Even I wasn't that imaginative. I was aware of mum's grip tightening on my hand as Paris emerged from number eleven. She had to be aware that all eyes were on her and yet, those long, slender brown legs strode straight towards George Granger again. He looked like he still hadn't gotten over the complete and utter shock of that first encounter with Paris Keller.

Harriet pointed the garden hose at Paris and frantically yelled, "If you don't get back to your own place, I swear, I'll turn on the water."

Paris stood with her hands on her hips laughing at poor, perplexed Harriet Granger and then she bent forward so that her top drooped open. George began to sweat profusely when he got the biggest eyeful.

"*You* can turn on the water, but I do believe *I* just turned your husband on," Paris called tauntingly to Harriet.

I didn't understand and was about to ask Mum to explain what tap Paris would use to turn on George like the water when she suddenly clasped both her hands over my ears in an effort to blot out the obscenities that had begun to fly. I was dragged inside the house as the screaming and shouting started. Our haven in the suburbs had been turned into a war zone.

Later that night, I crept out of bed and listened as Mum told Dad all about…well, what else but the Keller's latest episode.

"I bet you wish you'd stayed home today instead of playing golf. Jesus, it was a battle royal out there, Ralph."

Dad laughed really heartily. "Never thought I'd see the day a cat-fight would get you in such a tizzy. You've got to start getting out more, Gloria."

"What, and miss all the action? Not on your life." She sounded surprised that Dad wasn't taking this more seriously, but she carried on with the story anyway. "Well, Harriet did turn on the water and the force threw Paris on her backside and wiped the smile off her face."

The hilarity of it all must have struck Dad then and he roared with laughter at the picture his mind conjured. "So, it was handbags at dawn?"

"Oh, that was only chapter one. I think the best is yet to come. That little tramp is used to getting her own way and she's set her sights on George Granger. Ooh, there may be trouble ahead." My supremely sophisticated mother was actually savouring this.

I was still no wiser as to whether or not Paris turned George on and once more, I was left to wonder and as usual, make my own conclusions.

After that debacle, the Keller's were no longer made welcome in the community and I was warned to stay away from number eleven. "Why?" I asked and reasonably so.

All Mum said by way of explanation was, "Those people have been *ostracised,* Judy," and she used that warning tone for me to ask no more questions.

Problems and more problems, for since I was barred from asking, I now had to fathom out for myself what an *ostrich* had to do with this. It was all becoming too much for my young mind to take in.

Oh, to be bestowed with the gift of wisdom. Or at least a better understanding of grown-up logic, for I liked Daisy and it hurt when she waved and called, "HI, sweetie," and all I could do was what I'd been told—no, ordered to do. I now had to turn away with my nose in the air and ignore her. It hurt so much to see that sad look on her face, so when Mum wasn't looking, I'd smile and wave back at Daisy Keller.

After the Granger incident, Paris and Roman joined forces to bring mayhem to Juniper Drive. They were both endowed with the same malicious and absolutely wicked streak. There was no doubt about it, they were handsome kids and all the men, young and old, would sneak a glance at Paris as she strolled along Juniper, flaunting her perfect body in the skimpiest of outfits.

Roman too drew many admiring looks with that wild, gypsy allure that set hearts racing, but especially from Angelina Da Corsa, who lived at number three. She always seemed to be there or there about in her shorts and little bikini top that was two sizes too small and made her ample bust look like it defied the laws of gravity by staying inside.

When Roman walked slowly by, they made eyes at each other, and Mum said you could almost smell the lust. This gave me some cause to wonder—a lot of cause actually—because I definitely remember Angelina telling one of the girls in the cloakroom that the only perfume, she wore was Chanel.

Mr DeCorsa was a restaurateur and because his restaurant was so popular, he and Mrs DeCorsa worked long hours, which meant Angelina spent most of her evenings at home alone. They were in the throes of opening a chic new restaurant. Regular patrons had been invited to the classy new establishment for the grand opening. On that busy, but successful Saturday night everything was going so well. At around eight o'clock, Mrs DeCorsa decided to drive home and fetch Angelina so that she too could enjoy the party.

"Phone and tell her to get a taxi," Mr DeCorsa had said.

"No, no," Mrs DeCorsa insisted, "I want it to be a surprise and, on the way, back I can tell Angelina all about our wonderful success."

The house was unusually quiet when she arrived. There was no television and no music, only the sound of talking and occasional giggling from Angelina's bedroom. It wasn't a problem, if one of Angelina's friends had come to sleep over (which was often the case), she too could come and enjoy the party.

Mrs DeCorsa turned the bedroom door handle calling out, "It's only Mama," and then the most plaintiff shriek cut through the night air, "Santa Maria, holy mother of God."

The sound of Mrs DeCorsa's horrified screams ripped through Juniper Drive and from their windows, everyone watched Roman Keller, naked except for only a crumpled T shirt clasped in front of him to cover his dignity, run for his life with Mrs DeCorsa in hot pursuit, brandishing the most lethal looking cleaver and screaming, "The bastardo has defiled my daughter."

"What now?" Dad said irritably.

"It's the Keller boy…again. I think Mrs DeCorsa wants to kill him." Mum was so calm and matter of fact. With nothing more than the merest blush to her cheeks, she closed the curtains and told Dad, "I've been waiting for this, you know. I'm not exactly a founder member of the Keller fan club, but Angelina practically rapes that boy with her eyes every time he passes. It's disgusting."

My parents may have forgotten I was in the room, but I was determined to get my two-penny worth in, which I realised later wasn't the best idea I'd ever had.

With my arms crossed over my chest, in my best imitation of Mum passing on gossip, I related an incident from the school cloakroom that I was sure would be of interest.

"I heard Angelina talking to some of the girls in the cloakroom at school about Roman Keller," I announced in my most intellectual voice. Like a cat with a mouse, I waited for my mother's curiosity to kick in.

"And," Mum said eagerly, "what did Angelina say?"

"She said Roman was drop dead gorgeous and she'd like to get inside his pants."

I was aware of mum's mouth dropping open. I took this to be a sign of interest, so I began to relate every sordid detail of Angelina's lust exactly as I'd heard her tell it, only my mother hastily intervened.

"Judy! I'll say this only once, *be quiet*, we don't want to hear this."

"I was only saying…"

"Then don't!"

I was determined to have the last word. "Angelina said she has wet dreams about Roman Keller. What is a wet dream? Is it when you dream about swimming?"

That was when my shocked father jumped up and caught Mum as she went into some sort of seizure.

I was firmly rebuked and sent to my room. Although I honestly didn't know what I'd said and done that was so wrong. And then Dad came up and explained the dangers of repeating word for word other people's conversations. I made up my mind there and then to keep everything I heard to myself if this was all the thanks I got.

The morning after that right fracas, the Keller family hurriedly put suitcases into the Jaguar and as I skipped past, Daisy whispered to me that they were going to spend a month or so at the Spanish villa.

"See you soon, sweetie," she said, and then they sped off in the direction of the airport.

After almost two years of feuding, high drama and the Keller's heading for Spain every time Paris or Roman blotted their copy book (at this point I have to say the Keller family spent a *lot* of time at the villa), things actually began to settle down and for a short while a peaceful calm returned to Juniper Drive. Even the birds returned to warble their cheery message that spring was just around the corner.

It was reckoned by some that the Keller kids were growing out of that troublesome age, forgetting of course that Paris thrived on trouble and high drama. With her it was all dirks and daggers, that's what it was, dirks and daggers that were un-sheathed whenever someone invoked that inexplicable fury within her. Paris Keller watched, waited and sharpened her claws.

Chapter Six

It was the fourth of April, and I awoke to the glorious sound of a robin chirping merrily on my windowsill. Happy birthday it seemed to be singing. It was my tenth birthday. From my window, I saw all the spring flowers in every garden, and they seemed to greet me with open petals on this, the beginning of a new year for me, my special day.

I didn't know it, but tomorrow, Sunday, I would be saying goodbye to an era and closing yet another chapter in my life.

It would also be the most memorable of weekends for three of our highly respected residents for a long time to come. Unfortunately, it would be memorable for all the wrong reasons. For them, this beautiful April morning was to bring the most unexpected of surprises. These three letters on route to be delivered from no other than John Keller, were about to make accusations of the worst kind. Allegations set to mercilessly plunge them into an unbelievable situation.

But for one of these three accused in particular, Vince Robb, this letter from Keller would be the means of bringing closure to a time of tension and despair which for too long had doggedly clawed at his heart and shredded his soul. He had stupidly misread an innocent thing as a guilty secret and the consequences of this idiocy had been calamitous. Strangely enough, that incriminating letter would indirectly bring truth to surface, put an end to delusion and in a roundabout way revive the happiness and harmony Vince thought was lost. This harbinger of supposed bad news was to in fact turn the tide of fate and save him from making the biggest mistake of his life.

This Saturday would be a day of reckoning for all three, but more so for Vince Robb.

The postman delivered an array of birthday cards to our house. In his sack, he also had these three envelopes bearing the same handwriting. Mr George

Granger, 10 Juniper Drive, Mr Vincent Robb, 9 Juniper Drive, and Mr Leon Thomson, 8 Juniper Drive: three men who were about to enter purgatory.

When this particular scandal broke, and it emerged that the finger of suspicion had been pointed at these three there would undoubtedly be only one question on everyone's lips. "Which one of them *is* the father of the child Paris Keller was carrying? Surely, there was no smoke without fire?"

"There's a letter here for you, George. Mm, I don't recognise the handwriting. Could it be a client maybe settling an outstanding bill?" Harriet was overcome with the oddest, most unnatural edginess about the letter and when George reached out her fingers gripped the envelope as if she were fearful of it being opened. She said, "I have a terribly bad feeling about this, and I don't know why."

George's head crooked to one side, and he looked quizzically at the envelope, "Beautiful copperplate writing, only it's not a handwriting that I recognise either."

"Well, that handwriting positively screams, highly educated, top of the heap professional. Therefore, it's my guess this is from one of your posh clients," Harriet said informatively. "See if there's a cheque inside."

"I'm a bespoke tailor, Harriet. I create garments of quality and refinement for distinguished gentlemen. My clients not only praise my excellence, but they also pay for their goods on collection. *Not* when the spirit moves them to send a cheque." He ripped open the envelope and then stared limply at the single sheet of notepaper gripped in his shaking hand.

Harriet's feeling of fingernail biting unease rippled even more. "What is it? It's some kind of bad news, isn't it?" She asked fearfully.

"I'm not really sure what to make of this! It's some sort of bizarre invitation to the Keller's…tomorrow if you don't mind."

"Well, if they think for one minute that tea and scones on a Sunday afternoon is going to heal old wounds, they have another think coming."

Harriet stamped into the kitchen and filled the kettle, muttering under her breath all the while. She still smarted at the very mention of that name. "I'd rather stick pins in my eyes," she called out to George. "I told you I had a bad feeling about this."

George read the letter a second time. His eyebrows raised and he chuckled in a dazed, confused sort of way. "Don't worry! You won't have to go to that extreme."

"Why?"

"You're not invited."

"What do you mean I'm not invited? Let me see that." It must have been infuriating for Harriet: here she was, all psyched up to rap on their door and throw the goddamned invitation back at his feet. Only now to be told she hadn't been invited.

George held out the sheet of paper. "You read it for yourself, then tell me what you make of it because I'm stumped," he said.

Harriet snatched the letter from his hand and as she devoured the words her nostrils flared in temper.

Dear Mr Granger,

You are cordially invited to a meeting at number eleven Juniper Drive on Sunday at 2 pm. Since the matter under discussion directly involves you, it would be in your best interests to attend the meeting alone.

John Keller.

"Who the hell does he think he is? I'll put money on it that little tramp has something to do with this. I'll bet the over-sexed trollop is just trying to get you alone in that house. I'm going over there right this minute to thrash it out with them." Harriet was grinding her teeth in temper as she yanked the apron from around her waist.

"No, you're not!" George got to the front door before Harriet and barred her furious exit. "I don't know what this is all about, but on Sunday, we'll find out *together*. Whether or not they like it, you're coming with me."

"Was that the post, Leon?" Doctor Ruth Thomson was hurriedly checking her medical bag before leaving for the surgery. She called to Leon, "Anything of importance?"

"I'm not sure! Perhaps you should take a look at this before you go." Leon Thomson held out the sheet of expensive writing paper with the neatly written message. He didn't know as yet that two others had just received the exact same letter.

"In your best interests, huh," she sniggered and shook her head. "I suppose you noticed the invitation doesn't include me. What game is he playing now?"

She pursed her lips and made thoughtful kinds of clicking sounds with her tongue, shrugged her shoulders indifferently and picked up her medical bag. "Well, the mind may boggle, but I'll try to curb my curiosity. I'll be home straight after morning surgery. In case I'm held up, Leon, could you pick up one or two groceries?"

"No problem. Did you make a list?"

"It's on the kitchen table." Ruth was halfway to the door when she turned back. "Just a thought, Leon, but do you think you're the only one to get an invitation?"

"I was thinking along the same lines myself. I can't make up my mind if it really could be something important or just Keller trying a little male bonding."

"Male bonding, huh, after the two years of misery that obnoxious pig and the brats from hell has put everyone through?"

"Let's face it, Ruth, he hardly qualifies for a neighbour of the year award."

Ruth stopped halfway through turning the door handle. "I'll second that," she called back.

The incident with his car on the day they arrived was still very much alive in Ruth Thomson's mind. It still bugged her. It always would until the insufferable prick did one decent thing in his life and got out of Fairfield.

Vince Robb trudged wearily downstairs, picking up the mail on his way to the kitchen. How he wished Saturdays could be like old times. A lie in followed by a spot of gardening: and then the best part of the day, Emily and him lazily listening to their favourite music while sipping glasses of fine wine.

These bouts of nostalgia were becoming more and more frequent. He and Emily were in their autumn years, no longer youthful but not really old. Then after more than twenty years of marriage, Emily discovered the local gym. She became obsessed with tightening what she sorrowfully called 'the saggy bits' and recovering a youthful figure. Vince suddenly came into the category of lonely and alone fitness club widower.

It had been almost a year now since she took out membership to the gym. Vince thought—he hoped it was just a fad, a passing fancy she'd eventually tire of. He surmised that, Emily being of a certain age, it possibly could be something to do with that time in a woman's life—the dreaded menopause. Yes, when Emily started all this nonsense he'd read up on the signs and symptoms. Mood swings, hanging onto youth and for many menopausal dream catchers…toy-boys.

The last couple of months had created a dreadful feeling that his wife was ready and willing to abandon him and the wedded bliss they once had. Their marriage was now an empty shell without that spark, the lustre that once lit up their lives. He knew it was time to let go, to let her go and this was what urged Vince to take the final, painful steps. He had tried to find the right moment, the words to tell Emily that he had made a momentous, if rather extreme decision and after another sleepless night his mind was made up. It had to be today. The misery was too much to bear, and he couldn't go on any longer.

The letter lay open on the coffee table where Vince had left it for her to find. Emily read it when she came downstairs and gave a scornful snigger. "What's this invite for you alone all about?"

"*I* know as much as *you* do." Vince was all acid tongued and snappy. Making a fateful decision could do that to a man.

"You're not going?" It wasn't as much a question as an extremely blunt order.

"Well, pardon me, but I didn't realise I had to ask *your* permission." He bristled and the anger and hurt returned. "Look, just you go to your gym and forget all about me...you know," he said sarcastically, "the way you've been forgetting about me since taking out a membership to that place." His face was stony and stern. Their marriage had always been one of give and take until...This was a day Vince never thought he'd see. "Oh, and by the way I've decided to put the house up for sale." He was so composed and matter of fact it took Emily's breath away.

"What? Why? I...I don't understand, Vince." She was more than a little concerned now.

"Then I'll make it simple." It touched his heart the way she stood there in crumpled pyjamas, her hair all tousled, almost child-like. He hated being mean and spiteful, but it had to be said. "You've made it painfully clear that you no longer want to spend more time than you have to with me, therefore, I think we should make it a permanent arrangement. Don't you?"

It was an irrevocably harsh statement that came like an unexpected kick in the guts and Emily just couldn't grasp the full meaning. "Make what permanent? You're talking in riddles, Vince, and I haven't a clue what you're talking about."

"I'm trying to tell you I'm also starting divorce proceedings, which I'm sure you'll be delighted about." Vince ignored the shattered gasp. "You'll be free,

Emily, to work on that perfect body you strive for and spend your time with…whoever he is." The wry snort was packed with meaning.

The agonised look that distorted her face rather took Vince aback. He had expected another kind of reaction, relief maybe…elation surely, but not this hurt and silent shock as if she were waiting for the other shoe to drop.

Oh, to turn the clock back to the early years of their marriage when he would wake in the morning and just lay there watching her sleep, snoring softly in that state of unawareness. Unaware of how much he loved her. Then, as if she sensed his gaze, Emily's eyelids would flutter open, and she'd reach for him. Now, Keller's weird invitation for him alone was like a testimony that their marriage was over.

And then she found the will to speak. "You think that I…that I'd even contemplate?" Emily was aghast that he could blithely sit there and infer that she was unfaithful. "That's a cruel lie, Vince." Tears rolled down her rapidly paling cheeks. "Did you actually think I've been *enjoying* putting myself through a rigorous exercise regime at my time of life?"

"Oh, get off your high-horse and admit the truth."

Emily had smarted a bit at what was as good as an accusation. Now she was so raging mad both barrels were about to be fired.

"I'm on my high horse alright, Vince Robb. It's all been for *your* benefit—*for you"* she yelled irately. "It's true I wanted to be desirable, but you're the one I wanted to desire me, which I might add you haven't been doing a lot of lately," and she stamped her foot to add to the effect of her annoyance.

This wasn't at all what Vince had expected. It's true he had waited on the day Emily finally confessed something that would rip his heart out. It was true he had thought the worst, but now, seeing the pain in her eyes and those words, passionate and pleading. Like a mist had suddenly lifted it was all too clear. It wasn't Emily that was at fault…it was *him.* He had got the wrong end of the stick. He had been the one who pushed her further and further away. Emily was now giving up her secret that all she had been guilty of was simply being a woman trying to win back the husband she was so fearfully sure had lost interest in her.

With the weight of guilt on him, Vince watched her tantrum—but from a safe distance. "I'm to blame?" He asked, although it wasn't so much a question as an admission.

Emily huffed indignantly. "Oh lord, now you're going to play the martyr."

He was half laughing and half crying. "Not a martyr, Emily, a faithless fool. We should have thrashed this out at the start, fought like hell then tumbled into bed to make up. Just like we used to in the early years, remember?"

Emily raised a hand to her face, pressing the knuckles hard against her mouth trying to cover a secret smile that remembering those times always brought.

"Can't you see what's happened, Emily?"

"What?"

"Our life got so comfortable and content we forgot what passion was. I've seen you at your best and I've seen you at your worst, but don't you know my heart still pounds every time I look at you? I don't give a rat's arse if your figure is matronly, I'm not that shallow. As far as I'm concerned, you'll always be the most beautiful woman in the world."

"And I've never met the man who could lace your boots." Emily's eyes were suddenly sparkling and dewy, "So o o…" she said, slyly sidling towards Vince, "instead of killing myself at that damned gym every day, is it possible we can go back to taking those lovely long walks together like we used to?"

"Yes, oh yes please," Vince begged, "and maybe even a teensy tiff now and then, just for the hell of making up."

"Well, since this is a time for truths," Emily said. "I got it into my head you'd found someone else." She blushed at the telling of this shameful thought. "Now as it turns out, you were thinking the same about me. I suppose it's true what they say about no fool like an old fool. Just tell me one thing, Vince. Would you really have let me go that easily?"

"No!" Vince said adamantly. "When it came to the bit, I sure as hell would have fought tooth and nail for you." They fell onto the sofa, laughing together at the infantile foolishness of it all and the sheer relief of freedom from anxiety.

Crossed wires and cross purposes, that's what it had all been about. Emily thinking that Vince's love had died and Vince thinking Emily had tired of him. They had stopped communicating and in an odd sort of way, it was Keller's silly letter that forced them to communicate. In so doing, they had opened the door to truth and saved their marriage from ending up on the rocks.

"What about this?" Emily held out the invitation. "Will you go?"

"Yes, but as a happily married couple, we'll *both* accept the invitation."

"Well hooray for that! Whatever the slob has to say, he can say it to both our faces."

Chapter Seven

It was a strange sight that Sunday afternoon. I watched from my bedroom window as the three couples emerged from their respective houses almost simultaneously. Pleasantries were exchanged, yet suspiciously since they were all walking in the same direction, straight towards the Keller house. At some point, one of them must have asked the question on all their lips because all six heads nodded at the same time, like a row of these little nodding toys, you see in the back of a car.

High noon and gunfight at the OK corral rolled into one, that's what it was like. There was no rush to reach number eleven. They sauntered together in a group conversation, but with one important question in mind. Why had they all received the exact same letter? They each had not only a curious need to know, but the right to an explanation as to what urgency demanded their attention and their presence at the Keller's house.

Some intuition or sixth sense told me there was going to be fireworks. I held that thought and went downstairs.

Keller was momentarily surprised when he opened the door, and then without one of his typically rude comments, silently he ushered them into the lounge.

"Can I get you a drink?" He asked, "Tea or coffee?" His mouth twisted in a sick sort of smile but there was no humour in his eyes. "I think you'll find it wasn't such a good idea bringing your lady wives to hear what I have to say. Under the circumstances, perhaps you'll feel the need for something a bit stronger than coffee."

"This isn't a social visit, so dispense with the niceties if you don't mind and get to the point." Vince had made up his mind long before this hour came, he wasn't going to put up with being side-tracked or intimidated.

If it truly was only their best interests Keller had in mind, they each wanted to know only one thing—where did this sudden change of heart come from? Why the good neighbour now? Since that first day they arrived, Keller had oozed acrimony. It was highly unlikely this particular leopard would suddenly change its spots.

At that moment, Daisy Keller hurried into the sitting room. "Perhaps the girls would like to have coffee with me while you boys talk." She wrung her hands nervously which only increased their suspicion that something rotten was afoot.

"I think I speak for all of us when I say we're quite happy to sit here," Doctor Thomson said flatly.

Emily and Harriet nodded their agreement. Almost robotically, the three women slowly and deliberately lowered their very tense bodies side by side onto the sofa.

"Very well, if that's how you want to play it," Keller turned to Daisy and for the briefest moment there was the hint of a reassuring smile. "You can bring Paris in now," he told her.

Paris sauntered into the room wearing a self-satisfied smile and not much else. Harriet looked like she was ready and willing to scratch her eyes out. After all was said and done, she was the one Paris had antagonised the most with her constant attempts to seduce George.

"What part does *she* have to play in this charade?" Harriet blazed, and for a moment it looked as if she really might just leap from the sofa and punch the smirk from Paris's face. And then curtly she said, "By the way, did you know any vet would give you pills for a **bitch** in heat?"

It was Daisy's anguished gasp and sob that really angered Keller and brought the blood rushing to his face. He was ready with an equally uncivil reply.

"And cats too I believe, *sour puss*." He stared venomously at Harriet. "Now, since you *ladies* weren't invited perhaps you wouldn't mind keeping your mouths shut and your opinions to yourself for a moment because my daughter has something to say." Keller stood side by side with Paris and put his arm around her shoulder. "Don't be afraid, sweetheart. Tell them what you told us."

There was no trembling, no wide-eyed distress: Paris just came right out with it. "I'm pregnant and one of you is the father." Paris Keller looked as if she'd taken them all on in battle…and won. She stood there with glory in her eyes and an undefeated twist of her mouth, but not the slightest hint of a blush on those sun-tanned cheeks.

A surge of shocked surprise filled the room. Vince was the only one to remain calm. All along, he'd suspected something foul and had mentally prepared himself for whatever it was. Although he would later admit to this being the one thing he hadn't expected. Vince raised himself slowly from the gaudy red velvet chair, glanced briefly at Keller then turned to Paris. His narrowed eyes stared fully accusingly at her, yet with a kind of concern.

"Don't you realise how bad this thing you're doing is?" Vince asked, and a strange, almost pitying look flitted across his face. His voice wasn't filled with anger as you'd expect, only sadness. "You are threatening to destroy people's lives on a whim and for what, fun? Revenge maybe at the audacity of being rejected when you offered your, shall we say, *services* so willingly?"

George Granger squirmed uncomfortably. He would never forget that embarrassing encounter with Paris Keller. Neither would anyone else who saw and heard the abominable way she propositioned the good-looking man who caught her eye and took her fancy. And then that way she shamelessly offered herself?

In a profoundly patronising way, Vince concluded, "I'm truly sorry for you, *little girl*. I also pity you for having to do such an evil thing like this for excitement."

Paris's face paled and there was no longer any sign of that malice which was common to those dark and sinful eyes. And for the first time too there was no sultry pout and seductive come-hither look, only fear. "I'm…I'm…" she could only whimper. Vince's blaming reproach had truly curbed that adolescent impudence.

Vince showed no pity or guilt, only a determination to speak his piece. "I never laid a hand on you, but you already know that, and I have a sneaking suspicion the same applies to the others. Do your worst. I'm prepared to take every test available because I'm innocent, as you well know. And now my wife and I are going home to enjoy our day of rest." He took Emily's hand and then turned to face Keller. In not so much a threatening, but definitely assertive way he looked the man straight in the eye and said, "I'll see you in court."

"I think it's time we all left." Leon stopped right in front of Keller and following Vince's example, he too looked him in the eye. He shook his head with such spitting disgust it actually made Keller flinch with what could only be termed embarrassment. Then he turned his attention to Paris and in the same disgusted way said, "What a sad excuse for a girl you are. Did you wake up one morning and think what fun it would be to ruin some lives and then simply pick three names out of a hat?"

"That wouldn't surprise me in the least," said George Granger with spiteful revulsion. "Perhaps she's hoping one of us—or maybe all of us will offer to pay for her bastard's upkeep." And then as an afterthought he twisted the knife a little more. "Perhaps I was too much of a gentleman before, of course with your upbringing, I doubt very much if you would recognise a real gentleman, so I'll say what I have been longing to say since the day you arrived. *I personally wouldn't touch you with a ten-foot barge pole."*

As he listened to the cruel truth about his cherished daughter, for what had to be the first time in his life, Keller was at that moment robbed of speech as well as that ever readiness to lash out in anger which was his trademark.

"I'd like to say something before we all leave." Ruth Thomson waited until she had everyone's attention. "Now, you're a solicitor, Vince, and I'm a doctor, so between us we can start the ball rolling to clear your good names. I don't think these people have stopped to consider the power of our judicial system, but they will get the full force of the law when we begin litigation. You may not be aware of it, Mr Keller, but slander is a criminal offence in this country and your daughter will pay the price for her false allegations and her silly adolescent fantasies. Good day to you."

From the window, Keller watched that small band of neighbours, united in righteous anger, go into the solicitor, Vince Robb's house. Keller had expected a different kind of showdown, one where he cracked the whip while their morale…well, just cracked once they realised what the meeting was about. But this insurgence…and there was no trace of guilt in any of them at all. They were all taken by surprise alright and it wasn't surprise at Paris being pregnant either. It was indignation that they were being accused of something they'd never dream of doing.

"What have you done?" He furiously growled at Paris.

"It wasn't supposed to go this far, Daddy. I only meant it as a joke to wipe the smiles off their faces for the way they looked down their nose at us. It's true I flirted, but that's all that happened. Please, Daddy don't let them put me in jail." The frightened whining and pleading for mercy and salvation from the law was so different from the Paris who invited romance and passion with her eyes, her lips, and every seductive movement.

"If it wasn't one of them…who…?"

"It was Manuel!" Paris threw herself onto the sofa, buried her face in a cushion and sobbed bitterly at the shame of her deceit.

"Manuel? Not that fucking Spanish waiter from Jardine's restaurant? Christ almighty, I should have seen this coming. The way you were always disappearing to the ladies every ten minutes and him going missing at the same time. Just tell me one thing. Did he force you"

"No, no Daddy," she wailed pitifully. "I love Manuel and he loves me."

Beads of perspiration trickled over the protruding veins in Keller's temples. He took one look at Daisy crying like her heart would break and it was the last straw.

"I'm getting the first flight over there and then I'm going to hang him up by the thumbs until he rots."

"Wait, John, wait and think for a moment, but not with your fists." Daisy put her arms around Keller's waist and laid her head on his chest. "First you have to write letters of apology to those three men and then…"

"And then what?"

"Put this house up for sale. When that's done, we're all going to Spain." She pulled away and looked up at Keller with adoration in her soft blue eyes. Words of comfort were what he most needed now. "It'll be nice to spend time at the villa and relax round the pool. We should grab it while we can because when this little one arrives…Surely you haven't forgotten what it was like to have a baby in the house?"

Daisy watched the protruding veins disappear and Keller's moist eyes smile softly. To the outside world, he was this big, rough and ready hard man, but she remembered what he was like with his babies. The way he cried when those powerful, calloused hands held Paris for the first time. John Keller was a big softie at heart.

To say that the Kellers' stay on Juniper Drive had been a bumpy ride for the residents was quite simply a euphemism for 'hell on earth.' Therefore, it was with a little scepticism and a great deal of curiosity they watched the 'FOR SALE' sign go up at number eleven.

There were those who didn't really want the Keller's to sell up and go, for there hadn't been a dull moment since their arrival. There were also others who couldn't wait to see the back of them and an end to hostilities.

The three letters were delivered at about the same time as the black Jaguar drove out of Juniper Drive and Daisy blew me a kiss as they passed. I waved back, but little did I know this would be the last time I would set eyes on this woman who had shown me nothing but love and kindness. To this day, I still hold a place in my heart for Daisy Keller.

The written apologies from John Keller were sufficient to appease the wrath and emotional anguish caused by Paris's accusation and Vince, George and Leon graciously agreed to let it die a death. Not that it took much soul searching when they read those letters.

Dear neighbour,

It is with a great deal of pain in my heart that I write these words, not pain for myself but for the good people I have wronged.

My daughter has admitted to her mother and to me what she did was a silly, but nevertheless malicious prank and I apologise wholeheartedly for her disgraceful behaviour and hope you can find it in your heart to forgive a man who stands guilty of loving and trusting his only daughter too much and who will give the same love to her child, our grandchild.

We may not have been the sort of people you want in your community, but I can put my hand on my heart and say without fear of contradiction that we are good and decent people who only wanted to offer the hand of friendship.

I sincerely hope the new owners of the house are more to your liking.

John Keller.

If anyone had doubts or reservations about the manner in which the Keller's had been hounded out of Fairfield, it was too late. They were gone for good, and no amount of pathetic, apologetic excuses could alter the fact that snobbery alone had been at the root of everything.

There was an important lesson to be learned here. Wait until you know people before you judge them.

Chapter Eight

People from all walks of life came and went, looking, savouring and the hearts of all who saw number eleven were lost to its splendour and elegance. It was little wonder so much interest had been stirred since the flamboyant advertisement took up half a page in the property guide. But the Keller's were in no rush to sell. From a financial viewpoint, the money was of little consequence to John Keller. He had the wherewithal, and he was prepared to sit tight and hold out for top dollar.

Dad said you could separate the time wasters from the true house hunters by the car they drove. This intrigued me. Not so much that there were those who actually viewed other people's houses as a sort of pastime, but this concept that cars maketh the man and that the size of a person's bank account was reflected in the size, make and model of his car. So, I watched every car that drove into Juniper, but to be honest, I was more interested in the passengers and whether or not they were to be our new neighbours.

It was kind of exciting to watch a car roll up and wonder if they were to be the ones. I think in a way I was hoping that someone like Amy would move in because I still missed her so much. Or maybe even someone like Daisy Keller. How my sweet tooth still missed those daily chocolate bars.

It was an extraordinary cast of characters who came to view number eleven Juniper Drive. There were people who (I must stress that this was my mother's delicate turn of phrase, not my words) looked like they didn't have a pot to piss in. Of course, when she caught me earwigging with hope of an explanation shining in my eyes and questions ready to drip from my tongue as to the meaning of her colourful description, I was warned never to repeat her words to anyone. I think it was shades of John Keller, remembering that although a person looked poor, it didn't necessarily follow that they were.

There were young, there were old, there were the grimy and there were the overly grand. "Fur coat and no knickers," Mum said. What I hoped for was a family with kids my age.

Weeks went by and then it happened. The estate agent's car drove up the street and stopped outside number eleven and right behind it a long, sleek and top of the range Toyota. A well-dressed man got out of the Toyota, but the darkened, smoked glass windows obscured my vision, and I couldn't tell if anyone else was in the car.

The potential house buyer glanced casually at his surroundings and then walked to where the estate agent stood and talked for a minute or two. He didn't as much as speak or even glance at the obscured passengers in the car, only signal with nothing more than an indifferent crook of the finger for them to follow. The passenger doors opened, and a woman and two girls stepped from the car. They trotted at a distance behind him like minions. This was my first visual encounter with Richard LaVell, and I trembled without reason.

The woman was petite and pretty, with auburn hair that glistened in the sunlight. The two girls who followed her were about my age. They were so like their mother, but a mirror image of each other. Meredith and Maxine LaVell were identical twins.

All the other house hunters took only twenty or thirty minutes to view. Of course, this was mainly because estate agents have an instinct for picking out the time wasters and the just plain nosey. These types are given short shrift and a hurried excursion is the best for which they can hope.

I had closely watched the mixed responses. Some would stand for a moment outside looking wistfully back before getting into their cars and driving away. The unaffordable is like the proverbial carrot in front of the donkey, tasty, but out of reach. One thing was sure, there weren't many who came out of number eleven looking disinterested or displeased.

Quite often, I saw people who had already viewed the house come back for a second look. All those smitten, hopeless yet ever hopefuls were possibly clutching onto some dim possibility that with a little friendly persuasion the exorbitant price might be brought down to a more realistic figure. Dad said Keller was a hard man to bargain with and wouldn't budge on price. If anyone foolishly thought they could haggle with Keller's agent to accept a lower offer which was within their means, they were in for a big disappointment.

"What on earth is he doing?"

Ooh, something had irked Mum. I could tell by that abrasive quality in her tone and when I looked, the man who I'd later come to know as Richard LaVell was walking slowly down one side of the street, scrutinising every property. And then he walked up the other side doing exactly the same. My mother was positively blue in the face with indignation.

"The cheek of it," and she sucked in her breath through clenched teeth. "*We* are being inspected if you don't mind."

After more than two hours, the door opened and out they came. The estate agent beamed and vigorously shook hands with Mr LaVell.

"Looks like he made a sale," Dad said. "One good thing, they look like they have a bit more class than…you know who."

They were talking in adult speak again, but I wasn't stupid. I knew they were referring to the Keller family. I could understand them not mentioning names in case I repeated what they said to the 'you know who' in question, but since they were in Spain that would be a bit difficult. I was also a tad disgruntled at being treated like the eyes and ears of the world: the one who heard all and told all.

It seemed this was another cash transaction and without mortgage arrangements etc. the house purchase was signed, sealed and delivered instantly. One week later, all eyes were fixed on number eleven as painters and decorators moved in and went to work on the house. Mr LaVell came two or three times a day to check on the transformation. That was the one thing that struck me as strange. When our lounge was being re-decorated, Mum was the one who acted as gaffer. I came to the conclusion that perhaps Mrs LaVell didn't like the smell of paint and that was why she stayed away. One of my friends at school came out in blotches if she smelled new paint. She was allergic and perhaps Mrs LaVell had the same allergy.

They moved in almost unnoticeably. There were no shouts of, 'watch that,' or 'put this here and put that there,' and no packing cases littering the walkways. This was an exercise in how to move house with minimum disruption and maximum efficiency. An orderly, well-executed move from one house to another.

Harriet leaned on our front gate chatting to Mum. Well, they weren't actually chatting about anything in particular, it was more an excuse to see what kind of furniture the LaVell's owned. Mum maintained you could tell a lot about a person by their taste in furnishings.

"Just look at that gorgeous suite," Harriet said with impassioned envy as the huge, pale cream sofa was carefully manoeuvred inside. "And isn't it classy too?"

"The bedroom furniture and that display unit are positively breath-taking," Mum sighed. "Everything looks imported, don't you think?"

"Yes!" Harriet said dreamily, "I wonder if they'll have a housewarming. I'd love to have a proper look."

"Mm," my envious mum sighed, "perhaps they will. We can but hope that invitations will soon be coming our way."

By the time the removal van drove away, I was as jumpy as a kitten. I supposed it would only be a nice gesture if I introduced myself and offered to give the twins a Cook's tour of the neighbourhood. Alas, Mum said I had to be less impetuous and give them time to get settled, so I waited all of thirty minutes before grasping the brass doorknocker, rattling it twice and anxiously waiting for an answer.

"Hello, dear," Mrs LaVell spoke in a soft, almost melodic voice with a twang I didn't recognise: Australian perhaps or maybe American. I didn't know, but I'd sure make it my business to find out. "Is there something I can do for you?" It didn't escape my attention that she was edgy and unsmiling, almost hostile even. I was old enough to know this wasn't the way to treat a visitor.

"I'm Judy Vernon, we live at number four, and I was wondering if perhaps the…the twins…"

"Meredith and Maxine," she kinda filled in the blanks and waited to hear me out.

"I thought maybe it would be nice if someone showed them round and since I've lived here all my life."

Without as much as waiting for an invitation, like I'd been taught to do, I had blatantly crossed the threshold and was standing in the hallway beside Mrs LaVell without even realising I'd done it. That was the moment I knew they weren't my kind of people. It was polite and neighbourly to invite a visitor in, but Mrs LaVell rather warily and deliberately barred my entry into the living-room. I had after all come in peace, offering the hand of friendship. She was nothing like Amy with her welcoming smile. This woman wore a guarded and somewhat unfriendly frown.

Mr LaVell in particular was neither pleasant nor hospitable. He was a dour, angry looking man who stamped into the hall to see who had come to call at such an inopportune time. I could only stand motionless, for in that instant I felt threatened at the look on that scowling, thunderous face.

He waved his hand as if shooing a fly and said, "We've no time for this, Jean. Please see her out."

Like a dream that's forgotten the moment you wake, for a mini second, some kind of vision flashed before my eyes, too fast for me to see. Whatever that frightening sense of something was, it sent shivers up my spine. I didn't know what or why I was filled with such inexplicable terror. It was the strangest feeling, I was there—but it wasn't today it was another time. The sensation came and then was gone in the blinking of an eye. I didn't know it at the time, but this was the first real indication of what many called second sight. The doorway to a dormant sense had begun to open.

"It's time you were going home, little girl," LaVell told me sternly and when he put a hand on my shoulder, more to push me out rather than guide me to the door, that touch of his hand started a kind of trembling fit. I could feel the scalding heat of horror and fear, but it was without substance or meaning for me.

"The child…she only wants to make friends with our girls, Richard…" Mrs LaVell spoke hesitantly as if talking back was defiance that might bring some kind of punishment. She seemed…scared, swallowing hard and trying to force a smile.

His look, cold and steely, held no sign or even the slightest trace of affection. "You know my rules, Jean, no socialising," LaVell sniped. "The next thing I know neighbours will be trotting in and out of my house any time they feel fit, and I will not have my privacy invaded."

If this unsociable attitude were anything to go by there would most certainly be no housewarming. How disappointing it was going to be for Mum and Harriet.

My exit was hurried and forceful *and*…I hadn't even been offered refreshments. When Amy lived here, I had carte blanche to come and go and my visits were always accepted without even a hint of huffing annoyance. Not like these people who shuffled me out onto the street like an unwelcome intruder. Did they think I didn't notice?

In a situation like this, there was only one thing that helped…saying a swear word and the only one I could think of right then was, 'bitch,' so I said it…but under my breath.

I took a moment to look back to where Meredith and Maxine stood holding hands. They smiled wistfully and I just knew they wanted to skip with me down the street and play in our garden. I waved forlornly now that my hope of friendship and fun had been dashed. Richard LaVell wasn't just a disciplinarian; he was a tyrant and a bully, and I learned an important lesson that day. If his car was in the drive, I didn't go anywhere near number eleven.

That night I awoke screaming in terror and I couldn't explain my fear. Mum held me tightly in her arms to quell my hysterics, telling me over and over that she and Dad were there, and no one could harm me. But every time, I closed my eyes, I was consumed by the darkness of some unseen yet unspeakable horror. In this vision, nightmare or whatever it had been, all I could remember was being in a thick dark mist and some terrible thing was happening within that icy fog. The mist seemed to be crushing the breath from my body and I knew that if it cleared the most terrifying sight would fill my eyes and chill my very soul. The following morning when I awoke the sky was clear and bright and that suffocating nightmare which had haunted my sleep was forgotten.

At quarter to nine, Mum kissed my cheek and said, "Time for school, my darling. The bad dreams are all gone."

The pathway at the top of Juniper that skirted the estate was used by almost all the kids as a shortcut to and from school. It was the same pathway I had walked with Amy so many times when she took me to school and brought me home. The edge of the path was thick with lupin which had grown from seeds cast and carried on the wind. They had taken root, spread and multiplied over the years. Amy told me they were only weeds, but I loved the vibrant colours.

That Monday morning with my satchel on my back and fresh ribbons in my hair, I walked towards the path. Meredith and Maxine LaVell came out of the house wearing Fairfield High uniforms.

"I didn't know you were going to Fairfield High! Oh goodie, we can go to school and come home together," I called excitedly to them. "C'mon, I'll show you the quick way." I was filled with childish fervour at the prospect of new friend's right here in my very own street.

Like two frightened kittens they clung together. Their eyes darted scarily from me to the open door, watching nervously at their father walking towards us. His face still wore that engraved look of belligerence.

LaVell glanced warningly at the twins, then menacingly at me. "Where do you think you're going?" He snapped in that impolite, arrogant way I would come to know and hate.

"To school," I answered, pointing to the pathway.

"Judy offered to show us the quick way Father. May we walk with her please?"

Their eyes were sorrowful, loveless pools as they pleaded to be treated like normal children. Meredith and Maxine LaVell were bereft of fatherly affection, and it showed.

"You certainly may not! Sisters are company enough for each other. I have given you a strict code of conduct to observe and I expect you to adhere to my rules. I will as always drive you to school."

Rooted to the spot, I stared and stared at the man who I had encountered only twice, brief encounters, but both times I had felt like a fly caught in the spider's web. Yet the fear in me wasn't for my own safety but for the safety of Meredith and Maxine. It was impossible for me to explain the gnawing feeling of danger within me. A weird and totally absurd sixth sense that some kind of peril was linked to them, and their father is the only way I could account for this fearful sensation.

"You're not a nice man," I told LaVell defiantly. My neck strained to look up at him and for a second or so I saw in his eyes a definite look of either dread or alarm. Without another word, he pushed Meredith and Maxine towards the car, and I was left standing alone as they drove away.

I was too young, too naïve and I couldn't find the words to ask someone, my parents, my teacher, my priest, in fact any adult who could explain to me where these strange and hostile visions came from or what they meant.

I was troubled and confused without knowing why, so I made up my mind to do what had to be done. That evening I just came right out with it and told my parents, "I don't like Mr LaVell and I told him he's not a nice man."

Mum did that wagging finger thing when she wanted to stress a point. "It's wrong to judge someone without knowing them," she warned me with a smile, only the smile was nervy, like she was having a sudden bout of the shivers. "Is there a reason why you don't like him, Judy?" She nudged Dad and then said, "Tell me, Judy, what made you say he's not a nice man anyway?"

The only way I could describe my father's reaction at that very minute was—panic stricken. The words were a quiver in his throat, sort of croaky when he said, "Judy, my precious, did he say something or touch you in a way that's wrong?"

"He told me to go home, and I'd only just got there and then this morning he wouldn't allow the twins to walk to school with me even though they asked him nicely and…"

"Whoa there: if you keep talking so fast, you'll have no breath left. Now from the beginning, and slowly please."

Dad put his arm around me, and I immediately felt protected. I began telling them everything, emphasising the fact that I hadn't been made welcome in their house. At first, they looked amused, like they saw a funny side to my story.

Dad said, "It's an exhausting business moving into a new house, Judy. They were probably just tired."

It was when I described the dark feelings when LaVell was within two feet of me their expression changed to one of alarm.

"I think it's time we had a word with Mr LaVell," Mum said through clenched teeth. "He's not putting the fear of Christ into my child and getting away with it."

Although he himself didn't have an argumentative nature, Dad could see through people. He knew how minds worked. "Well, we're not going up there to be intimidated on their home ground," he said assertively. "You sit and calm yourself while I phone LaVell. If he's a man at all, he'll do the right thing and come down to discuss the matter with us right here."

I saw the anger rising in my father and reproached myself for starting this and perhaps saying too much. Although I couldn't begin to imagine exactly what was going through their mind, one thing was sure. My parents were now thinking the worst.

Surprisingly, he came. Richard LaVell looked meek and mild as he sat in our lounge offering platitudes to excuse his behaviour and begging forgiveness if he had caused offence. I listened from the hallway to the mealy-mouthed explanation he gave.

"To let you understand, a few years ago my wife had a breakdown and began drinking rather heavily. At times, for no apparent reason she…flies into a fit of temper and has to be…restrained," LaVell said in a martyred, whining way.

It was patently clear that La Vell's bleating failed to either move or impress my father. "Oh, really," Dad said. "And you feel that gives you the right to bully and frighten the wits out of other little girls whose sole objective is to make friends with your own daughters?"

"I certainly do not!" His answer was sharply defensive. "My reluctance to allow Meredith and Maxine to make friends isn't based on any kind of sinister motive. I simply can't take the chance of Jean having an episode with other children in the house."

Mum clasped a hand over her mouth in horror. "You poor man," she wailed. But then again this was a woman who would believe there were fairies at the bottom of the garden if it were told to her with even the slightest credibility and oh how credible this man sounded.

"There is treatment for mental illness, you know. Or haven't you sought medical advice?" Dad's manner said it all. He was in his own way telling LaVell if he cared, really cared about his wife, finding the proper treatment was the best and only course of action. "Physical restraint each time your poor wife lashes out in frustration at her own ineptitude and shortcomings isn't the way."

"I hear what you're saying, and I understand why you may think I'm lax in my duty to help Jean, but I can't just watch her being taken away and locked up in one of those places for the mentally ill."

The pathetic crocodile tears were already in place and ready to flow. LaVell was a man of the world, he had pushed me quite forcibly and he knew that was wrong. He was trying now to appease the situation by gaining a sympathy vote. Richard LaVell would soon find out that crossing swords with my father over family issues was an exceedingly bad idea.

"Alcoholism and mental illness aren't a criminal offence and doctors no longer use barbaric treatments on mentally ill patients." My father stayed coldly unflinching. "Your wife would not be locked up in what archaically used to be called a *snake pit*. These days we are more understanding and perhaps you should be too." It was touché, Dad! The smarm didn't wash with him. "I can put you in touch with an excellent psychiatrist." This was a challenge, not an offer and LaVell immediately caught the inference.

From where I sat at the foot of the stairs, I observed everything through the half open door. LaVell hastily and brusquely concluded the meeting with an angry retort about people not being able to mind their own business. As he walked by the balustrade, his hand brushed against my face and it happened again, the nightmarish thing I could sense but not see.

"Judy! Judy!" My mother was gently shaking me from my trance and all I could do to feel safe was cling to her until my heart stopped pounding. Mum assumed I had fallen asleep sitting there and I didn't make her any the wiser about what had really happened. She would either misunderstand or tell me I was imagining things anyway.

My parents never ever browbeat me or made demands, all they asked was that I be sensible in my approach to life. They instilled in me the necessity not to repeat everything I heard and if I harmed no one then hopefully no one would harm me. It was a simple philosophy, one that I would carry with me through life.

It had been made painfully clear that Mr LaVell didn't appreciate me socialising with his daughters, so I made a point of standing at our gate until his car passed before walking to the path that led to school. That way, the twins wouldn't have to employ the contemptuous attitude taught by their father and hurtfully ignore my attempt at friendship.

It puzzled me, this insistence on segregation. They (or rather he) didn't welcome any kind of social intercourse. What next, a plaque to say, *no visitors*? Perhaps, a big sign that said abandon hope all ye who enter here would be more apt.

Number eleven had become like an island amid the community where callers were neither welcomed nor tolerated. And then for good measure, LaVell had a sort of palisade erected. The house was now surrounded by fancy swirls of shiny black iron that to me looked insurmountable: even the gate, tall and austere like LaVell, commanded seclusion. I wondered if these wrought iron rails were meant to keep people out—or his family in.

Chapter Nine

Mum's birthday came four weeks after mine, the first of May, and as usual, she insisted on no fuss saying, "I'd rather just forget about the all too rapid passing of the years, Ralph, if you don't mind." She repeated this same thing every birthday.

Dad just laughed and told her, "I don't mind at all, in fact, I'd be only too happy to forget…if you're prepared to forget about presents, that is."

But that was a different kettle of fish. "Don't you dare," she warned him.

"Would I ever?" Dad laughed even louder and grabbed mum, dancing her around the room and singing, *"I've arranged a surprise for you."*

"What is it? Tell me," she pleaded.

"Mr DeCorsa has reserved a table for you at his restaurant and I've also asked Harriet, Ruth and Emily to share a birthday lunch with you—my treat of course."

"You are a clever, clever man," she said with a little mousy squeak and wrapped her arms around his neck. It was a hug of gratitude, a thank you, not one that made me blush thank goodness. I found it *so* embarrassing when they went all gooey.

"Ah but that's not all," Dad said gallantly. "We're throwing a party on Saturday to celebrate your birthday and I've organised everything, caterers, drinks the works. All you have to do, my darling, is relax and enjoy it."

I watched them, happy and carefree, waltzing around the room and I could feel the abounding love. But more than love and adoration, my parents had respect, one for the other, along with a commitment to always do what was right and decent for each other and for me and my brother.

That day, the LaVell's moved into number eleven, I took it for granted they would be as friendly and welcoming as all our neighbours, past and present were. But right from that very first encounter, I felt something was missing and now, seeing the way my parents were with each other I knew what it was—respect—LaVell didn't have a shred of respect for his wife and family. But there was another thing that worried me. I had never seen three more frightened people than Mrs LaVell and her daughters.

That evening, I heard my parents talking and although I could hear the chatter and giggling as Mum related every detail of her girly luncheon party, well, I wasn't really concentrating and hanging onto her every word. Getting my homework finished was my first priority.

Mum obviously had a fun day the way she talked about her lunch at the DeCorsa. She spoke all fluttery and excited about her birthday treat. I just knew her cheeks would be pink and glowing, eyes moist and dewy and hands emphasising every word. My ears pricked to the sound of pure delight and excitement that raised the tone of her voice.

"And, Mr DeCorsa," she gave one of those elated gasping sounds, "what a kind and generous man, Ralph. He put two bottles of the finest wine on the table—on the house as an extra birthday treat."

I could almost taste her elation. This unexpected, pampering gift had obviously touched her heart.

"What a really nice and caring thing to do," Dad said, "I must remember to thank him."

It was then her tone changed and my mum's excitement became more secretive in a, *can you believe this,* kind of way. The sudden lowering of her voice stirred my natural curiosity and once again my ears pricked. I dropped my pencil and crept to the vantage spot at the foot of the stairs. If there had been more to that lunch than three courses, I wanted to know.

"It wasn't nice to watch," Mum said, dramatically holding a hand to her heart. "I was shocked! We all were to see the way LaVell behaved with that woman. We saw them, yet although we were in plain view, LaVell and the fancy bit didn't see us, they were so engrossed in each other."

A whole new avenue of imaginative thoughts opened up for me on hearing those words my mother spoke. Now, as I tell this story, you're probably starting to see me as a nosey child, and you might well be right. I, on the other hand, prefer to be remembered as an inquisitive if somewhat precocious child who was simply interested in everything and everyone.

The gist of mum's story was that Mr LaVell had been seen lunching at the DeCorsa with a woman who wasn't Mrs LaVell. The connotation being that he was up to no good.

"I could have told you there was something going on," Dad said knowingly. "It's obvious he doesn't consider the current Mrs LaVell to be worth a tuppenny liquorish stick and in my estimation that usually means only one thing—another woman."

"And secret lunch dates," Mum added.

If they thought I wouldn't put two and two together and recognise the subject matter of their conversation, they were wrong. I was now eleven years old and knew about the birds and the bees. Well, some of it anyway, thanks to cloakroom gossip.

Mr LaVell must be having an affair with a fancy bit. There was a time I wasn't exactly sure what that meant, but I discovered the true meaning, thanks to one of the older girls using this terminology. I overheard her unashamedly tell other girls in her year how she'd spotted her own dad with a fancy bit. My curiosity was stirred, so I asked her what a fancy bit was.

She laughed and said, "A bit on the side…a brazen hussy, you stupid twit."

So that was it! LaVell had a brazen hussy. My curiosity deepened, because with the mental picture drawn by the older girls, I now had a vision in my mind of this other woman as flamboyant, dressed in red with peroxide hair swept up and piled high on her head.

Then I heard Dad ask, "What's she like anyway, this mystery woman?" It was the perfect opportunity to find out if my intuition was well founded. It wasn't.

"She's sophisticated, elegant and quite beautiful actually, *and* she was all over LaVell like a rash."

"What about him?"

"The same utterly shameless behaviour; they finished lunch and went straight across to the Windsor Hotel, so you know what they were having for dessert."

This was where they lost me. DeCorsa is famed for its deserts, so why would LaVell take the fancy bit to the Windsor? It was on the tip of my tongue to ask, but then they'd know I had been listening and it wasn't worth another lecture.

When Saturday came, Mum was all a dither about her party. She made me promise to stay in my room and if Charles woke (which was highly unlikely since he now slept so soundly, a bomb going off couldn't stir him) anyway, I had been put on guard to make sure he didn't wander out of his room and come downstairs.

"You see, Judy," Mum said in that worldly wise fashion grown-ups adopt when explaining something to a totally indifferent child, "adult conversation becomes stinted when a child is in hearing distance. What you must understand is that some subjects just aren't meant for young ears."

My promise was given with fingers crossed behind my back. To my way of thinking, adult conversation was…educational.

As the evening went on and the wine flowed freely, the laughter grew louder. I could say the noise kept me awake, but it wasn't so much that as my inborn defiant streak which didn't take kindly to orders. There was of course that burning passion within me for listening in on conversations, even though at times they were a bit nonsensical to me. I crept from my room and sat at the foot of the stairs where I could watch and listen.

When the alcohol loosened tongues, it wasn't long before the question of LaVell's infidelity was raised (as I hoped it would.) I have to admit that was the current issue that intrigued me and activated my wild imagination. I was at an age where the reckless way adults behaved mystified me. I just had to find out more.

Harriet Granger looked as tipsy as she sounded, teetering to the kitchen to have her glass replenished. "I don't normally partake of grape or grain," she slurred, "I'm only drinking tonight to ease the shock."

"What shock was bad enough to turn you, a self-confessed abstainer of alcohol no less, into a dipso?" I heard Mum ask, and reasonably so considering Harriet was drinking wine like it was going out of fashion and she had reached the talking gibberish stage.

Harriet's face took on that wide eyed wonder look. "You were there, Gloria, you and Emily and Ruth." She slurped a whole glass of wine in one gulp. "Don't tell me you weren't all shocked that old strait laced at number eleven has a bit on the side?" She staggered drunkenly and spilled most of her drink down her front when she missed her mouth.

"He's a bastard, well, aren't all men bastards at heart?" Emily grunted drunkenly and they all laughed so riotously they had to hold onto each other in a kind of group hug to save from falling over.

I personally didn't see the funny side, but everyone else seemed to think it was hilarious, especially when Mrs DeCorsa said, "You're talking about the beautiful brunette? I shouldn't be saying this, but LaVell lunches with her at least three times a week and then they go straight across to the Windsor."

Mum added, "For dessert," and once more, the room erupted with laughter.

I grew tired of the conversation that was beyond my comprehension and having lost interest, turned my attention to the men. Perhaps, with a bit of luck, I'd understand at least some of the things they talked about.

Vince Robb was saying, "There's some sort of work going on in the garden at the rear of the LaVell house. You have the best view of their back garden, George. Any idea what he's having done now?"

"Well, the builders are in and there's a lot of clanking from shovels at the rear of the house, but even from the upstairs window, you can't see their back garden properly with all those high shrubs secluding it." George valiantly puffed out his chest. "I just walked out and challenged him as he was getting into his car, asked outright what all the noise was about."

"And you've still got your nose?" Dad said in feigned surprise.

"Well, strange as it may see, he was unusually polite actually. According to LaVell his girls—now don't laugh because I tell you no lies, this is his exact words—*have requested an ornamental fishpond.*" It was on the tip of my tongue to ask if the request was typed, double spaced and in triplicate. "Anyway, to cut a long story short, he's having one built, complete with a mermaid fountain in the centre."

This snippet of information was the one thing to make me gasp. It sounded spectacular and so wonderfully exciting; my imagination went into over-drive. I could just picture myself languishing by my very own fishpond as the gurgling fountain sprayed the golden carp, shimmering in the sunlight as they swam among the algae and water lilies. What glorious scenes my mind conjured of a fishpond with a real mermaid fountain too. Perhaps if I asked nicely Meredith and Maxine might show me their fishpond…when the LaVell person wasn't at home of course.

I yawned and my eyelids were suddenly very heavy, so I crept upstairs to my bed and fell fast asleep.

I wasn't at school the following Wednesday morning. I had a dentist's appointment and we just got back when Harriet Granger came to see Mum. To say, she was a little upset would be an understatement. This woman who was normally aloof and in control of her emotions was crying her eyes out and shaking from head to toe.

"I've done a terrible thing, Gloria," she wailed pathetically. "Now the postman's been and she's breaking her heart and I feel awful. It's a catastrophe."

"Who's breaking her heart? And what have you done to cause this catastrophe?" Mum looked panicky. It obviously distressed her to see the state Harriet was in. I was told, "Go into the other room, Judy, while I speak to Mrs Granger," but as usual my ears were flapping.

Harriet's trembling hands covered her eyes as if this would blot out the wrong and make it right. "I wrote an anonymous letter to Jean LaVell telling her that her husband was having an affair and that he frequently had lunch with his lover at the DeCorsa then spent the afternoon in the Windsor."

"Aw, sweet Jesus, what possessed you? I'm sorry,, Harriet but if you're looking for absolution, you've come to the wrong person. What you did isn't just vicious it's downright evil. What the hell made you do it…jealousy? That's it isn't it? You're jealous because Richard LaVell has a lover."

"Maybe…. perhaps I was jealous of that beautiful woman he was with, and I know it didn't give me the right to…to…"

"To what, turn into a bunny boiler? For all you know, this could simply be an infatuation that would one day fizzle out and what Mrs LaVell was unaware of wouldn't hurt her." My mother had reached a point where fury made her screech the words. "You didn't just put the knife in you, rotten bitch," and I winced as my mother did what I had never heard her do before—she used the F word, "you fucking twisted it too." I had never ever seen her this irate, and it terrified me.

Harriet wailed her feeble excuse. "I thought she had a right to know."

My mother's anger and disgust was there in the tone and level of her voice. "People who write anonymous letters make me sick," she roared. "If you were so intent on breaking the poor woman's heart, why didn't you just go and tell her you saw her husband with another woman? That at least might have been less painful than a cruel poison pen letter."

Harriet sobbed frenetically as she kept repeating over and over, "What have I done, what have I done?"

The scary scene made me feel very afraid, and in that moment, as I listened to Harriet confess to a stupid and selfish act, the door to that dormant sixth sense creaked open a little more and took my breath away. Suddenly, I was plunged once more into the realm of cold black mist where my very sanities were prey to that intensely horrific sensation, but still, I couldn't find the courage to look deep into the fog. The fear in me was so strong, in an effort to break the spell and let go of the terror within me, I must have screamed and gone into a faint. The next thing I knew, Mum was kneeling by my side, her face twisted in anguish.

Our GP said my (as he put it) dizzy spells were down to the onset of adolescence. Mum pointed out I had only just turned eleven and a bit young to be entering puberty. His argument was that I could simply be maturing faster than normal and there was no cause for alarm.

"It's not all that unusual, Gloria," Dad assured her, "but if you're uncomfortable about discussing sex with her, I'll bring a couple of explanatory manuals."

"No! Definitely not," I heard Mum stress as I listened from my much used third step from the bottom. "When the time is right, *I'll* discuss the facts of life with Judy."

My first thought? If her discussion was going to be anything like the discussions in the school cloakroom…I couldn't wait.

Chapter Ten

The day after Mum and Harriet's quarrel over that letter, Thursday, it was late that evening when LaVell's car drove into the street. Rather than go to sleep, I had sat by my window watching and waiting. This fearful thing I was experiencing had only begun the day LaVell arrived, and I had to see if it was the sight of him in that black suit and expensive black cashmere coat he wore that triggered this threatening, intangible thing which had begun to unlock a door and release whatever was buried deep within my subconscious. A door I desperately fought to remain closed. I needed to know if my own mind was willing these fits to occur or if they happened spontaneously at the sight or mention of LaVell. But he passed by and this time I felt nothing.

In the small hours of Friday morning, I was awakened by the sound of shouting. From my window, I could see the door to number eleven lay open and there were suitcases in the hall. One by one, the lights went on in the street and windows opened as Mrs LaVell's voice, high pitched and convulsive, carried the length and breadth of Juniper.

"Don't try to deny it, Richard. It's here in black and white." (She was obviously referring to Harriet's letter.) "I telephoned the Windsor Hotel," she screeched, "and when I introduced myself as Mrs LaVell, do you know what? They thought I had a complaint about the service **this afternoon.** It appears you and **Mrs LaVell** frequently used the best room in the hotel. How do you explain that?"

"For God's sake, Jean," LaVell sneeringly called out as his wife threw another case into the hall. "You're making an exhibition of yourself *again*."

"Me? You're the one making an exhibition of yourself. The way you've been wining, dining and bedding her with no expense spared she must be a costly whore."

There was a lot of crashing and banging then Mrs LaVell shouted, "You'll pay for this, Richard. I'll find the best lawyer money can buy and I'll take you for everything. Forget about the DeCorsa and the Windsor, by the time I've finished, you won't be able to afford a McDonald and a room at the YMCA."

I watched Mrs LaVell run from the lounge with her husband close behind. They were silhouetted against the hall light, and I saw LaVell's shadowy form yank Jean LaVell roughly backwards by the hair and with great force, his open hand slapped the left side of her face then in a reverse volley the back of that hand connected violently with her right cheek.

The twins were crying loudly, "No, Daddy, no," and then the door slammed shut.

After a few minutes, the hullabaloo stopped rather abruptly. No more shouting and no more wailing, just deathly silence. Mum said, "Good, he must have managed to calm her down. Maybe we'll get some sleep now."

The next morning, I overheard that LaVell had apologised profusely to George Granger for the disturbance. He explained that his wife had been greatly upset by a poison pen letter she'd received and had become quite hysterical.

George had no idea it was Harriet who had sent the letter when he venomously decried the person who had done such a cold-hearted, insidious thing. "Some people," he said disgustedly, "hanging is too good for them. Anyway, pass on my kindest regards to your wife."

"I thought under the circumstances, it might be best if Jean took the girls to visit her family, so I phoned the airport and managed to get them three seats on a flight to Canada. I drove them to the airport myself early this morning." Then in answer to George's questioning look, he added, "Jean's Canadian you know. She's originally from Toronto."

"Well, it's a small world! My brother moved to Toronto some years ago. What part of Toronto does Mrs LaVell hail from? Who knows, he may even know your wife's family…" George was unaware of the disturbing effect his questioning had on LaVell, even when the man cut him off mid-sentence.

"Jean had no family! Could you excuse me one moment?" LaVell asked with a kind of courtesy which was normally scarce in his vocabulary. The workmen had arrived and were enthusiastically telling LaVell that, all going well, the structure would be finished by late afternoon.

"Their own fishpond and fountain to sit by on a nice summer's day will be a nice surprise for your girls to come home to." George smiled warmly. LaVell smiled back and nodded his head in a vague sort of way as he followed the workmen into the back garden.

Almost a year went by and still Mrs LaVell, Meredith and Maxine hadn't returned to Juniper Drive. Mr LaVell let it be known that Jean had decided to remain in Canada and the girls would be staying with her. He put on a magnificent show of deepest sorrow, telling the Grangers that, thanks to the poison pen letter, his marriage was over. Harriet's shame and guilt deepened, although she never told George that she was the one who had wielded the poison pen.

LaVell made a point of informing anyone who as much as looked in his direction that the house, as opposed to selling, was going to be rented out just in case circumstances changed and his dear wife returned with the children. But until then, he had decided to stay with a friend as he couldn't bring himself to live alone in the house any longer. Did he really believe anyone gave a damn about his feelings?

The leaving of a friend and neighbour is normally a sad occasion, but LaVell's departure was quite the opposite. You could almost hear the collective sigh of relief, for it was his own pomposity that had made him so unpopular.

Many times, I peered longingly through the fence at the rear of number eleven where there was a space in the shrubbery which allowed me to see the mermaid standing forlornly in the centre of the carp filled pool with water bubbling and spouting from the shell she carried on her shoulder. I prayed that the new tenants would allow me to see the wonderful structure at close hand with nothing to obstruct my view.

In the same orderly fashion as when he arrived, LaVell took his personal possessions and moved out.

The residents waited with bated breath to see who would take over the tenancy of number eleven. The bets were on a professional person, possibly a doctor who was coming to work in Dundee on a temporary basis. At any length whoever took up residence, there had to be reasonably well off to afford it.

I think, all things being equal, the residents of Juniper Drive preferred that the new neighbours had some social standing, an enhancement to the area if you like. What I'm trying to say is that people like the Robbs, the Grangers and yes, my parents too hoped for neighbours with refinement that bordered on snobbish. They were after all, entering the realms of Fairfield.

Chapter Eleven

"Aw, Mother of God, would you look at this beautiful place, Danny. Sure, I must have gone to sleep and woke up in paradise." The woman stood with her arms outstretched, just the way Julie Andrews did in *The Sound of Music*. For one brief moment, I half expected her to start singing.

The brogue was unmistakable. Our new neighbours were Irish. They were the Raffertys, and they were the next chapter in the colourful history of number eleven Juniper Drive.

They arrived in a white transit van. There must have at one time been a distinguishing name plastered on each side in bold red letters. For some reason or other, the lettering had been removed leaving unrecognisable bits of red here and there. More than likely the van, having passed its best, had been sold and the new owners had removed almost all of the company's personal logo. Anyway, it was a normal Saturday morning in Fairfield with the harmonious sounds of lawnmowers, hedge clippers and the hissing spray from hosepipes. Or at least it had been until that van drew up.

There seemed to be so many of them, I was sure the van had revolving doors and they were going in one and out the other.

Mrs Rafferty called out to anyone and everyone in hearing distance, "Good morning to you and a fine one it is too."

The littlest one was about five or six and I'd later come to know him as Daniel. He was the youngest of the Rafferty brood and the sweetest, gentlest little boy.

Daniel went over to where George and Harriet were weeding and hoeing their immaculate garden. He walked up the path, and much to George and Harriet's amusement, contentedly went around smelling the flowers as he went. And then without warning, little Daniel Rafferty pulled up a clump of begonias, roots and all then happily skipped down the path and handed the flowers to his mother. George and Harriet stood in open mouthed shock and disbelief.

Mrs Rafferty just smiled proudly then bent down and hugged the little boy. "My sweet child, Mummy loves flowers, but not someone else's," she cooed. "Now give them back to the fine people and tell them you're sorry."

Daniel clasped his mother tightly, his little arms around her neck and his cheek resting against hers. Mrs Rafferty gave his bottom a gentle, playful pat and said, "Off you go now."

Skipping merrily back up the path, Daniel stopped in front of the Grangers' and announced, "I have to put these back," and then slowly scrutinising the garden until he found the void that until a moment ago had held the cultured blooms, Daniel plonked the begonias back into the space where they belonged. His chubby little hands patted the soil then he gently touched the pink petals and said, "There now, all better."

I watched Harriet and waited for her to throw a fit at any given moment, but surprisingly, she smiled tolerantly, and Mrs Rafferty acknowledged the kindness by offering an explanation for Daniel's behaviour.

"The sweet child's backward, do you see. The passing years won't make much difference to him for the dear Lord has seen fit to keep him a child," she said sadly.

And Harriet Granger uncharacteristically sniffled and dabbed her eyes with a handkerchief. "He's such a darling child I…" Harriet reached for George's hand, "we could never be angry with him over some silly flowers."

Mrs Rafferty smiled and said, "Thank you for indulging the child, and thank you too for putting up with me talking of sorrowful things when there's enough sadness in the world." Then she called out, "Molly, Noreen, put the kettle on, your ma's dying for a cup of tea."

Their worldly possessions consisted of three large suitcases and a box of groceries, bringing speculation that the Raffertys were only on a short-term lease. Their arrival had been enlightening, but unspectacular in the respect that three suitcases were hardly fuel for gossip and as the house had been let fully furnished, they had virtually no belongings of their own.

After little more than a week, everyone had formed their own conclusions about the family. The general consensus was that they were pleasant and the five children, rather than running wild and making a nuisance of themselves, had impeccable manners.

If someone were taking shopping from the car then as surely as night follows day, one of the Rafferty children would suddenly appear with an offer of help. It was the same if there was a sudden shower when washing was hung outside to dry. It was safely gathered before the rain could do its worst. All in all, they passed the good neighbours test with flying colours.

Eamon was seventeen and the eldest, Michael was a year younger. Molly was fifteen and Noreen was the same age as me, eleven, but it was little six-year-old Daniel who was the sweetheart of Juniper Drive. His innocence, borne from lack of wit and the ability to learn gave him an endearing quality. Daniel Rafferty was also a supremely beautiful, cherubic child.

The Rafferty children all had the same type of hair, dark and wild—except Noreen. Her hair was the same as her siblings alright. Wild tendrils that curled like springs of wood shavings, only hers wasn't black as night, it was titian. A glorious mass of flaming, untamed curls held together with a mother-of-pearl clasp. How I envied her.

At the time, I didn't realise Daniel was backward. I simply saw him like my own little brother, a contented little boy who smiled a lot. It was overhearing talk that made me realise Daniel wasn't like normal children.

"Such a shame, I wonder if his condition was caused by an accident or if he was born like that," I heard Harriet say to my mother.

They were only just on speaking terms again. My mum was the kind of woman who could never be real friends with someone capable of writing a poison pen letter. She put up with Harriet and that's all it now was, an impartial, detached friendship.

"I don't believe Mrs Rafferty is the type of woman who'd take offence, so I might just ask her outright rather than speculate." Mum shrugged her shoulders in a, *no harm in that* way. "A friendly interest can hardly be termed prying and I think everyone has enough affection for the little mite to want to know."

So, there it was and now I understood, but I wondered how Mum would get round to asking what happened to Daniel. With the best will in the world, *friendly interest*, no matter how diplomatically shown, could easily be misinterpreted as prying.

It was the next day when an opportunity presented itself and Mum seized it. She had dropped Charles off at the nursery school, then practically ransacked the supermarket. The car was laden with Tesco bags.

Mrs Rafferty called out her usual greeting as she passed, "A glorious day to be walking this earth."

And Mum wearily replied, "I've been shopping all morning and I'm dying for a coffee. Would you by any chance care to save me from total boredom by joining me?"

I think more than anything, Mrs Rafferty had too much dignity to refuse a genuinely kind invitation. Happily, she answered, "If you're sure, I'll not be holding you back from preparing your husband's lunch, I'd love a cup of coffee," and in her own helpful way, she picked up some of the shopping bags from the car.

"Ralph eats lunch in the hospital cafeteria," Mum explained. "That way, he's on hand in case of an emergency."

It was all small talk at first as Mum put out her best China coffee mugs and brewed an aromatic pot of her favourite Brazilian coffee. Then she cut to the chase. "Would you mind if I asked you a rather personal question, Mrs Rafferty?"

"I will answer your question if it's decent and you start calling me, Win. That's short for Winifred but no one ever calls me that," she said in that soft, soothing voice. "If we're to be dispensing with formalities, what Christian name were you given?"

"My name's Gloria," and in that moment when they clasped hands the two women of genres so distanced, one from the other, sealed a friendship. (To this day, when my mother softly sings, "When Irish eyes are smiling," I know she's thinking of Win Rafferty.)

"Now, Gloria, if you ask your question, I'll give you an honest answer," said Win in that sweet, lilting voice.

Quite simply my mother asked, "What happened to make Daniel the way he is?"

It didn't startle Win to be asked this question. She sighed deeply and said, "The moment he was born, the angels touched my baby and claimed him for their own. I care for Daniel until the time comes for him to join his celestial family, for the medical men have told me his time on earth will be short."

"That's your belief?" Gloria asked incredulously, "That…"

"It's best I tell you the whole story and then you'll understand." Win held out the mug and when it had been refilled, she added sugar and cream and slowly stirred the coffee in silent thought. The coffee had begun to cool before she spoke. "I was eight and a half months pregnant with Daniel. Aw, we were all so excited about the new baby. Why, Danny was like a dog with two tails to wag and I was at the stage where I had the urge to feather me nest. With the great need on me to buy everything, all the essential things for my baby's arrival, I went into town. I remember walking towards the escalator with the list clasped in my hand, the mother and baby shop was on the upper level do you see. That was when the bomb went off."

"This was in Ireland?"

"Oh, yes, and it was done in the name of patriotism by sick, perverted men and women who call themselves soldiers and get there point across by murdering innocent people."

"You read about these things, but it never seems real because the mind can't accept that anyone could do such a cowardly thing in a place filled with women and children."

"There are many cowards and few heroes! It shames me to admit that because I'm talking of my own countrymen."

"How frightened you must have been, Win, ready to give birth and caught in a…a…war zone."

"I came to amid the rubble with the wailing and crying of injured and dying people all around me. I lay there, too shocked to realise that the pain I felt was the labour started and my Daniel was born while I lay trapped. I listened to his first cry but couldn't reach my baby to hold him. The rescuers came, only not soon enough. For a few minutes, the baby's brain had been starved of oxygen. If they'd got to me sooner, a few minutes, that's all it would have taken, then Daniel would be…"

"I can understand now why you must have been desperate to leave Ireland, but why here? Is this a stop-gap, a sort of extended holiday?"

"You could say that. With respect, Gloria, you'll have heard of the troubles in Ireland but believe me, you don't know the half of it. My Daniel's a casualty of a mindless war and if I sound bitter, it's because I am."

My very staid and composed mother didn't cry very often, she wasn't a weepy person, but that night as she recounted the story to my father, she wept buckets.

I was overcome by the strongest sensation that the Raffertys were in some sort of danger, not danger past, but danger yet to come and I still had no idea what these premonitions meant or where they came from. Maybe abhorrence at hearing the awful way Daniel came into the world had stirred my senses. Yet why did it only happen the moment I picked up and held the gloves Win had left in our kitchen? I knew, I just knew that something really bad was lurking, and not just in the shadows of my mind.

Chapter Twelve

Once more, I had the privilege of being warmly welcomed into number eleven and I blended into the harmonious family atmosphere. Noreen and I had hit it off immediately and become best friends. It was hard to believe that only a short time ago, we had been separated by an ocean and were unaware of the others existence. We were the same age, but also alike in so many other ways. We had the same likes, the same dislikes, on the same wavelength so to speak.

There were many times I would answer a question before Noreen had finished asking it. Mrs Rafferty would laugh like she didn't believe her ears and say, 'now that's scary.'

Each time I rang the shiny brass doorbell or rattled the equally shiny letterbox, I was filled with such utter contentment, like a wanderer returned. I told Win all about Amy and Paul and how Amy had always kept fresh flowers on the hall table. Win said, "Then I'll carry on that tradition in memory of your friends," and from that day, she did keep her promise.

There was no standing on ceremony in their home. Mrs Rafferty would say, "Sit yourself down, Judy, and tuck in, there's freshly baked scones and homemade strawberry jam."

I bathed in the love that flowed and I loved this family that had taken me to their hearts. Don't get me wrong, my mum, dad and little brother were the world to me, but inside that house on Juniper Drive, there was a different sense of belonging and I was captive to the feeling.

With each passing day, the feelings within me were growing stronger and I couldn't explain them to myself, let alone anyone else. I pushed aside the flashes that came and went. I can only explain it as like pretending you hadn't seen a person you didn't particularly like when they tried to catch your attention. Was that it? Was I ignoring what I didn't like and couldn't understand? Equally, I didn't want to face the fact that a word or a touch opened an invisible door and I stepped into a time yet to come and witnessed what was still to happen.

It didn't happen all the time, but I was beginning to realise these occurrences were significant. Like the time I gave my friend at school a book I had promised, and she put the book in the same hand as the little purse with her dinner money that she carried. In that instant, I had a sense of *my* hand grasping the book and the purse and they felt as one. I had a feeling of loss and knew that with the book in her grasp, she would be unaware of that purse slipping from her grasp. I knew that unless I did something to stop it happening, she was going to lose her dinner money.

"Put that purse in your pocket before you lose it," I told her. She did as I asked without question, and I knew it was safe. The sensation of loss was no longer there.

I wasn't sure whether it was a blessing or a curse, but I was sure of one thing: if God had given me this gift, there had to be a purpose and I was about to take advantage of my gift in a spectacular way.

It was a day that will always live in my memory. We had an appointment with the dentist and Mum picked me up from school. It was to be another turning point in my life. I was about to attain acceptance and understanding that this sixth sense, second sight, call it what you will, but it was not shameful or bad, only the blessing of a higher power.

We were stopped at traffic lights and Mum being a driver who didn't charge off on the amber, waited on the lights turning to green, put the car into gear and as it began to ease slowly forward, she patted my knee and asked, "Any suggestions for tea tonight?" I don't know if it was her touch or her words, but there and then I knew we were seconds away from a disaster.

"STOP," I screamed, and she instinctively slammed on the brakes.

That was when a joy rider come speeding through the red halt light followed by a police car in hot pursuit with warning siren and blue flashing beacon. We would have been exactly in line with them right at that precise moment. A fatal crash would most certainly have been inevitable had I not seen in my mind what was about to happen before it happened.

"What made you do that, Judy? How did you know?" She was breathless and her pallor was deathly with shock. Her white-knuckle hands gripped the steering wheel so tightly like she was terrified to let go. People who had come to their windows and doors at the heart stopping sound of a police siren were traumatised by the sight of what looked like was about to be a most horrific fatal crash…had our car not slammed on the brakes and stopped only seconds away from certain tragedy.

A man tapped on the window and asked if we were alright. "Christ, that was a close thing," he gasped. "How lucky you braked when you did."

When she regained her breath, my mother asked again. "How *did* you know, Judy? I heard a siren coming from somewhere, but never for a minute did I imagine that a police car was going to come through the red light at that speed…Yet you knew it was going to happen. How could you have known?"

I realised there and then the time had come for explanations. "I sometimes see things happening before they do." What else could I say to account for my irrational action? Truth was the only way. She deserved that much.

"Well whatever premonition you had saved our bacon." She sounded ready to burst into tears and her shaking hands crashed the gears a couple of times before the car moved cautiously forward.

She didn't do as I expected and disparage my explanation or put it down to the wild imaginings of an overly imaginative juvenile mind. Neither did she make light of it. But all the way home, I was aware of the snatched glances as my mother tried to fathom out this rather freaky occurrence.

It wasn't going to end there, not with the need for credible answers that gnawed at my parents like hunger that just had to be sated. They cared enough to want to know the why, what, and how about the premonition that had saved our lives only, I had no viable answer. They believed in scientific fact, not hocus-pocus. All I knew was that Richard LaVell, for whatever reason, had been the catalyst that stirred something dark and scary within me. I was frustratingly trapped in this quandary that no one seemed to understand or even care to question.

"Well, you see…" I started to explain, or at least try to explain the inexplicable-and then a thought quietly crept into my head. If I were to maintain credibility, I had but one option. Give no more than only enough information to satisfy their need to know.

"Chasing that car, sirens going and everything, maybe that's how I knew they wouldn't stop at the traffic lights. Is that what you call logical?" I asked innocently.

"Well, so much for my logic that it's safe to go on the green light," Mum wheezed. "I'll never again trust traffic lights."

To effectively ease the moment and change the subject, I childishly told them that one day I was going to own number eleven. And then with blithe innocence that was for their benefit only, I asked, "Do you think it's one of those premonitions?"

Naturally, they were sceptical, but amused and content to believe I was simply daydreaming. My father laughed, my mother was still spooked, but at least both of them were relieved now to put it down to nothing more than the castles in the air fantasising of a highly-strung child rather than something more sinister. In the end, my parents reached their own conclusions and were happy to categorise our *near miss* as a lucky escape.

Win Rafferty sat contentedly in the back garden; her knitting needles click clicking almost in time with the poignant Irish melody she quietly hummed. Her watchful eyes constantly darted from the work on her needles to where Daniel playfully splashed Noreen with water from the pond.

"He's gone and got me dress all soaking wet, Mam," and Noreen squealed with laughter as she splashed Daniel back, calling to me, "let's duck the little imp, Judy." That's when Daniel took off, running as fast as his little legs would carry him to hide in the folds of Win's dress.

Molly was sprawled on a tartan blanket on the ground, lying on her belly with her chin resting in the palms of her hands while she serenely read a book. She called to Daniel and happily he ran to her, throwing himself onto the blanket and mimicking her pose with a pretend book.

An effective scolding tone was for Daniel's benefit. "Don't you worry," Molly promised, "the very minute Dad comes home, I'll be telling him of this carry on and he'll wallop our Noreen."

Daniel's laugh was an infectious chuckle that was without any trace of fear because this happy brood had never known physical punishment. The Rafferty children had never experienced an angry slap; an angry chiding maybe, but only if it was deserved.

That beautifully landscaped back garden at number eleven was a truly wonderful place to spend afternoons and warm summer evenings. More so with new friends in the richness of affection that was freely and wholeheartedly given. Shielded by the high fencing and foliage it was a sun trap and Mrs Rafferty said the gurgling of the fountain had a soothing effect. "Why, if I close my eyes, I'd swear I was sitting by a brook in Donegal," she'd sigh wistfully.

Noreen skipped around the pool, calling me to join in her game. "Come and count the fish with me, Judy." But the fishpond and fountain I had once been so desperate to see held no particular fascination for me now. I was apprehensive about the way the mermaids pleading, tear filled eyes seemed to watch me.

When I told Noreen the mermaid was crying, she said, "Don't be daft, it's only the spray from the fountain." Yet it scared me somehow and I swear, there were times when I looked in the water, the reflection looking back at me wasn't my own, but a face from the past.

These summer afternoons were a delight that I never wanted to end. I never gave a second thought to the fact that Win and Danny might one day move on. Perhaps, my love of this family was such that I was in denial and my mind refused to believe that, like Amy, one day they would disappear from my life, my world.

The feeling that danger lay ahead was growing stronger by the day and I knew by the intensity of the feeling that it was close. And then at some point— and for the life of me, I can't remember how it came about—but some instinct, like a whisper in my mind, told me *I* had nothing to fear. There was no threat to *me* here at number eleven; if there had been then I would have sensed malice, not this calm and gentle touch of warmth and safety within these walls.

I was in no danger, but I was more than ever certain the Raffertys were. The doorway was where I felt it most. As soon as I stepped over the threshold, it hit me with such force-a suffocating sensation of dread, fear and sorrow that robbed me of breath. The only way to describe that threatening sensation was like one minute relishing the warmth of sunshine and next minute, the icy chill of dark storm clouds. That chill was on me, and the pace of intuition was quickening. My awareness told me some awful thing was about to happen to them right there at that doorway. If all it took was for me to open my mind and take a peek into the future to stop it, why should I be afraid? Whatever peril they were in was close, it was coming, and I had to be a willing vessel for the apparition. The Raffertys' salvation might very well be in my hands.

Chapter Thirteen

"I know milk is good for you, Judy, but *must* you always use every last drop? It irritates me when you think of no one else but yourself," Mum irritably lectured.

She *was* extremely irritated and rightly so. I had come home hungry and thirsty and if truth be told, I hadn't given a thought for Charles or anyone other than myself when I drained the carton by filling my glass a second time.

"I didn't think," I told her apologetically.

"That's the trouble, you never do and you're old enough to know better," she snapped.

I bridled and snapped back. "Well, you're the one who does the shopping. *I* can't be blamed if you don't buy enough milk." I immediately regretted that fit of pique when instead, I should have been offering an apology for my selfishness. Quietly and rather shamefaced I asked, "Shall I walk to the corner shop on Main Street and get a carton?"

The little storm in a teacup passed and Mum smiled and soothingly stroked my face. "If you would please, Judy, I've had a busy day, but I shouldn't have taken my frustrations out on you. I'll make sure there's plenty milk in the fridge from now on."

I hurried down Juniper, turned the corner into Maple Road and collided with two strange men who were too busy scrutinising a sheet of paper to watch where they were going.

"Whoa there, girlie, steady on, anyone would think the devil himself were after you." The one who spoke had that strong Irish brogue I had come to know so well. "We're looking for an old and dear friend who recently moved to this part of the world. Aw, you know how it is, the name crops up in conversation and Jesus would you know it, here they are, living in the very town you're going to be passing through; small world, eh?" He spoke with a sincerity that took me in…for a moment.

I was about to say, "Do you mean Danny Rafferty?" But then he laid a hand on my shoulder and once more, I was in another day, another time, a spectator in an event that hadn't yet happened. I saw the gun, heard the crack as a bullet left the barrel, the bullet that would take the life of Danny Rafferty when he opened the door in answer to the brass knocker's rat-tat-tat. These men had come here with murder in mind. The revelation left me with a look of alarm that the other man noticed immediately, and he nudged his accomplice.

"You shouldn't be laying a hand on her," he said in a low, sly way that supposedly I wasn't meant to understand. "Listen, Jimmy, if she starts yelling…do you catch my drift? What I'm saying is you could be accused of assaulting her."

The one called Jimmy let go of me like his fingers had just been burned. Too late, I'd seen what was in his mind.

"Who did you say you were looking for?" I tried—hoped I appeared to be a willing helper in their search for missing friends.

"The estate agent says he rented a house on Juniper Drive to the Rafferty family, would you happen to know them? The family we're looking for would be a couple with five youngsters."

I scratched my head and furrowed my brow, looking thoughtful, but vague. "Are you sure it was Juniper Drive? I live on Juniper and there's no family called Rafferty living there." How I prayed they didn't see through my lies and deceit.

"Be sure, girl, because it's very important." His tone was no longer pleasant. There was anger and frustration in his voice. "Could the estate agent maybe have made a mistake about the address?"

His cold, merciless stare burrowed through me and for a brief moment, I had the strongest inclination to turn and run.

"Apple Blossom Walk," I snapped my fingers as if I'd just remembered, "I'm sure an Irish family moved there just recently."

"Would you be kind enough to direct us?" His murderous eyes shone victoriously with the belief his quarry was now within reach.

"Carry on along Maple until you come to Rowan Drive," I pointed in the direction they were to take. "Apple Blossom Walk is right at the end of Rowan." I had deliberately picked the farthest away street to give me time to think of what to do while they searched fruitlessly.

If they knocked on doors, hopefully, people would be too wary of the strange, burley Irishmen to tell them anything, even if they knew. It was unlikely anyway that people five streets away from Juniper would know who lived where. It was even possible that some law-abiding citizen might call the police and report strangers who didn't belong in Fairfield acting suspiciously. What then? A hasty retreat surely since they couldn't very well admit that they had come to take the life of a countryman.

Breathlessly, I burst into the kitchen, startling Mum. "We've got to help them. I don't have time to explain, just trust me when I say two men are looking for Danny Rafferty and they're going to kill him if we don't do something."

Mum held my shaking body. "Did you have one of those funny turns, Judy?" I nodded my head frantically and softly she said, "Hush now, it'll be alright," and I felt her acceptance of this thing she didn't quite understand.

Mum took one side of the street, and I took the other, knocking on doors as we went and telling every one of our neighbours that if and when two Irishmen came looking for the Raffertys, they *must* insist they had never heard of any such family. No one questioned such an odd request. Perhaps, it was the desperation in our voices, or perhaps it was simple trust.

"This is a nice surprise, Gloria." Win greeted us on the doorstep, and she stood aside, her arm bidding us enter, but the absolute agony on my mother's face told her something was terribly wrong, and the smile waned.

Mum hugged Win awkwardly. She was trying to find a way to explain to these people what she didn't understand herself. "Win, two of your countrymen are close by and they're searching for Danny," Mum said with some reluctance. "Now you may find this hard to believe, but Judy had a premonition they were here to harm him and there's not much time…"

"I've known from the first day we met she had the gift. Your Judy is a very special child. Thank you for the warning, but we can't change our destiny."

"Then why was Judy given this…this gift if not to change what was wrong or bad? You can't stand idly by while they rob you of a husband and your children of a father. I don't know what you did, Danny," she spun round to face the trembling, white faced Irishman, pleading with her whole being for him to make sense of what she was trying to say. "Whatever you did, it doesn't warrant the taking of your life. If there's a snowball's chance in hell you have to take it."

Danny's drooped head shook in a defeated way.

Suddenly, mum's body stiffened in defiance. "Win, give me your apron and a bag of flour, then all of you go upstairs and stay very quiet," she demanded.

Even I didn't know what my mother had in mind, but her desperation sparked some survival instinct and without any more argument, Win and Danny herded the children upstairs. I watched curiously as Mum hurriedly tied the apron around her waist and rubbed flour on her hands. She was preparing to act out a part. It was right that minute I heard the rat-tat-tat from the door, and I took off upstairs too.

"Whatever you're selling, I don't want any," she snapped irritably, facing the two men, and looking suitably aggrieved at the inconvenient timing.

"Pardon the interruption, missus, but we're not selling anything. We've been making enquiries trying to contact one-time friends of ours do you see? We're searching to find Mr and Mrs Rafferty." The one called Jimmy looked questioningly at mum's blank stare. "We were informed they were tenants here?" He squinted around her, trying to see inside the house.

"Then you were given the wrong information," she said bluntly. "My husband and I recently moved to this town, he's a police inspector. (Gloria thought this part of the lie a touch of genius since their kind didn't take too kindly to the law.) We only rented this property short term until we find a house of our own, so we'll be moving out very shortly. Now, as you can see, I'm busy! My husband will be home soon, and he *doesn't* take kindly to uninvited strangers hogging our doorstep. As a matter of interest who told you these Rafferty people lived here?" The feigned indignation and rasping tone were so realistic anyone would have believed her.

"The estate agent, Bryce and Gray," they answered looking totally confused. Gloria had been very convincing.

"Then I suggest you go back to the estate agent," she advised in a way that left them in little doubt her patience was running out. "They've obviously made a grave error." The righteous tone, floured hands and this is *my* home was a stance that worked.

Somewhat taken aback, they muttered, "Sorry for intruding," and hurriedly left in even more confusion than when they arrived.

Gloria watched from behind the curtain until they were out of the street before giving the all clear to come downstairs.

Halfway down the stairs, Win stopped and sat on a step with her head in her hands. She seemed war-torn and totally defeated. "It's no use, Gloria. Sure, they'll be back once they speak to the agent."

"They won't be back, trust me. You rented through Bryce and Gray, well, Roland Bryce is a very good friend of ours and I think this is as good a time as any to call in a few favours." Gloria was dialling the number even as she spoke, but surprisingly, Danny put his finger on the cradle before the connection was made.

"You need to know what this is all about first, then if you're still of a mind to help us…" Danny Rafferty didn't look afraid, just accepting and when he smiled at Win, she smiled back through eyes that were now tear-laden.

"Tell her, Danny. Get it off your chest."

He worried for a moment at the words that had to be said, but he knew there could be no holding back now.

"I was at one time…still am a qualified accountant," Danny gave a wry snigger, "diplomas, letters after me name and everything. I earned a handsome salary, and my employers were the organisation I believed in. We each in our own way did our bit for the cause and I'm ashamed to say, I turned a blind eye to many things, atrocities. But do you see I was armed with a pen, not a gun."

"You mean, The Irish Republican Army, the IRA? Let me get this straight, Danny. Are you saying they were your employers?"

Win sat on the arm of the chair, her work-worn hands fidgeting in her lap. "Aye, Gloria," she said ruefully, "that's the bitter truth. Danny was paid well. We had a nice home and food on the table, so it was easy to make excuses. Until that bomb went off in the shopping centre…" Win's lip trembled at the recollection.

By this time, Danny's hands were covering his face, hiding the shame that was written all over it as he readied himself to relate the events that led to their exodus from Ireland. He got up and walked round the room as if being on the move might make the telling easier.

"Wait a minute," Gloria said, her face rapidly paling. "All this is about Daniel, isn't it?"

"Our poor wee boy," Danny said mournfully. "Of course, Gloria, everyone in the organisation was sorry about Daniel, but it was God's will they told me. Only the God *I* believed in didn't condone the murder of innocent women and children."

"And that's my thoughts exactly," Gloria agreed. "Then, what was it you did?"

"I carried on day to day as normal, although now I saw the people I had regarded as my friends in a different light and knew I wasn't and never could be one of them. But to let you understand, Gloria, once you're a member of the organisation, they don't easily let you walk away. It's not like giving up a membership to a club or getting a divorce, this really is for life."

"Danny's a good, God-fearing man and he would never willingly harm another living being." Win trenchantly defended her husband. "For two years, he kept the secret of what he was planning from me. I knew there was hatred in his heart, and I worried that a day would come when it turned to violence against those who had wronged us."

At that moment, the thought uppermost in Gloria's mind was that Danny must have harmed, even killed those he blamed for what happened to Daniel and this was the reason they were after him. She had visions of this peaceable man picking up a gun and exacting revenge and now the organisation was seeking retribution.

Hesitantly, she asked, "What terrible thing did you do to make them come after you with murder in mind? Did you kill someone, Danny?"

"I took from them what in their eyes was more important than any life." Danny pulled a wry face and there was no humour in the laugh that burst through his taut lips. "Before I say another word, Gloria, you must believe that I am an honest man, not a thief. What I did wasn't motivated by greed."

"I believe you, Danny! I've only known you and Win a short time, but I trust my instinct and I trust you."

"You may change your mind when you hear what I have to say." Danny ran his fingers nervously through his thick dark hair, pushing back the stray wisps that, damp with perspiration, clung to his forehead. "We were funded by patriots all over the world, but the big money came from the United States, and it was always cash, brought by couriers and delivered by hand. I bided my time, for you see, St Patrick's Day was when Catholics were at their most generous and three shipments were due at the same time, over half a million pounds in total. As the accountant, I was entrusted with the job of counting and logging the money before distribution. This was how their arms and ammunition were funded and I'd be damned if I were going to stand by and let it happen."

"It was blood money, Gloria! And all to help them rob women of their husbands, mothers of their sons and children of fathers." Win neither tried nor wanted to hide her disgust and disrespect for those who more than likely were at one time welcomed into their home as friends.

"Wait a minute," Gloria's eyes widened as the full meaning of what they were saying hit home. "You mean to say you *stole* half a million pounds from the IRA?"

"I did that, and I feel no shame only triumph," Danny said defensively.

Win jumped to her feet at Gloria's shocked intake of breath. "My Danny is a professional man, Gloria, respected. *He,*" she stressed with pride, "was *not* a terrorist who gloried in war and insurgency."

"But obviously a man with the heart of a lion; what I feel right now isn't contempt, Danny—its admiration and, dare I say it, respect."

"Ah but I'm no hero, simply a man who took retribution for a terrible wrong without spilling a drop of blood. I waited until Friday afternoon and pretended to feel really bad with the flu."

Win pressed a clenched fist against her mouth to hold back the laugh. "He sniffed pepper to make his eyes water and start a fit of sneezing to make it look like he really was full of the flu."

"They were all gathering for a meeting that afternoon, so I said I would lock up and leave early, have a few days in bed to get over the flu rather than have everyone else come down with it. I promised to finish the job when I was better. When everyone was gone to the meeting, I fetched a valise from the car and packed it with all the money from the safe. I slipped out unseen and almost broke the speed limit to get home."

"You must have been greatly trusted, Danny."

"I was, and because of that no one suspected a thing. Four or five days would give us a head start. I had prepared well ahead for this day with a false driving license and all our documents in the name of Rafferty. Under my assumed name, I went to another town and bought an old van from a junkyard. In the dark early morning hours of that Saturday, we took the children, a few personal things and that valise full of their money and I don't regret it."

Win covered her mouth to stifle an involuntary giggle and her bright eyes twinkled. She said, "My only regret is that I couldn't see the daft looks on their faces when they realised we were gone and so was their money."

"I knew they'd come looking for me, but I thought by now they'd have given up. In the first year, they came close to finding us twice, but with God's good grace, we were always one step ahead of them."

"And now they've caught up with you again."

"Who knows what alerted them we were here? It could have been a careless whisper that set them on our trail. The life of a soldier in the IRA is built on lies so that they can mingle and pose as old friends when asking after someone. Their network is far-reaching, and they have ways of tracing a person on the run."

"Then your name isn't Rafferty?"

"No! And it's best for you, safer if you don't know our real name, for what you don't know you can't tell."

"Who knew you were coming here?" It seemed logical to Gloria that someone they trusted had unknowingly—or worse still—knowingly given them away.

He knew immediately what Gloria was saying, maybe not in as many words, but it was nevertheless there in those unspoken words. Danny told her emphatically, "Only our immediate families, brothers and sisters who would give their own lives rather than risk ours."

Gloria listened to the extraordinary tale with her elbows resting on her knees and her chin resting in the palms of her hands. She smiled easily and stretched her arms in the air saying, "I'll use your phone now, if I may. Do you trust me?" She asked them and without waiting for an answer, dialled the number,

"We trust you with our lives," Win said with hand on heart.

In the most superior tone, Gloria asked in a way that bordered on demanding to speak to Roland Bryce on a personal matter, and then spent what seemed an immeasurable length of time chit chatting aimlessly about nothing in particular before getting to the point and asking the favour that was after all the purpose of the call.

"You see, Roland," Gloria wheedled, "it's only a little favour but since it would mean so much to my friend, Win, it means so much to me too." In a flash of inspiration she added, "Remember you told us how Samantha (Roland's wife) cringed when that cousin she couldn't stand paid an unexpected visit, and the two of you hid and didn't answer the door? Well, it's the same for Win and since they'll be leaving Dundee very soon anyway…Oh I'm sure you get the picture, Roland. No one appreciates the black sheep of the family hovering around begging for hand-outs."

Roland was now in a position where he couldn't and wouldn't refuse now that he could relate to the situation. "You say this Irish person will undoubtedly come back to the office to enquire about the tenants of number eleven Juniper Drive?"

"Yes, yes, Roland, and all they need be told is that a mistake had been made. You could simply make the excuse that although Mr Rafferty did originally agree to rent the house, he cancelled the following day because he had decided to accept a job opportunity up north. You won't be breaking the law or anything Roland. All you are saying is another family took up the tenancy and apologise for the mistake."

"I have a feeling there's more to this than meets the eye, still, what are friends for, eh?"

Gloria tittered girlishly. "Doesn't a bit of secrecy and subterfuge just make you feel like a movie hero?"

"You can count on my discretion! All I'll tell my secretary is that I messed up on the lease, but I'll handle it personally and sort it out. I'll make out a new lease and change the name from Rafferty to…oh, I'll think of a name, something less Irish. Showing them the new lease should, shall we say, put them off the scent. It's all a bit James Bond, Gloria, but still the most excitement I've had since Samantha shocked everyone by actually passing her driving test."

"You're a treasure, Roland. The name Rafferty won't show in your books and LaVell will still get paid for the lease, so everyone's happy." With the phone still to her ear, Gloria signalled to them with thumbs up.

"Is it true?" Danny asked with a flicker of hope. "The estate agent is really going to cover our tracks and buy us some time?"

"One thing about dear old Roland, he's as good as his word." Gloria exhaled as if she had just held her breath for the longest time. "You won't have to run now; you can stay here."

There was no denying it, Gloria was clutching at straws, but only for a moment and then she saw it. The solemn look on those two dear faces said it all and she knew in her heart of hearts they had to go.

"Do you really believe they'll come back even if they think you went up north?" She just had to have one last try at convincing them it might be safe to stay. Then she realised, it was selfish and unfair. Juniper was now a danger zone for them. It was time to let go and bid farewell to this remarkable family.

"We can't take that chance of making you a target, for if they found out you'd helped us, there would be a price on your head too." Danny looked weary and heart sore, too tired to run and too afraid to stay. "Every day, I ask myself if this could be the day I get a bullet in the head. I open my eyes of a morning with the thought, could this be the day I'm paid back for my betrayal? Maybe it would be best for everyone's sake if I…if I had the courage to…"

Win suddenly jumped to her feet and began slamming her fists against Danny's chest. "You're not giving in to them," she wailed like a hurt puppy, "that's what you were thinking wasn't it? I won't let you, not after all we've been through."

Suddenly, the flaying stopped and as Danny held her close, Win did something very rare, she wept. The sound of her pathetic sobbing brought great sorrowful tears rolling from Danny's eyes and Win's dark brown hair absorbed the wetness of his weeping.

Danny held her in his arms and the fists that only a moment ago had rained blows now clutched desperately at his jacket to keep him beside her. Gradually, the hysterical sobbing became soft sniffling, and he was able to whisper in her ear, "Listen to me, Win, we'll stay here for one more week. That should give me enough time to do all the arranging, but we can none of us set foot outside lest someone's watching, and they will be watching."

Win made a gasping sound like she'd just been kicked in the guts and frantically her trembling hands clasped both her cheeks. "The children are content here, how will they cope with more upheaval?"

"They're old enough to understand what we're running from and little Daniel, well, we'll tell him it's a game of hide and seek and you know how he loves playing games. Now hear me, Win. I know these people and how they think. They'll accept the agent's story to a point, but they're not stupid and they'll watch every house in turn until they're sure we're not in this area."

"Then we stay prisoners inside these four walls and not set a foot outside?"

"Aye that we will, but if Gloria were to come and go with bags of shopping—sorry, Gloria, but we'll have to rely on you to help us even more—they will be watching all the goings on unseen, but without a trace of us, they'll think they got it wrong and go away."

"But what if…"

"No more what ifs, Win. I'll leave here with Eamon and Michael under the cover of darkness, take the coach to Birmingham and get on the first available flight to Calgary. I'll phone you from the airport when it's settled. You wait a couple of days and do the same with the girls and Daniel."

Gloria said, "Don't worry, Danny, when it's dark, I'll get them into my car and drive them to the airport myself."

"I'll be waiting for you in Calgary, my brave family, and we'll start a new life."

For a moment, Win just sat there without moving and then she was suddenly filled with the fear that Danny might be planning to do something heroic, although stupid, to rescue his family from what had become a nomadic existence.

"Why, Danny?" She wailed, "why can't we all go together?"

"Because wouldn't a family of seven stand out like a sore thumb and draw attention?" Danny tried to reason with her, but Win was so afraid. "It will work, but you must have faith, for only the good lord can decide our fate now."

Gloria tried to imagine herself in their position, running, hiding, always having to look over your shoulder. It took a special kind of courage to live like this and their fortitude had to be admired.

"What Danny's saying makes sense, Win. With me coming and going like I lived here, why it's perfect," Gloria said positively. "Even when I go into my own house, it's only going to look like I was visiting a neighbour."

"But won't it look funny you leaving your own house every day to come here? They'll be alerted to the trickery for sure." Win still had that squirming uncertainty.

"We have to play the hunch that they'll only be watching the front. I'll slip out my back door, onto the path behind Juniper and in through this back door. All they'll see is me going out through the front door and returning with some shopping."

"But when you knock on your own door, if you're outside, who's going to answer?"

"They'll only be able to see my back, so I'll knock with one hand and slip the key in the lock with the other, wait a moment then push the door open. That way, it'll look like whoever answered is on the other side of the door."

Slowly, the uncertainty dissolved, and Win nodded her head acceptingly. "God help us all," she said, slowly and deliberately crossing herself. "I remember hearing it said once that if you must dance with the devil make sure you're flameproof. Is that what we're doing, Danny, dancing with the devil?"

"You've got that wrong, dear friend," Gloria said, "*God* will help you and your family. The devil only looks after only his own."

The great escape did work and in less than two weeks, my beloved friends had vanished in the night without as much as a proper goodbye. I was only told that if anyone asked about them, I must insist that no Rafferty family had ever lived in Fairfield. I was being asked to banish them not only from my life, but from my mind, as if they never existed and it was the most painful thing I ever had to do. It would be years later that I learned the truth behind their sudden departure.

The dark malignant feeling of danger which for weeks had haunted me faded into a quiet calm. That pair of gloves Win left in our house, I put them in my dresser drawer since there was no chance of returning them and periodically, I would hold them to my cheek and sense Win near to me, unafraid and content. I knew that wherever they were they were safe from harm.

Their escape had been a success and periodically, a postcard would arrive with the message, *enjoying the holiday, wish you were here, lots of love from your favourite aunt.* It was Win's way of telling us not to worry, they were safe.

Chapter Fourteen

The restless seasons changed. That glorious summer spent with the Raffertys now drifted in and out of my thoughts like a recurring dream. Or perhaps it was a chapter in my book of memories which I read and re-read so as to never let go that time of perfect contentment. And yet, the sound of Daniel's happy chuckling and the appetising aroma of Win's baking will be branded on my heart and mind for all eternity. I will forever re-live and remember in glorious colour and depth of detail the pleasure in those happy days which time and circumstances could only lend me for such a short time.

Summer became autumn and as autumn turned into winter, my house still lay empty. No warm glow from lamps illuminated each room in the dusk of evening as winter descended and now, only darkness expressed the bleak emptiness. I waited and lived in hope that one day soon, another happy family might move into number eleven and then the sound of laughter would once more drift through open windows. But it didn't happen, and I wondered if it ever would again.

I began to wake every night to the same sound of a voice, distant and yet near, frantically, and desperately calling my name, *'Judy, Judy.'*

The sensation was so chilling, so macabre that in desperation I'd call out, "Who are you? What do you want?" A cold sweat would wash over me when my frenzied pleading was left unanswered and I felt as if I were left in a kind of limbo, dangling between make-believe and actuality.

My mother gave her own considered opinion that it was no more than the wind rustling the trees or raindrops falling against the window with a whispering pit-a-pat that played tricks on my much too vivid imagination. I may have respected this basic explanation, but how could I subscribe to it when *my* innermost feelings contradicted *her* reasoning?

I became more and more convinced that in the darkness of night, some lost soul was reaching out to me for help, and it took every ounce of energy to overcome, not just the distress, but the feeling of ineptitude that gripped me on these occasions. If my help were needed, then why could no one tell me what I was supposed to do or what task I was expected to perform?

My self-confidence was destroyed, shredded by frustration. Like a tidal isle when the tide had ebbed, I felt cut off from mainstream life and so alone. Eventually, close to breaking point and overcome by exhaustion, both mental and physical, I was admitted to hospital for tests.

"We can find nothing physically wrong with Judy," my parents were told, "all in all, she's a healthy enough child."

"She used to be, but not anymore. Look at her," my mother demanded. "Our child goes to bed exhausted and wakes the same way. Can you honestly say that's normal; that there's nothing wrong with her?"

"That's not at all what I'm saying, Mrs Vernon," the doctor reasonably and objectively tried to explain. "I'm trying to tell you there is nothing *physically* wrong with Judy."

"What then, what?"

"I think rather than the physical we should turn our attention to the mental aspect of Judy's trouble. It's obvious she has deep emotional problems. What I'm trying to say is that a child psychologist might get to the root of the trouble."

Well, you can imagine my mother's reaction to the implication that the problem was mental and not physical. She blew hot and cold for a few minutes until the doctor managed to calm her down enough for him to fully explain his prognosis.

"What Judy is experiencing, the sleeplessness and the voices in her head, all points to some underlying fear. She needs psychological help in order to get to the bottom of whatever frightens her so much. That's the only way we can tackle the problem and begin to heal her troubled mind. It's entirely up to you whether or not you take the advice offered, but I strongly advise you to consider it."

"What are the options?"

"There are no more options," the doctor said, frankly.

With reservations, Mum agreed to a consultation with another doctor.

Right from the first moment I met Dr Sophie McGraw, I knew she understood me in a way that didn't come from her training, but from her own experience. I liked her, but more than that, I trusted her because we were two links in the same chain.

Sophie looked at me with such deep intent when she said, "I'm here to help you, Judy, but first I need you to open your heart and your mind. I need you to tell me everything that's been troubling you."

Holding nothing back, I told her about the premonitions, the voices and Sophie's gentleness and sympathetic ear gave me the motivation to give vent to my anguish and fears. I told her of every strange, unfathomable occurrence and wept tears of simply relief to have someone listen with credence, not cynicism. "They're not faces I can see, just this calling out for help—my help. I don't understand what it is, and no one will tell me."

"Is it your innermost feelings, Judy? What you sense rather than see and hear, is it that which frightens you?" She asked.

"Yes," I answered honestly, "but not all the time. *You* know what I feel, don't you?" I wasn't asking a question; I was telling what I saw in her.

Sophie's head nodded. "I do, Judy," she answered. "I can relate to your concern because I've been in the exact same predicament."

Her admission was what I already knew. We were two of a kind and now we were bonded by a clear and present affinity. Sophie reached out and clasped my hands and, in that grasp, I felt a great surge of strength as if I had just awoken from a long, restful sleep.

"I found a way to accept without fear. I'm going to help you to do the same." Her reassurance and honesty offered me hope as well as a crutch to support my wearied mind.

"Tell me, please!" I had been living in the shadow of my fears and now Sophie's expertise was introducing me to the first trickle hope.

"I want you to think of it in this way. You and another girl start reading the same book at the same time. You read faster than the other girl, so you know what's going to happen before she does." Sophie didn't talk in terms that were beyond my understanding. Her approach to my problem was pragmatic. She set a scenario that was easy for me to relate to.

"Yes, yes, that's what it's like." At last, an explanation with which I could associate.

"You see, Judy, there's nothing wrong with your mind, you're just—well, one or two pages ahead, that's all," she said with a knowledgeable directness. "It's important for you to know that many people have this psychic energy. It holds no disgrace."

Her words opened a shutter in my mind. "You're one of those people, aren't you? You can tell. You can see something happening before it does."

"People call what you…what *we* have by many names. There are those who fake the gift and take money from vulnerable folk with the promise of miracles. Never be tempted to gain financially from what God has gifted you. Listen to me, Judy, clairvoyance is one of those things that others treat with suspicion or contempt. People are only believers when it suits them."

I listened intently to Sophie, the only person I had ever met who could connect to my anxiety and give me encouragement with the words of wisdom that poured from her heart because…she knew. Sophie was to be the architect of my healing. She didn't just quote from textbooks. She spoke from experience.

It was my third session and I had asked Sophie one of those 'why' questions. I seem to remember it was something like, "Why don't I know how to use this gift properly?"

As always, she offered a logical explanation. "Fledglings have to learn how to fly. Babies have to learn how to walk. What you must learn is significance. Let's say, for instance, at the school lunch break you and a friend are enjoying fish and chips when you have one of those seeing ahead visions. Your friend is about to choke on a fish bone. The significance isn't the relishing of fish and ships; it's the fish bone that's about to lodge in her throat."

"Yes, I see that, but if I gave her a warning, told her I knew because I'd seen her two minutes from now choking on a fish bone, she'd think I was some kind of loony."

"Well, for a start, you wouldn't say that you'd just had a vision. All you'd have to do is quickly make up a fib that you think you see a bone in her fish and warn her to pick it out in case she happens to swallow it. Emphasise the horror of how easy it would be to choke on a bone. Let imagination do the rest."

It was the dawning of reason. "Then what would have been a scary thing didn't happen," I said.

"Exactly, because you had the advantage; you knew what she didn't. Unfortunately, people like us are considered freakish by those who consider themselves normal. It's easier to put a tag on what they can't comprehend- oddball, weirdo or freak."

At that moment, I had the strongest feeling of sorrow, but also bitterness and I asked Sophie, "Do you hate the people who call you horrid names?"

She looked at me strangely and then answered, "No, no, Judy! Hate is too strong a word to use. What I feel for the ignorance of anyone who labels me a freak of nature is pity. A heightening of the senses doesn't make us freaks, it makes us unique. Think about it-if what we have is a bad thing which mindless bigots believe to be something the devil has bestowed, doesn't it stand to reason it would be given to bad people and the world would be lost?"

Time and effort were to be the instruments to make me realise that it wasn't only the visions that frightened me, but more the fear of being shunned by school friends and neighbours were they to become aware of this so-called gift and see me as freakish. I was able to talk freely and openly to Sophie. The fear in me subsided and I began to smile again as contentment replaced confusion.

In the months that followed, she taught me how to understand and control this profound twist of nature. Slowly, I learned and came to accept that it was neither alarming nor fearsome. Sophie McGraw taught me not to close my eyes when I stepped into the future, but to observe and use what I saw advantageously, as in the fish bone hypothesis.

Once I understood, well, acceptance and the ability to keep a tight rein on my emotions came naturally. The only thing standing between me, and a full recovery was the anomaly that began with my first encounter with LaVell. He was responsible for whatever fearsome thing was lodged and locked in my mind. Even his nearness made me feel like he was dragging me into hell. I made a promise to myself that one day I would stand face to face with this man and demand answers.

In what seemed like the blinking of an eye, a year had passed since Win and Danny Rafferty closed the door of number eleven for the last time and vanished into the blue. They were the last people to live there, and it became a never-ending puzzle to me why the house had lain empty for so long.

Finally, I learned why the house on Juniper Drive was still vacant. I overheard Mum tell Dad that she bumped into Roland Bryce in town. Seemingly, Richard LaVell had ordered Bryce and Gray to take the house on Juniper Drive off their list of properties for lease. He gave no reasons for this inexplicable decision. They tried to sway him into changing his mind, but Roland Bryce said it was as futile as holding a candle in the wind. LaVell was deaf to all recommendations.

Roland had gone on at some length about LaVell's order to close up the house. "How ludicrous to leave a beautiful property like that vacant when it could command a handsome income," he had ranted.

"Of course," Mum sneered, "as an estate agent, he's more than likely mourning the loss of his percentage."

Dad was immediately interested. "I do hope you pointed out to Roland what an eyesore it was becoming with the garden more like a jungle and how unfair it was to other residents."

"Don't worry, he got both barrels from me on that score," peevishly she bit her bottom lip, "and then I had to apologise profusely."

"Apologise for what?"

"I suppose you could say for shooting the messenger."

"I don't get it."

"Well, Roland insisted he did stress the importance of maintenance to LaVell. He pointed out that residents of Juniper were now furiously complaining on a daily basis that the house, being in such a state of rack and ruin and the garden nothing more than a jungle of overgrown weeds, it had now become a disgraceful blot on a refined landscape. Roland offered his professional services as an estate agent to see that the property was adequately maintained. Either that or put it on the market with a view to selling…if that was what Mr LaVell preferred."

"Well, thank God for that!" Dad gave a relieved sort of gasp. "That garden is like a scene from Day of the Triffids, not only that, but also it really does look like it might become the means of ruining a beautiful street."

"Well, don't get your hopes up. LaVell is adamant that it remains exactly as it is—vacant. He has no plans to sell the property now, or in the foreseeable future. It seems LaVell acted with what Roland described as furious indignation at the suggestion and said, quote, 'that house was a sorrowful place for me, and no one is to set foot inside as long as I am alive.' The be all and end all is…we're stuck with that blot on the landscape until LaVell either dies or sees sense."

"So, it's nothing to do with Bryce and Gray after all? Here we are blaming poor Roland when LaVell's the one we have to blame for turning that beautiful house into the biggest eyesore on the estate."

"Roland says we can approach the council or environmental health, make waves if you like, but it won't make a blind bit of difference. Its private property and the council have no authority."

"Well, I hope he's proud of himself that's all I can say. The man's a lunatic."

LaVell was a misery maker. Weren't his own wife and children's victims of that misery he gleefully compounded with sheer badness? It was little wonder Jean took off with the twins when she did.

It was that touch, that laying of his hand on my shoulder which opened the door to some hellish scene so terrifying that, for the sake of my sanity, I had to lock that door and never allow myself to look beyond the dark mist. I'm now sure that was the day, the time, and the place when he knew I had seen the depths of his wickedness and immorality. Looking back, I realise that the feeling I evoked in him wasn't so much dislike as some kind of intense fear of whatever it was, he had sensed in me.

My house wanted to be filled with light and love, yet with madness of mind and acrimonious spite, LaVell shuttered the windows and left it in darkness. I might never know what motivated that man to do such a selfish thing.

So, there it was! And now I felt robbed and cheated that perhaps never again would I have the chance to make friends with new tenants. People like Daisy and Win who gave me affection, or Noreen who came with the gift of friendship. I might never again have the opportunity to sit by the fountain and try to discover why the mermaid wept.

I held onto the faith in my heart that one day, I *would* turn the key in the latch, walk through the door of number eleven as the new owner and fulfil my destiny. I also had faith that one day, the house would disclose the secret torment within its walls. Or perhaps in its soul, if there is truth in the myth that houses do have souls. Would the day ever come when the house on Juniper Drive shared its secret with me?

Chapter Fifteen

In what seemed no more than the clicking of my fingers or the blinking of an eye, it was the fourth of April and my eighteenth birthday.

"There's our birthday girl, happy birthday and many, many more, Judy."

A chorus of birthday greetings and good wishes rang in my ears, and I was encircled by happy smiling faces. Everyone on the guest list seemed to arrive at the same time and all wanting to give me a congratulatory hug—which was becoming more and more difficult since my arms were fast becoming laden with gifts.

"This is a sign of just how much affection people have for you, Judy," my mother whispered to me as one by one she relieved my arms of the beautifully wrapped packages and laid them neatly on a table.

The church hall in Fairfield was emblazoned with balloons, streamers, and banners. Music played and champagne corks popped. Mum squealed with delight when old friends she hadn't seen for ages turned up bearing gifts. Mind you, she did the same with people she had seen only the day before.

My eighteenth birthday was celebrated with gusto because, not only was it a sort of coming of age, but it was also in fact a double celebration. I had also been informed of my acceptance into the highly prestigious Dundee University where my teacher training would begin.

One thing about my mother, she was a living legend when it came to organising parties and this one was no exception. With all the glitz, glamour and frolics of a Hollywood party, this birthday bash would be remembered for a long time to come.

When the party ended and it was time to go home, Dad made a little speech, thanking everyone for the beautiful gifts, their good wishes for my future, and for taking part in this joyful celebration.

When the hall had cleared and we were last to leave, Mum gave one of her subtly rhetorical yet classically brief opinions of the party. "That went well."

And then the Easter break was over. The time had come for me to enter the great seat of learning to be educated and fulfil my dream of becoming a teacher.

The next three years were spent on life's trampoline as I juggled the highs and lows of university life. The will was in me to work and study like a demon. I had set my own high standards with one ambition—to achieve my goal. And I did it!

On graduation day, my eager hand clasped the *Decree With Honours* I had gained through sheer hard work and determination. I was well and truly following in Amy's footsteps, just as I always knew I would.

And now my teaching career was about to begin in no other than the one school which I had set my heart on teaching in: Fairfield High.

How proud Amy would be when she got my letter. I had all but lost contact with her after David became vicar of a new parish and they moved way down south, but she never, ever forgot my Christmas card, which *always* arrived for the anniversary of Paul's death. Amy never forgot to draw a heart in the corner of every card with Paul, xx within and I knew the meaning in this. I could still hear the promise her gentle voice made to me. "I will never forget Paul because he's always in my heart." Dear Amy, she knew how much this meant to me.

Over the years that saw me grind through a somewhat hectic childhood and adolescence before emerging into a genteel and more or less sedate adulthood, I still retained that one routine which had become more of a habit than anything. Looking to the top of Juniper Drive last thing at night and first thing in the morning was like taking off make-up and brushing teeth, it was up there on the must do list. But how painful my visual visits now were to see that once beautiful house become a decaying abhorrence and it maddened me.

"I swear we'll wake up one morning to find a heap of bricks where number eleven used to be," I ranted. "Why doesn't he do something to stop the rot from setting in?"

"Oh, I've given up looking in that direction. It just makes me so angry," my mother said with a cry in her voice. "That pig of a man doesn't give two hoots about anyone but himself."

Perhaps I hoped for a miracle, a turning back of the years, but that miracle never happened. I was forced to sadly witness the woeful deterioration of number eleven as it slowly fell into a state of dilapidation. The peeling paint and the now tarnished brass letterbox and door knocker which had once gleamed so proudly on the front door were now green with Verdigris. I could imagine behind that obscured glass picture window; the once pretty white lace curtains must now be yellowed with age. Careless time was doing its worst and day by day, month by month, year by year, my sadness deepened.

Before I knew it, fourteen years had elapsed since I last set foot inside the house on Juniper drive.

Dreams and aspirations never really die. The glowing embers of a special dream are always there just waiting to be rekindled. For some time, I had fostered an idea that might bring my lifelong wish to fruition, and I was now old enough and wise enough to do something about it.

We all have choices to make, some good, some bad, some right and some wrong, but they are consequently *our* choices, and no one has the right to dictate what another should or should not opt to do. I was almost twenty-six and my parents were still treating me like the child of twenty years ago who acted in haste, not wisdom. Still, there's a right way and a wrong way to do things and, in retrospect, perhaps I could—perhaps I should have been a bit less bumptious and a little more cautious in my approach when sharing with my parents and little brother the plan which I had in mind. Well, Charles wasn't exactly my little brother anymore. He was now out of his teens, six foot two and following Dad's footsteps into the world of medicine.

I ought to have shown them more consideration-why didn't I stop to think instead of blazing a trail of fear and hurt through their feelings? That time of my therapy was still fresh and very much alive in my parent's minds. Not just the therapy, but the reason for it. They never spoke a word about LaVell, not openly in front of me anyway, but there were times when I sensed my father's mind drift into the past and knew what was in his thoughts at that moment. He was remembering the frailty of my mind through the terror LaVell had put me through and to him it was every bit as repugnant as the taste of bitter almonds. They never stopped laying my troubles at LaVell's doorstep and who could blame them.

There were, to put it mildly, angry recriminations when I finally told Mum and Dad of my stringent, but as yet, futile efforts to find the one and only person who just might now be ready to rid himself of a white elephant by agreeing to sell me the long vacant house on Juniper Drive. Unfortunately, and somewhat ironically, that person was my adversary, the originator of my nightmares…Richard LaVell. There were lots of ranting and raving, but I remained tight lipped and resolute.

"I forbid you," and my mother's eyes were pools of torment.

That order really got my dander up and I retorted angrily, "You seem to have lost track of the fact that I'm a grown-up now with a mind of my own. I don't need your consent to live my own life."

"You're acting like a spoilt child demanding the biggest cake."

"Well, that's rich coming from you."

The dispute was becoming heated and had every indication of being endless but now it had reached the point where my father's tolerance gave out. He didn't roar in anger. He didn't even raise his voice. "Stop it, both of you," was all he said.

"But, Ralph…"

"Judy is determined to do what *she* wants, Gloria, so…just let go the reins."

I don't know if she was taking Dad's advice or just too damned tired arguing, but with the inability to accept each other's viewpoint, we reached stalemate. They couldn't understand this compulsion which in their opinion was just foolishly chasing rainbows. I knew that no amount of arguing could douse this passion to own number eleven. It gave me no pleasure to renounce their clichéd advice that it was a dead in the water, over-ambitious plan which, after all these years, surely didn't have a hope in hell of ever bearing fruit.

Even although it was very much against my parent's wishes, I remained a girl with a mission. Over the following five or six months, I tried in vain to trace the whereabouts of Richard LaVell. The man was virtually untraceable and for all anyone knew he might just as well have fallen off the face of the earth and taken up residence on Mars.

My determination, rather than waning, grew stronger and stronger with each passing day and I refused to accept defeat. I was like a marauding bull, ploughing my way through every obstacle. There was this desperation, an overpowering need to find LaVell and beg him to sell number eleven to me so that I could raise it to its former glory before it crumbled and decayed beyond repair.

And then, a year into my search, the man of my dreams came into my life. I didn't and never would give up my quest; I just felt it right to put Jack first. We were—as my mother so quaintly put it—courting. I knew right from the start that Jack was the real thing. We met and there was an instant rapport between us that was fast growing into a binding love. We had even discussed (in a matter-of-fact sort of way) the benefits that investing in property would bring, especially if the house and all the costs were shared. Jack was tired of staying in a rented flat and

I wanted, not so much to break free of family ties, but to be independent. In truth, we were two minds with a single thought. What we really wanted was for the two of us to move in together as a couple. And that was when I told him it must be number eleven, no other house would do.

Jack understood I was past the stage of living with my parents. Apart from the fact that they needed their own space, I too needed mine to live and love without restrictions. He understood the logic in squirreling away every penny I could towards my goal. What he *didn't* understand was this lifelong obsession with the house on Juniper Drive.

"Why that house in particular when it needs so much work?" He kept asking.

"Because I've set my heart on it," that was my honest answer. It was the only answer I had.

He would bring me the property guide with bold black circles around a few of the advertisements and it must have been so frustrating for him when I refused to even look. Then one day, Jack told me bluntly, "I'm beginning to think you're afraid of commitment." He pointedly folded the property guide and threw it in the waste bin.

I knew he was ready to give up, walk away from me and end it unless I removed the blinkers. Desperately I pleaded, "How can I explain this obsession, Jack? Tell me truthfully that there has never been something in your life that you'd willingly give your eye teeth for."

And my gentle Jack smiled acceptingly saying, "I would for you, Judy, only you. Do what your heart tells you. I'll go along with whatever makes you happy."

With Jack's blessing and backing, I resumed my search, but my patience was running out and so was time, for one day LaVell might be made a tempting offer for the derelict property. An offer perhaps he'd gladly take to rid himself of it. I could only watch, wait, and pray that I got to him first.

For the time being, I would go on living with my parents.

Chapter Sixteen

"Judy! Judy, why are you not ready yet? My appointment at the hairdressers is for 9.30 and you know how I feel about tardiness." Frantically, she tapped her watch.

My dear mum had this thing about being late for an appointment. Since my childhood, she had instilled in me that keeping someone waiting wasn't just bad manners it was downright selfish, but there were times when she was inclined to take this obsession a bit too far.

"Mother, it's only seven thirty," I called to her in pure exasperation, "I'm meeting Sophie at half nine, that gives us two hours and it only takes ten minutes to get into town."

"I know, dear, but you have to allow for traffic."

"Traffic, what traffic on a weekend morning when normal people are still in bed? I can't believe you actually expect me to get up at seven thirty on Saturday morning to shower and dress."

"Well, I thought the clock read eight thirty. Besides, you really must remember what Dad keeps telling you. Always expect the unexpected."

I took my time showering and dressing before ambling to the kitchen. All through breakfast, Mum made it clear she was clock-watching. "We've still plenty time," I told her, but with the respect she deserved.

She usually had an answer for everything, except for now. My dear mum just sat there, silently, and impatiently tapping her toe while looking ever so sweetly righteous.

I reneged and laughingly said, "Ok, let's get you to Pierre's before you blow a gasket." Oh, the exasperation of having a parent who only truly functions when her commands are being obeyed. "I only hope you appreciate that getting you to Pierre's much too early leaves me twiddling my thumbs while I wait for Sophie."

We both knew I'd take my time driving into town and she'd still get to Salon Pierre with time to spare.

I was silent during the drive into town, not morosely so, more contemplative. With all that was going on in my life I did have a lot on my mind.

"Penny for them," my mother enjoyed idle chatter, not quiet contemplation. In her book, silence wasn't golden, it was an irritation.

"Oh, I was just pondering on how strange destiny is. I was thinking actually about that day you told me I was going to see a very special doctor called, Sophie McGraw. You said she was a doctor who could take away the bad thoughts in my mind."

"Oh yes, I remember that too. How could I ever forget? The way you screamed the place down because you thought she was a doctor who cut your head open to see what was inside." Mum tittered in a nostalgic way. "We can laugh now, but at the time…"

"I took one look at Sophie and knew she was the one to help me find peace of mind and now, how long is it, fourteen…fifteen years later who would believe we still maintain such a close friendship?"

"It was a worrying time for us, Judy. You seemed so ill; we were afraid of losing you."

"Then Sophie made me whole again."

"Yes, and we'll be eternally grateful. In what seemed no more than a heartbeat, Sophie healed your misery and gave us back our happy little girl."

Her eyes misted and her pink lips trembled the way they always did whenever we spoke of that time. I often think that if I'd had parents who were less caring or more inclined to ignore the obvious symptoms of my troubled mind, I might easily have slipped into madness.

In Sophie, I found an ally who was herself psychically gifted and understood my frustration when I couldn't explain to anyone, least of all myself, the emotional turmoil within me. When my disquiet left me teetering on the brink of despair, it was Sophie who reached out and pulled me back and through her guidance, I learned control. So, I made a vow never to allow anyone to question my indebtedness to this woman.

From the very first, I had faith in Sophie, and the consultations with her that lasted almost a year were for me the most important time in my life. It was more than a healing of the mind. It was a uniting of kindred spirits. Sophie taught me to believe that right was right and wrong was wrong and what I had was in no way wrong. Neither was it an illness of body or mind. I talked, she listened and explained and bit by bit, the barriers crumbled until my arduous struggle with those strange and often baffling images which pervaded my troubled mind could be put up with and finally accepted. With Sophie, my mentor, and the help she gave me, I rose above the haunting time where for me there was no in-between, no gentle passage from one stage of growth to the next and for the first time, *I became me*. I eased into a natural interest in clothes, make-up, and boys. All those things that make up the wondrous time of adolescent wants and needs which filled normal teenage girls with tingling excitement.

One thing had always puzzled me and even Sophie had no answers. What I saw in my mind's eye was usually clear and I could relate every detail. Yet those first visions which happened with LaVell's touch were still only vague shapes in a very thick mist. Try as I may, and I did try with every ounce of willpower I could muster, my mind could not break through that fog and see what horror lay beyond. I could only ever get as far as seeing shapes forming, fearsome shapes that my mind refused to take in and the shutters came down. It was Sophie's belief that LaVell had in the past or would in the future commit some atrocity and his touch had unwittingly made me a witness to whatever it was. But my young, innocent mind was unprepared and unable to deal with such abject fear and had therefore shut out whatever vile scene I was testimony to. And that's how it had stayed from that day to this.

The car park was virtually empty at that time on a Saturday morning, so I parked and then walked the short distance to Pierre's Salon with Mum. "If you're not here by the time I finish, don't worry," she sighed forlornly, "it's really no bother for me to take a taxi home. You have a nice day out with Sophie though and remember to give her my love."

She might as well have screamed, "Look, world, I'm an abandoned parent."

I kissed her cheek and said, "Martyrdom doesn't suit you, Mum. You're much too young and pretty, but if you must be a martyr what better place to suffer than the best beauty salon in town?"

"How right you are, I am rather pretty aren't I? When Pierre's finished with me, I'll be downright gorgeous." Like a goddess of the silent screen, she theatrically clasped her heart and slyly watching my reaction from the corner of her eye, she sighed sorrowfully, "But alone…and lonely."

I mimicked her theatricals in the same melodramatic way and feigned remorse that I must now go and leave her to the mercy of a beautician.

In her best Bette Davis, southern belle accent she drawled, "Well, honey child, an expensive new dress is the only way to ease ma suffering."

I watched my mother trot lightly down the street towards the salon until I could no longer hear the click clicking of her heels on the pavement. She didn't begrudge me a life of my own, I knew that. All the folderol and showboating were simply the way she was. Being dramatic was all part of her make-up, but I nevertheless thanked God that she was *my* mother.

Chapter Seventeen

The dusky pink suit that was Sophie's favourite caught my eye. She was standing outside Marks and Spencer where we'd arranged to meet. As if she had felt my presence, Sophie turned and hurried towards me. "I don't know about you," she said, "but my body is crying out for caffeine."

Single minded and without another word, we made straight for the coffee shop which had become our favourite stop-off. We much preferred to do all our catching up over a mega cup of frothy cappuccino. Sophie had been in France for the past six months. She had taken this gap in her working schedule to supervise work on the holiday home she recently bought. Sophie had her dreams too, and that was to one day retire and live in her own idyllic corner of heaven: a village in France. After six months, we had a *lot* of catching up to be done.

Sophie watched me over the rim of her cup. She seemed amused with that crooked smile and those devilishly twinkling eyes. I asked her outright. "Why are you staring at me with your famous gotcha look?"

"Because *you* have the look of a little girl who's just been kissed for the first time-smug, surprised and obviously very excited." Sophie grinned from ear to ear. "Go on, tell me about him," she said in that probing, analytic way.

Most young women my age would have reservations about telling their innermost secrets to someone almost twenty years their senior, but not me. Sophie had steered me from the negative to the positive and willingly shared my sadness and my gladness. I could tell Sophie things my lips would never speak of to another. Now, I was suddenly fumbling and stumbling awkwardly with the words to tell her my very own love story.

"I'm aware of your heart racing. Only a special *him* could do this," she said with that link to my senses I had come to know so well. I'd admired Sophie McGraw's blithe and carefree style for as long as I'd known her. But so too did I admire how serious and caring she could be. Sophie clasped my hand. "I can sense a profoundly deep attraction. Yet that pleasant rippling I feel right now is more than simple attraction. This is absolute passion, isn't it?"

I blushed and said, "His name's Jack, Jack Wayne," then giggled as I handed Sophie a paper napkin and advised her to wipe the frothy moustache from her top lip. She'd done this on purpose, and I knew it. I knew she'd seen that blush creep over my face and the frothy moustache bit was simply to lighten that moment of quandary she sensed in me. The exact same thing happened on our first meeting, only not deliberate, not then, but it did break the ice. It had made me laugh and this simple act of genuinely carefree laughter was to begin the easing of my fears. She must have remembered it too and this was a reminder that I could trust her whenever I needed to talk things over in confidence.

The cappuccino I sipped appreciatively was creamy and welcoming. Sophie was speculative, but patient. She never was one to rush me. I put my cup down, rested my crossed arms on the table and looked Sophie in the eye. Sophie did likewise, but with her elbows on the table and chin resting on her clasped hands. "The whole story from the beginning if you please," she said casually.

"Well, Mr Phillips who teaches maths was off ill and Jack was the supply teacher who filled in for him," I began. "Anyway, Mr Phillips decided to take the early retirement that had been offered him on health grounds and Jack was offered the job permanently."

"That explains how you met, but it doesn't explain the rush of blood to your face when you say his name. What was it, Judy? What image did you see the first time you met?"

"It was so weird, Sophie. We were introduced and I held out my hand the way you do to greet a newcomer. This perfect stranger smiled and then when he clasped my hand in his, it was the strangest thing. In that instant, it was so clear."

"What *did* you see and feel?"

"I clearly saw us standing before an altar and wedding bells were ringing. How nonsensical does that sound?"

Sophie made a dramatic circling motion in the air with one hand and in the same dramatic theme said, "You've seen your own destiny. You've seen the man who'll walk side by side with you along life's highway."

"You should have been an actress, Sophie. Such a romantic. You wouldn't put it in simple terms like, oh, you've just met your intended, oh no, not you."

We laughed so heartily heads began to turn. There and then, my mind was filled with a memory that curbed my laughter. It was like turning back the pages in a book and re-reading a sad and poignant chapter.

Perhaps it was because Sophie had used those very same words Amy Royle spoke that day so long ago and it brought back a painful memory my mind had chosen to forget. I remembered the sad way Amy had tried to explain her loneliness without Paul beside her on that mythical road through life. I had pretended to understand, but I didn't, not really. And now, in that one brief statement, came the realisation that the strange crushing sensation which took my breath away at that time was what Amy felt at that very minute too. She must have been so lost and alone knowing Paul was never coming back. What I had experienced was the sorrow and suffering of her breaking heart. I had felt her pain.

"What is it, Judy? Did I do or say something to hurt you?" There was such guilt in Sophie's question. "A moment ago, you were laughing fit to burst. Now suddenly you've gone all silent and sad."

"I just remembered something-another piece of the jigsaw so to speak."

"Don't hold anything back, Judy, speak to me. I know you're suffering frustration and fear of losing something. I can feel a tremendous sense of loss. What is it you're so afraid of losing?"

"I'm afraid of losing the house!" I watched Sophie's sympathy turn to puzzlement as she slowly put the cup back onto the saucer.

With the deepest concern she asked, "What makes you think you're going to lose your home?"

"Not my home!" It struck me then what Sophie was imagining. "That house belongs to Mum and Dad. Strictly speaking, I'm merely a lodger. Let me explain. Since I was a little girl, I felt I was in some way connected to number eleven Juniper Drive. That big house at the top of our street? Remember I once pointed it out to you?" She half nodded as if trying to recall that time. "All my life, I've been in no doubt there was a bond between myself and that house, a link. I always believed, truly believed it was my destiny that one day number eleven Juniper Drive would belong to me and discovering I had second sight strengthened that belief."

Sophie tap, tap tapped a finger against her lips in a thought-provoking way while I waited until she spoke her words of wisdom. "I truly believe that some houses are more than just bricks and mortar," she admitted. "That house is the centre of every incident you told me about. I even underlined 'connection?' in my notes. There is a long history of houses that appeared to have a soul. Quite rightly, in the early days, people were less inclined to tell of strange disturbances for fear of being condemned as a witch."

"Of course, historical facts are a passion of yours." I had all but forgotten this. "I remember you once told me that your hobby was researching ancient landmarks and the customs and beliefs of our ancestors."

"Still is, Judy! I've always been fascinated by how barbaric our race was in earlier centuries. Witch finding was big business way back then and ignorance caused many innocents to be burned at the stake or condemned to the ducking stool. The irony being that if they survived, they were guilty and if they drowned, they were innocent."

"A bit like heads I win, tails you lose."

"It was more than ignorance or fear of what they didn't understand, it was open season. If a person was in debt to another and wanted to get out of paying the debt, or someone simply didn't like a neighbour, all they had to do was denounce them, point a finger and cry 'witch' and the kangaroo court did the business. Anyway, enough of times past: are you afraid you've lost the house because LaVell is still the owner, and you can't stomach the thought of approaching him with an offer to buy?"

"I would gladly bite the bullet, steel myself and make him an offer on the house—if I could find him. Fifteen years ago, the house was locked up, abandoned and left to go to seed and no one—least of all LaVell—has set foot in it since then."

Sophie sat there tapping her lips again, the way she always did when deep in thought and then she asked the obvious. "Why don't you just ask the estate agent to put you in touch with LaVell?"

I sort of snorted when I said, "If only it were that simple," and then began explaining (or rather confessing) that for weeks I had been frantically, obsessively trying to locate LaVell. "Every time I thought, progress at last, a step forward, it was always just another dead end. In short, Sophie, it's an impossible task."

"Why?" She quizzed.

"Bryce and Gray were the agents who originally handled the leasing and since Roland Gray is a friend of the family, I thought all I had to do was ask him, easy peasy."

"But it wasn't?"

"When I made enquiries about number eleven with a view to buying it, he politely told me that the property in question had unfortunately been taken off the market and as far as they were led to believe, Mr LaVell had intimated his intention to one day take up residency himself, therefore their agency no longer had any interest in the house. According to mum, Roland suspected this was a deliberate lie on LaVell's part to get them off his back about letting *or* selling."

"What did he have to say when you brought up the subject of the house lying empty for all these years?"

"Since the owner had dispensed with their services, Bryce and Gray were no longer interested."

"What about a contact address?"

"In typical LaVell fashion, he refused to leave a contact address. Instead, he arranged to contact Bryce and Gray himself and personally settle accounts."

"He's suspiciously like a man with something to hide." I was aware of Sophie beckoning the waitress, "Two more coffees please," she said without taking her eyes off me.

Her interest and her imagination had been well and truly stirred and before we parted company this afternoon I knew, I felt it. Sophie would find the answers which evaded me.

I carried on telling the story of my search. "I remembered that he, LaVell that is, owned some kind of engineering company, so I looked through yellow pages and in alphabetical order began phoning each one asking if a message could be passed to the owner and director, Richard LaVell. I was almost at the end of the listings and giving up hope. Each time the answer was the same, Richard LaVell was neither owner nor director of that particular company. I was ready to give up as the list grew shorter and then I came to the last one, Valiant Engineering, and what do you know. I was asked to hold while they put me through to the manager's secretary."

"You've traced him?" Sophie interrupted.

"Well, yes and no. She told me Mr LaVell no longer took an active part in the business, but she would pass on my message, and it would be at his own discretion whether or not he replied. When after a week I hadn't heard from him, I went to the factory, introduced myself and asked to speak with the managing director on a matter of great importance. I fully expected to be turned away and waited for another door to be slammed in my face, but instead I was politely shown into a rather grand office."

"Well, good for you." Sophie kind of proudly and approvingly patted my hand.

"LaVell's portrait hung on the wall and though I tried to ignore it I was drawn. Oh, Sophie! When I looked, I swear those scowling eyes were watching my every move. The dark mist surrounded me again and even after all this time the terror returned."

"But you still couldn't see what was so terrifying?"

"No…I…I can't…"

"That's alright, Judy, don't force it. One day that mist will clear, but not until you find the strength to see. Now, what happened next?"

"The spell was sort of broken when the secretary brought in a tray of coffee and asked if I took sugar and cream."

"How very civilised, promising too. Why then do I sense defeat?"

"They wouldn't—or rather couldn't help. In answer to my communication, LaVell had given his managing director strict instructions that if and when I contacted them, I was to be treated with the utmost respect, but under no circumstances was I to be informed of his whereabouts. They were to pass on the message that the house was **not** and never would be for sale and the decision was final. I tried to argue the point that if I could only speak to LaVell face to face I might just convince him to change his mind. It was like banging my head against a brick wall."

Sophie sat there with narrowed eyes and furrowed brow. "I've dealt with many strange cases," she told me, "But none as strange as this. Unless he truly does intend coming back one day, there's no sense, no logic in his actions. Who in their right mind would lock up and shutter a valuable house? And why refuse point blank to even consider selling? Something isn't right."

"Mr Bell—that's the manager's name—did let it slip sort of accidentally on purpose that LaVell had now moved to a, quote, *remote and secret location*, his excuse being that he needed seclusion because he had never really recovered from the break-up of his marriage."

"I get the feeling your Mr Bell is a loyal employee who likes his job, but not his employer."

"He also told me, in confidence of course, that every three months, a substantial amount of money from the business was paid into a numbered bank account."

"Well, LaVell may be in seclusion, but he's obviously still in circulation," said Sophie.

"I asked which bank was used as perhaps they could help me. He got a bit hot under the collar. I think Mr Bell realised he may have let out more than he should have and immediately insisted that what he had accidently told me was a confidentiality that a manager daren't break. He said that even if he could tell me, it would be a waste of my time. Banks too have a strict code of confidentiality. There's no way they would give out personal details. So, that's that, Sophie, my last hope."

"Not necessarily so! There are more ways than one to skin a cat. I have legitimate access to hospital records. On Monday, I'll request the records of one, Richard LaVell. He has to have medical records and his address is bound to be on them." Sophie looked delightedly rebellious. What I called her gotcha look.

"What if someone questions it?" I had one of those panic-stricken thoughts. I imagined Dr Sophie McGraw being frog-marched unceremoniously from the hospital for breach of confidence.

"My dear, Judy, there is nothing suspicious about doctors requesting medical records, it's allowed, it's a perfectly normal procedure. Don't worry, LaVell started a battle, but we'll win the war."

There was still a grain of hope, the merest chink of light at the end of a very long tunnel.

Chapter Eighteen

I was a typical Aries, born under the sign of the ram, headstrong and pushy. Waiting and patience—they were words that didn't apply to me; everything had to be done…yesterday. Yet strangely enough when I hadn't heard from Sophie the week after our meeting, I wasn't in the least perturbed. I didn't do the frantic thing either, like tearing my hair out in frustration because things weren't moving fast enough for my liking. I had other things on my mind. Perhaps nothing as nail-biting as my endeavours to trace the whereabouts of the mysterious LaVell, but most definitely less chaotic. More the actual joy of simply taking time out for some peace and quiet.

In my inimitable, talk now think later way, with neither regard nor thought for hurt feelings and inferiority complexes, I had made a silly, thoughtless joke about Jack and how spontaneity wasn't his strong point. My shy, mindful Jack gave me cause to take back my careless, but nevertheless callous remark. He booked a room—a double room—for a romantic weekend break in a quiet country inn.

We drove to The Hollies Inn on Saturday morning and spent that entire day in ardent bliss of just being alone together. On Sunday after breakfast, he took me on a ramble along the quaint country lanes, a stroll along the riverbank, then lunch and a slow drive home. Oh, Jack wasn't all that shy, as I discovered on that weekend alone with him. He could be excitingly spontaneous when he put his mind to it.

I was in love and what's more, Jack said he loved me too. It was still early days and we agreed to give our newfound love time to grow. We needed time to learn about each other before making any lifelong commitments.

Our weekend break had eased my tension and drew rein on my stress. I was relaxed and still dreamily treading cloud nine on Monday evening when the telephone rang. I knew even before I picked up the receiver it was Sophie.

"Don't know where this will lead, Judy, but I have an address for you. Let's hope it brings an end to your search." I could tell she was elated about her discovery and thrilled with the anticipation of where it might lead. "Six years ago, while moving into a new house at fourteen Grand Mews, you know the place almost in the heart of town? Well, while opening a packing case, Richard LaVell badly gashed his hand and required stitches. That's the last entry of him having attended hospital for anything. I hope and pray for your sake, he's still at that address."

"Mr Bell did say he was living somewhere remote and secluded." That feeling of utter dejection, like a storm cloud hanging over me was back. "Grand Mews isn't exactly remote. Thanks anyway, Sophie, I do appreciate it." I wanted to curl up in a corner and cry. Sophie had done her best so why let her taste my disappointment? I put on a happy face because she would sense my smile and it would give her peace of mind to think she'd helped. "I'm probably clutching at straws, but if he has moved within the past six years who knows? It's possible the people who bought the mews apartment might have a forwarding address."

I vaguely heard Sophie say, "That's my girl, think positive," just before I hung up.

I stood outside the aptly named Grand Mews hoping that the people who now lived there were receptive and not hostile. Although they had every right to be hostile when a stranger came knocking on their door questioning them about something as private and personal as the purchase of their home. Perhaps when I explained the necessity of finding the previous owner…

The musical door chimes played *welcome home* and I smiled easily, confidently. Surely, only nice people would install this kind of door-chime. I was right. Chrissie Dalton opened the door and she smiled chirpily saying, "Can I help you?" But then her smiling eyes saw this nervous wreck standing on her doorstep. Without hesitation, she immediately invited me inside.

"I need to know…it's really important." I stammered like a jittery schoolgirl trying to find the right words to say. "What I'm trying to ask is if you have no objection to telling me that is."

Her face turned quite pale, she was uneasy and who could blame her. Kind of fearfully she asked, "What is it that you need to know so badly?"

"The person you bought this beautiful apartment from, was it by any chance Mr Richard LaVell?"

She was suddenly wary and suspicious, as well she might be. Chrissie Dalton demanded an answer. "Why would you want to know that?" She stepped back worriedly, as if contact with me might burn her flesh.

Hastily, I assured her, "Oh, I'm not the law or a debt collector, nothing like that. I'm only an ex-neighbour whose sole objective in finding LaVell is to ask him to sell me a vacant house he still owns, but obviously has no intentions of ever returning to."

Chrissie heaved a great sigh of relief, and I felt her trust. "It *was* Mr LaVell who handled the sale of the apartment. He wasn't the owner though. He was only acting on behalf of the friend he shared the apartment with. A Miss Weston? I'm afraid that's as much as I can tell you."

Miss Weston, ah, now I could put a name to the fancy bit. But I mustn't let my mind wander into the past. Every scrap of information was essential, so I concentrated on what Chrissie was saying.

"Did he by any chance say where they were moving to?" I asked hopefully.

"My husband and I came here to finalise some of the details and unfortunately, I asked that very same question. I wasn't being nosey, only interested in a courteous way. And then in total innocence, I asked if they were moving to a bigger house for children. What a mistake that was. Oh my God, the exception he took when I mentioned children. It was so rude the way he told me in no uncertain terms to mind my own business."

Right then I could feel her bitter anger. It was like bile rising at the recollection and I made a humble and hasty apology for reminding her of something best forgotten.

"What's worse," she went on, "when I tried to explain that I'd only been making polite conversation, he opened the door and asked us to leave, saying from now on any business should be done through his solicitor."

"He is a rude, aggressive and not very nice person," I told her. "Unfortunately, if I'm to have any hope of buying his house, I will have to firstly, find him, and secondly, speak to him."

"Then good luck with that—you'll need it," Chrissie hotly advised.

At the door, before leaving I said, "Thank you anyway for kindly allowing me to invade your privacy and please accept my apologies for barging in on you this way."

What a downfall! I had not so much expected as really hoped for so much more, only to be left deflated again. Perhaps, it was time to end this dream, for that's all it was, all it had ever been—probably all it would ever be. Not a glimpse into what was to come, only a silly childish fantasy. Metaphorically speaking, I'd fallen off my horse, but then Chrissie Dalton had an afterthought that put me right back in the saddle.

"Why don't you speak to Mr Burrell? If anyone can give you information, it's him." Her hand gripped my arm, holding me back. "Wait, wait," she said, "I have his card somewhere."

"What does this Mr Burrell have to do with it?" I was just a tad perplexed, but the most sensational feeling of hope began to stir within me.

"Burrell, Sheen and Thomson are LaVell's solicitors. It was Mr Burrell who personally handled the sale." She handed me the business card and proudly exclaimed, "I keep everything like this for future reference. Look, that's even Mr Burrell's private number."

I held the card that might possibly take me a step further on my journey. "I don't know how to thank you," I said gratefully to Chrissie. I truly was grateful, but it was much more than gratitude. I had a good, positive feeling about this.

"Oh, go on, I'm just glad to help," she said with a blush creeping over her cheeks, and I thought, how strange the way helping another embarrasses a kind and thoughtful person such as Chrissie Dalton. And then caringly she said, "I hope you find him and manage to buy your dream home. It's a wonderful feeling." That very special young woman kissed my cheek as I left and told me, "Be lucky," and I just knew that with the help she had given me I would be.

That evening, as dusk was gathering, I stood outside number eleven, peering through the now permanently locked wrought iron gate. Time had cruelly taken its toll and the garden was sadly, but not hopelessly overgrown. Not if loving hands could restore it. The beautiful rose bushes that once filled the air with perfume so sweet were now briar, wild and unkempt. I reached through and picked what appeared to be the last surviving yellow rose. A single tear dropped into the soft petals as I raised it to my face. A sudden soft breeze brushed my cheek and I swear at that moment I heard the house sigh my name. "Soon," I whispered, "soon," and right at that very moment, the strangest thing made me gasp. The once exquisite lace curtain seemed to part ever so slightly as if someone was peeking out at me. It was a sign.

I was prepared to do whatever it took to get the information I needed and if that meant grovelling then I'd grovel like a professional. If—and that was the key word—if Mr Burrell agreed to see me and he turned out to be as bumptious and overbearing as most of the solicitors I'd met, well then, I would be nice as pie then maybe that would stir his conscience.

I still bottled-up the fearful thing that haunted me, even as the flashing images grew stronger. Sophie was stepping up her efforts to persuade me to undergo hypnotic therapy, but I was adamant that actually seeing what lay beyond might be more traumatic than imagining. In short, I was terrified to face whatever demons were in my mind.

Next day, during mid-morning break I telephoned Mr Burrell's direct line number expecting…well in truth, I didn't really know what to expect. I told myself, "Hey, the worst he could do was hang up the phone, not hang me."

It was more of a shock than a surprise. His attitude was sensitive and kindly; that alone was like a refreshing breath of fresh air on a hot and humid day. Brian Burrell didn't rush me through the speech I had spent half the night rehearsing. He listened with patience and what seemed to me like real interest as I told him about my search and lo and behold, I was invited to his office to discuss the matter in full.

Standing outside the grand red brick edifice that housed the offices of Burrell, Sheen and Thomson, I suddenly had doubts and reservations. Why had Burrell been so kindly sympathetic to my plight? He didn't know me. I was sure we'd never met. Yet, when I mentioned LaVell and Juniper Drive, he seemed strangely accepting, almost as if I was an expected visitor. There was only one way to find out if he was genuinely sympathetic to this need for knowledge as to LaVell's whereabouts. Or did the invitation and the information come with a price tag?

I wasn't asked to wait, which to say the least was unusual, but shown directly into a rather smart office with filing cabinets lining the walls. The first thing that struck me about Brian Burrell, he could easily have doubled for Robert Redford. His light brown hair, greying at the temples, was well trimmed and there was a smile in those blue eyes. Past the first flush of youth I thought, but handsome nevertheless—for an older man.

"I called you about number eleven Juniper Drive," I stammered.

The first thing Burrell said was, "I must admit, your telephone call did intrigue me." He rested his arms on the desk and those blue eyes held one of those not quite knowing looks, more-quizzical.

"It was pure chance I got your number-either that or divine providence."

"Well, it's been so long since I've heard from Richard and when you showed such interest in buying the house on Juniper Drive, I thought, what house on Juniper Drive? As far as I knew that house was long gone. Years ago, Richard made it perfectly clear he had no desire to live in what he called a mausoleum, and he was getting rid of it. I took it for granted he'd sold the house. Look, I'll try to explain why I'm so bewildered."

By then, what I felt was more like a befuddled irritation, like just missing the last bus home. "Oh, I wish you would," I said through clenched teeth.

"For reasons I prefer not going into, Richard LaVell stopped dealing with our firm for about a year and put the house in the hands of an agency with the intention of renting it out. Well, to cut a long story short, he eventually brought all his legal affairs back to our firm, but there was no longer reference to this property in his list of assets. I never had reason to question it, just took it for granted he'd sold it through…that other agency." For some reason, he appeared to be perhaps a shade guilty over whatever problem he had with, *that other agency*.

"Bryce and Gray," I said.

"Yes, Bryce and Gray! Of course, that was years ago after Jean took the girls and went back to Canada when she found out about his affair with my secretary."

"The woman who…who…" I stammered in embarrassment and my heart thumped, "she was your secretary? I'm sorry I had no idea, but then I was no more than a child at the time."

The revelation left me gob smacked. He obviously thought I knew all about the sordid affair and in all probability, Burrell, was letting me know the identity of the other woman in case I made some hard to take, snide remark about her without knowing the facts.

With forced light-heartedness, Burrell said, "Maybe he had a thing about secretaries, first Jean and then…"

At that point, I made a hasty swerve onto another subject since my unease was showing. "You know, I haven't even introduced myself yet," I said briskly. "I'm Judy Vernon and as you've probably guessed, Mr LaVell was our neighbour." He grasped my outstretched hand, and I was immediately overcome by sadness like I've never known. "She…the woman…your secretary, was she your wife?" The words were spoken without thinking.

"Not my wife," he replied with a calmness that only comes with breeding—and years of practice. "Amanda Weston and I were at one time engaged to be married."

"Forgive me," my backside shifted uncomfortably in the chair. "I've learned to live with this phenomenon of seeing into another person's life. Unfortunately, I still haven't learned to zip my mouth."

My feeble apology seemed to amuse him and without recrimination or hostility, he replied, "Condemnation is due only when a hurtful remark is made with the knowledge that it will cause pain. As you didn't have that intent, Miss Vernon, you are blameless."

I thanked Burrell for his kind indulgence and wondered then if Amanda Weston had any idea that she had let go a kind and decent man in favour of a cold-hearted brute such as LaVell.

"You may not know it, but the truth is Richard became a recluse, completely cutting himself off from the outside world." Brian Burrell opened the desk drawer and took from it a buff folder which he placed on the patch of green leather that served as a base for writing materials. He reclined back in the chair, elbows on the arms and hands clasped in front of him. In a dreamy kind of way he said, more to his own self than to me, "What I never understood was why a beautiful woman like Amanda, with such a zest for life and a real addiction to socialising, all at once accepted being snatched from that life and shut away? No more dinner parties, no more dressing up, which I might add she loved." Burrell's head drooped sadly, and I suspected he had done this many times over the years when, for one reason or another, the name of Amanda Weston cropped up in conversation. This kind of pain was a private thing. He ran his hand over the buff folder and sighed sorrowfully, "Yet she did so willingly, such was her love for that man."

The admiration in his voice, the love that obviously still lingered, led me to suspect that LaVell was the one with the least human emotion out of this, ménage-a-trios. A man incapable of love and yet, Amanda Weston had stayed by his side all these years in a situation that for most women would have been not only difficult to bear, but almost intolerable for a woman with such an aptitude for socialising. Impossible surely?

"What possessed him to plunge into obscurity? I've tried every way to trace him, estate agents, the electoral register, even hospitals, but they either couldn't or wouldn't give me information." The frustration building inside me was like a pan drop lodged in my throat. Hoarsely I said, "My efforts led me here, you are my last hope."

"Let me put you straight on one thing, Miss Vernon…"

"Please, call me Judy." Perhaps in the back of my mind, I was hoping that the familiarity of using first names might induce Burrell to yield and give up the location of LaVell's hideaway.

"Well…Judy, to let you understand, LaVell is the kind of man who never, ever acts spontaneously. The reasons for his anonymity are a mystery to me. I myself have only met and spoken with him twice over the past ten years." Burrell's eyes darted uneasily round the room as if the weight of conscience were becoming too much to bear. Without looking directly at me he muttered, "Personally, I suspect he has a more sinister reason for hiding from the world. Then again, I confess to being biased."

"But is it possible for a man to carry on a successful business and yet be virtually untraceable?"

"It is! If every purchase, every transaction is done in someone else's name."

"Amanda!" Suddenly everything slotted into place. "Of course, that's the reason I couldn't find LaVell's name anywhere. That's why there was no trace of him. Accounts, title deeds, everything was in **her** name." I suddenly felt uneasy and shivered involuntarily as if I had just unearthed something that was best left buried.

All this time, LaVell had hidden behind the façade that the cause of his reluctance to face the outside world was the infidelity that cost him his family. But I remembered the cruel, inhuman way he treated Jean and the children. There *was* no love there. He barely showed affection for them. I also had a clear recollection of the night Jean left him. The memory of the way he hit her and the obscenities he used were still vivid in my mind. Mr Burrell broke into my train of thought.

"I wish I could help you more, but you must understand my hands are tied, client confidentiality and all that." There was a sort of twisted smile on his face like he was about to get his own back in some way. Then he said, "You don't mind if I leave you alone for a few minutes while I have a word with my secretary? By the way, the folder on my desk is marked private and confidential." He secretively winked an eye and gently, reassuringly patted my shoulder as he moved lithely towards the door.

It was an invitation which I gratefully accepted. I leaned across the desk, the buff folder marked LaVell/Weston lay facing me and I hesitated momentarily before opening it. Brian Burrell must have thought long and hard before coming to the decision to allow me the opportunity to see this. Perhaps, he saw it as divine retribution, or perhaps he just felt sorry for me, but it was there staring me in the face. A single sheet of paper with LaVell's address.

I had turned the metaphoric corner, but as for LaVell, I still had the unenviable task of coming face to face with him and the best I could hope for was civility. Who knows, he may have changed, mellowed with the years, but was a change of heart possible in someone without a heart?

Chapter Nineteen

Détente cordial would definitely not be the order of the day when I finally came face to face with LaVell. I had no illusions on that score. He appeared no more than strangely wary of me the very first day I went to their house. But I really hit a nerve the day we crossed swords over the twins walking to school with me. What I sensed in him that day wasn't wrath, but alarm when angrily I told him he wasn't a nice man. Perhaps because I did what his own daughters were too afraid to do—I stood up to him and his bullying ways. Why then had he ordered his factory manager to treat me with the greatest respect? I haven't the faintest idea why. Since it's highly unlikely LaVell would treat me like a long-lost friend, I'd happily settle for the man himself indulging me with the same respect.

It was almost three weeks since I'd spoken to Mr Burrell and in that time, I had been feverishly putting my finances in order before approaching LaVell. I had geared my mind to the expectation, the certainty that my parents would almost surely pressurise and try to dissuade me when I told them of my intention to use the power of persuasion and engage in a battle of wits with my nemesis. I was unprepared for the fury that spilled from my gentle dad.

"This is stupidity in the extreme," my father yelled in a furore that brought tears to his eyes. "All you're doing is stirring up old and painful memories. We don't know and we probably never will know why this man had such a devastating effect on you. Why, why, Judy, would you risk your sanity by going to see him?"

"I'm not risking my sanity or anything else," I yelled back defensively. "For heaven's sake, please, please, will you *stop* treating me like a child." And then I sensed their concern and humbly said, "I don't want to put you through this anxiety; all I want is for you to trust my judgement."

"At least let us go with you, or at least one of us." Mum had resorted to pleading and that in itself was unusual. I had never before heard her plead. Demand yes, but pleading? It just wasn't in her nature.

Dad then pointed out what he obviously thought I had carelessly overlooked. "Have you given one single thought to what that house is worth? Even with its state of disrepair, the value must be at the very least £150.000. I don't think you've really thought this out, Judy. The mortgage and cost of putting it right will be crippling and you still have furnishings to consider."

He had rather disparagingly raised a point. How was he to know I had already taken all that into consideration?

"Did you really think I'd blindly go into this without first doing the maths?"

"And have you done the maths?"

"Yes! Along with the money Auntie May left me, I also have considerable savings of my own…and let's not forget, Jack's a partner in this too. I'm not getting my hopes up, but on the other hand, LaVell is a businessman and he's sure to see the sense in offloading what's become little more than a white elephant that will only decrease in value as dry rot and decay takes its toll."

"Aw, you're just spitting in the wind, Judy," Dad yelped frantically. "Couples starting out look for a small flat to begin with, but you don't want one chocolate, you want the whole bloody box."

"I don't cherish the thought of speaking to LaVell, but I'll do whatever it takes and be very diplomatic in pointing out what all those years of neglect has done when I offer a much lesser sum than it's worth." I felt I was drowning in a tidal wave of mixed feelings, but my determination was armour that no bullet could pierce. "I'll also point out that, as he clearly doesn't want the house, why keep paying taxes on it?"

"Your mother and I can't understand this obsession you have with that house, Judy. It's only bricks and mortar for Christ's sake, and with so many nice properties on the market…"

"Why can't you at least try to understand *I don't want another property? I want that house.*" Was I being over emphatic? Probably yes.

They looked at me with shock horror when stubbornly I stood my ground. It was the pain in my mother's eyes that made me cringe with disgrace and sorrow that it was no other than I who put that pain there. She sat side by side with Dad on the sofa, her frail hand clutching his hand so tightly as if she'd fall into some bottomless pits were she to let go. There and then I knew that fear was for me, not for her own self.

In the past when I said or did something that puzzled them, my explanation was always meagre and hollow. It was preferential (from my parent's point of view that is) not to look this anomaly in the eye and I respected that. Right then I did what I should have done a long time ago. I told them truthfully that I was well aware their logic decreed the inexplicable to be no more than tommyrot. While it was their right to believe there was no such thing as the paranormal, from experience I knew differently.

Calmly I put a question to them. "Please, will you just listen to what I have to say and keep an open mind?"

My parents only nodded, simply because they were out of words to speak and criticisms to shout.

"For reasons that I don't yet understand, I do and always have known it is my destiny to own that house and that's why I have this compulsion I can't control." I needed them to understand the truth and honesty in my words. "My senses are purely and simply on a different plain from yours and that's all. Let me ask you to recall one very significant event that might help you to understand…"

"We do understand!" Mum was oblivious to her conceit. The way she saw it, people who gave vent to weird notions, what she called improper thoughts, simply weren't decent. That was her inspired opinion. It seems I had fallen into the category of indecent. "What we can't understand is why you persist in trying to make something out of what are no more than purely coincidences."

"No, no, no, you *don't* understand because you never really wanted to. I've lived with this thing that used to scare the hell out of me. All you ever did was made me feel like a…a freak." I was yelling and I knew it, but I was determined to put an end to the pretences. "Dad, have you any idea how frustrating it was for me when Mum piously referred to it as funny turns or dizzy spells?"

As if I had just lanced a very sore boil or doused him with ice cold water, Dad drew in his breath sharply. "Aw, Judy, sweetheart, you actually believe we thought you were a freak?" The truth hurt!

My dad, the man I'd idolised and looked up to for as long as I can remember was gutted by my tirade. Pain was written all over his face and right there and then I wished it hadn't gone this far. I wished I had kept to myself the plan to go and speak to LaVell face to face. But now, I was out of options and had to finish what I'd started.

"If it weren't for this *thing* as you so delicately put it, mum, you and I would be a heap of bones rotting in some cemetery. All those years ago, cast your mind back to the near miss we had when that joy rider ran the red light. How do you think I knew that if you drove on when the traffic lights changed to go and if I didn't do something, that speeding car was going to crash straight into us? My only option was to make you brake. What I'm trying to say is this foresight gives me options." It might just have been no more than a flash of inspiration bringing that day to mind, but it was the pill that eased their torment.

"Remember, Ralph, how badly shaken I was? That stupid joyrider was doing a lot more than sixty and if Judy hadn't screamed at me to stop neither of us would have survived."

His head slowly nodded in agreement. "And that night you told me we must have a guardian angel looking after us."

Mum sniffed and dried her eyes and suddenly there was acceptance. "We did, Ralph, we did. Our guardian angel was our own little girl."

"Do you see it now, Mum?" I said, and the frustration in me subsided. "That wasn't just another coincidence. I stepped momentarily into the future and that's why we're here today to tell the tale. Now please, can we call a truce and just agree to differ?"

In that moment, a kind of peace descended over our house of fear. Her tear-filled eyes looked straight into mine and my mother, very softly said, "You do what you have to, my darling. We'll be right here if you need our help in any way."

"I'll need your help when I move into number eleven." It was as if the sun had come out after the rain. Suddenly, everything was clear. I was in no doubt it was going to happen.

Chapter Twenty

And then the working week was behind me, and it was Saturday at last. Dad left for the hospital, Mum went shopping and I waited to speak to Jack before leaving on my mission. He had phoned to say he'd done his own reconnoitre and was coming to give me explicit directions to LaVell's hideaway. I think he must have had visions of me driving lost and alone through the countryside and he was only making it easier and less frustrating for me to find the place.

"I know this means a lot to you." Jack handed me the sheet of paper with the carefully drawn directions. Tenderly, he stroked my face, and I held his hand against my cheek. "I accept it's something you want to do alone, Judy, but I wish you'd let me go with you." It sounded almost like he was begging her to have a change of heart. Then he pointed out, "I have a vested interest too. All going well, that house is where we'll live together one day."

"Was that a proposal or a business proposition, Jack Wayne? I can't quite make up my mind whether or not you're serious."

"I'm deadly serious!" He blushed and began fiddling with the sheet of paper. "I had a special evening planned, wine, roses, soft music playing in the background and instead I go and spoil it all by…"

I knew right then that Jack felt let-down in some way. Maybe it was botching what he intended to be a proposal, or maybe just disappointment that I wanted to do this on my own, so, thinking it might ease his anxiety I made a silly joke. "For a minute there, I thought you were about to burst into song." Jack just stood open-mouthed and slightly befuddled. "Frank and Nancy Sinatra," I explained. *"Then I go and spoil it all by saying something stupid like I love you."* My warbling was totally unmelodic. My throat was oh, so dry with excitement and my singing voice was more like the croaking of a crow.

A smile flitted over Jack's face. He'd caught my meaning. "Maria Callas, eat your heart out," he said in a frivolous way that I think was for my benefit. "I never guessed you had such a…unique singing voice, Judy."

I pretended to be cut to the quick by Jack's sarcasm and he laughed. I laughed too in that free and easy way when your whole being is filled with gladness. It wasn't Jack's arms holding me or the words he spoke either. Or that I had known from the very moment we met, it was our destiny to marry. It was none of those things, only the ground shaking anticipation that, with God's good grace, my lifelong ambition could be fulfilled by the end of this day.

Jack said, "Tonight! We'll have a long talk tonight. There are things I have to say, but they can wait." He gave one of those nervous coughs and hurriedly got back to the business in hand. "I've written everything down." There was a noticeable tremble in his hand as he went over the sketched map of the road I had to take. "When you hit the A9, about two miles on, the village of Benvie is signposted. Go through the village and just past it, you'll see another signpost for Benvie farm. Don't be misled, there's no farm any longer, it's LaVell's residence and that's where you make for."

I waved from the open car window until the car turned out of Juniper Drive and Jack disappeared from my sight. With Fairfield behind me, I joined the A9 and just as Jack said, only a short drive away, the signpost for Benvie. I turned left onto a more scenic route and drove slowly through the quaint little village. I probably would have passed the farm signpost but for Jack's warning. All the searching, all the speculation and only a short, ten-minute drive from where I lived brought me to the very location that for gruelling, tension filled months I had so desperately sought to find.

About a hundred yards of bumpy and dusty dirt track took me to the front of what had once been an old farmhouse and stables. It was quite awesome the way they had been converted into this rather sumptuous, quietly picturesque dwelling place. I could only imagine the considerable cost of this undertaking.

My index finger sort of hovered over the doorbell. Was I doing the right thing? Was I opening another can of worms? I could turn away now and after all the months of striving to reach this point forfeit my only chance to realise an ambition. Or should I go ahead and risk coming face to face with the only person who had ever caused me to feel such gut churning fear? I considered the options before resolutely and firmly pressing the doorbell and almost immediately, I could see through the ornate stained glass door panel the figure of a woman approaching.

She stood in the open doorway, regal and as elegant as a thoroughbred. This woman was possessed of a beauty that defied her advancing years. This was **the**

Amanda Weston, the woman LaVell had wooed with a mystique that unbelievably captured her heart. Or was I perhaps wrong in my assumption, and it was the other way round? I had seen in LaVell something ugly and frightening. This woman must have seen him in a totally different, a kinder and obviously loving light, for she had willingly given up everything to be with him. She said nothing, just looked at me questioningly with sorrowful eyes.

It was time I introduced myself.

"I'm Judy Vernon and Mr LaVell used to be our neighbour." I was careful not to mention **Mrs** LaVell.

"You've come to pay your condolences. How kind, please come in." She wore a simple black jersey dress which swirled around her ankles as she stood aside to allow me to enter. Other than a single strand of lustrous pearls with a diamond and emerald clasp, not fake either, these were the real thing, and other than this she was without adornment. She didn't need baubles to enhance her elegance.

Condolences, it suddenly struck me what she had just said, and I froze briefly before querying, "You said condolences? I'm sorry, Mrs LaVell, but I don't understand. There seems to be some confusion. I'm here in the hope of speaking to your husband."

"I am Amanda Weston, Richard and I never married. The confusion is now mine. I took it for granted you had heard of Richard's death and that was the purpose of your visit."

I reeled, teetered slightly, and muttered, "Oh my," before plonking myself onto a sofa.

That was when she saw the utter shock on my face. "You didn't know?" She asked, curious now as to what purpose had brought me there. Slowly, she lowered herself next to me on the sofa. "It appears we have been talking at cross purposes. I think perhaps we should start again, Miss Vernon…"

"Judy, please call me Judy, only my students call me Miss Vernon."

"You're a teacher?" She asked with admiration but just a hint of envy.

"I'm proud to say that's my vocation."

"Your pride is well and truly justified. In my youth, I wanted to become a teacher. I loved children and saw myself developing young minds and firmly guiding the children in my care so that one day, hopefully, they might become responsible adults." Her voice was soft, like velvet, and her diction cultured. "Unfortunately, I achieved nothing of what I set out to do. Fate took a hand, and my life took a different direction. To my regret, I never had children of my own." There was unmistakable resentment in the way she said it, but only for a fleeting moment and then she smiled. "Tell me, Judy, what urged you to go into teaching?"

"My parents moved to Fairfield before I was born and when I was a little girl, Amy and Paul Royle bought eleven Juniper Drive, the house Mr LaVell subsequently bought. Amy was a teacher at Fairfield High and in my eyes, she was a heroine. In fact, it was at a very young age I made up my mind to mould myself on her. But then a terrible thing happened. Paul was manager of the village bank, and he was shot and killed during a robbery."

"Oh, how awful!" she gasped. "What a devastating effect that must have had on a child of…how old were you?"

"I was six."

Tears like tiny jewels rolled from her eyes and sat momentarily on those high, classic cheekbones before tumbling onto the black dress.

In a moment of remorse for speaking of that sorrowful time while she was in the midst of her own grief, I laid my hand comfortingly on hers. Instantly, I had a vision of a beautiful, lost, and forlorn child kneeling beside a young man lying on a lawn edged with begonias, weeping and desperately pleading, "Daddy, Daddy please wake up."

"The man who died in a garden when you were a child, he was your father?" All my life I had been berated for doing this thing that was in my nature. Speaking without thinking and now I'd done it again.

"How…what…I've never spoken of that day so you couldn't possibly have known." Amanda spoke with awe, not anger. Considering I had quite possibly encroached on a very private time in her life, other than a slightly ruffled composure, there was absolutely no trace of malice in her words or her manner.

"Were you remembering that day right then when I touched you?" I asked.

Guardedly she answered, "Yes, why?"

"I am so sorry for coming out with it like that but let me explain. You deserve that at least. When I was about ten, I discovered that sometimes, not all the time just now and then, physical contact, a touch opened the door to someone's past— or future. It can be very upsetting you know, like just now for example. I actually felt that piercing agony of the sorrow you were feeling."

"I'm no stranger to the pain of that memory. That day my father and I…" She gave an involuntary sob. "We were playing in the garden. Like you, I too was only six at the time, Judy, but I still remember like it was yesterday." She twisted a lace trimmed white lawn handkerchief in her delicate, trembling fingers.

I ventured a rather frail apology, "Please, don't distress yourself anymore," but she didn't seem to hear me. It was like she had a need to talk about that day.

"We were playing my favourite game, hide and seek. I remember how my father used to pick a flower, hold it up to his face and pretend to be hiding behind it. Sometimes, he'd put a buttercup or a daisy on his head and lie on the grass, supposedly hiding and then I'd run all around pretending to look for him."

I smiled nostalgically, remembering how my own dad used to play these same silly games with me.

"That day, I came from behind the garden shed and he was lying on the grass in the shadow of a sycamore tree. I ran over shouting boo, boo. His head was resting in a clump of begonias, and I still thought it was all part of the game. He didn't move although his eyes were open. Only, they weren't smiling. They were staring glassily at me. I was too young to understand death, yet I felt very afraid."

"It must have been very traumatic for you to witness something like that. What was it, a heart attack?"

"A cerebral haemorrhage they said. He didn't know a thing about it. One minute he was there and the next minute—gone. My mother gave me the usual excuses each time I asked where my daddy had gone. Her answer was always what you'd tell a child in the hope of easing their pain. Daddy was now in heaven with the angels. I still searched endlessly for him anyway. Even got stuck up a tree that I'd climbed trying to get to heaven and fetch him home."

"Please believe me, it wasn't my intention to open old wounds."

"You didn't! Wounds like that never really heal." There was no recrimination, just an aura of gentle, captivating sweetness that surrounded her. "Now please," she said, "it's been a long time since I've had a decent conversation with another woman and your being here has brought a breath of fresh air into my rather dull existence. You were telling me about Amy and Paul, the people who lived in the house before Richard bought it."

"Oh, but Mr LaVell didn't buy the house from Amy. He came later."

Amanda didn't speak with discontent or sadness, but there was a kind of hurt kitten look in her soft hazel eyes. "I only ever saw it from the outside, you know. Richard told me to wait in the car while he went inside to secure all the windows and doors. I never did understand why he adamantly refused to sell a house he freely and openly admitted to hating."

I liked Amanda Weston. I liked her very much. She proved to be nothing like the femme fatale I had imagined all these years, but a warm and sensitive lady, for she *was* every inch a lady. I could see now why that torch Brian Burrell carried for her still burned so brightly.

Did LaVell really, really know the beauty on his arm, the gregarious woman who walked by his side, smiling and confident? Did he ever take the time and trouble to notice her warmth, her intellect or was she simply a chimera of his own making? Was it her vivacity and the very essence of a rare and beautiful orchid he wanted to keep to himself, to lock away in seclusion until the flower wilted? Or did he selfishly only want the company of a stunningly beautiful and sensuous woman in his self-inflicted solitude?

"Come, let me show you around." Amanda was suddenly filled with a sort of frivolous excitement. "We bought this when it was no more than a shell. It was a blank canvas, and I was the artist. I told the architect exactly what I wanted, and this was the end result."

We moved from room to room and the taste and elegance took my breath away. The sitting room with its deep sofas, plush pile carpeting and a huge Georgian style fireplace was enough to make anyone melt with envy. The dining room was so spacious the hand carved dining table and ten chairs seemed to take up hardly any space. But what really captured my attention was a truly exquisite silver rose bowl in the centre of the table. It looked so forlorn and empty. How sad that something so lovely should be without the blooms it was made for. Or had it been that LaVell was such a strict and stern being he had simply protested that roses were an unnecessary indulgence? It was obvious this house with all its grandeur had only ever been a fancy shell for just himself and Amanda.

Without thinking I said, "You must have had lots of lovely parties here?"

"Ah, how I would have loved to hold candlelit dinner parties and play mine hostess." Her hand lovingly stroked each dining chair as Amanda walked by. "Unfortunately, Richard was a very private person. He wasn't in agreement with socialising." Her hand frustratingly thumped the last chair as we passed.

I mumbled a slightly embarrassed apology for the faux pas. Amanda was politely forgiving about it, and we moved on to the rest of the house. Oh, how her style and grace shone through in every room.

"With flair and imagination like yours, you should have been an interior designer," I told Amanda. "People would have paid a fortune for your services."

"Oh, I could just picture Richard's face if I even hinted at going out to work." Her eyes widened at the very idea. "He would have died…" In that instant, realising the words she had thoughtlessly spoken, Amanda bit down hard on her bottom lip. Somewhat abruptly she said, "Talk to me while I make coffee," and more than likely steeped in embarrassment at having forgotten so easily that Richard was already in the hereafter, she hastily swished towards the kitchen.

We sat in the lounge, drank coffee, and talked. Well, at Amanda's insistence, I did most of the talking. I saw now that Amanda Weston was a woman who had never in her life known what it felt like to be deprived of anything. And then, LaVell's refusal to allow her entry to the house on Juniper Drive? Of course, with him being the type of man he was, stingy with affection and miserly with explanations, LaVell gave Amanda no account for this denial, and it must have been like an itch she couldn't scratch. My filling in the blanks was what she needed and I willingly obliged.

Her laughter rang throughout the house when I told her about the Keller family. I related the stories of Paris's mischief and Roman's naked escape from Mrs DeCorsa and her lethal cleaver. She smiled wistfully and even shed a heartfelt tear when I told her about little Daniel Rafferty.

But when I came to relate Win's story and what she said about how the sound of the gurgling fountain brought back such fond memories and her mind ventured back to a place by a brook in Donegal where happy times were lived, for some reason that sad look of longing returned to Amanda's face.

Amanda sighed and softly said, "There are times I think about a time or place, and I too have these very same sensations." She spoke with a kind of yearning, and I sensed that she was back in that garden of her childhood, playing hide and seek with her father.

There were tears in my eyes when I told her of the sorrow and disappointment it had been when the Raffertys moved away. Naturally, I didn't disclose and never in my life would I ever give full details of their sudden departure, or the fact that the real reason they had left in a hurry was only a daring escape to take shelter in the safe haven of another country.

"What a wonderful family they must have been, Judy. How I wish I had known them."

It was all too clear that Amanda had been starved of company for years, the way her face shone when I recalled incidents. She positively oozed rapture at the release from solitude and begged me to tell all. She clutched the moment like an excited child being taken to the seaside or the zoo for the first time.

It wasn't until she started switching on lamps that I realised the lateness of the hour. The afternoon light had faded, and we were into evening.

"My goodness is it that late?" I jumped to my feet. "It's time I went. I've kept you captive long enough."

"I haven't enjoyed a day so much for…such a long time and…" There was an ache in her voice as if she verged on crying, but then her natural composure took over and she said, "I haven't even gotten around to asking the real reason for your visit since you were unaware of Richard's death."

"Would you believe I came to **beg** Mr LaVell to sell me his house on Juniper Drive?" I could only laugh at the irony. All my searching, the anxious sleepless nights, dashed hopes and then I finally found him…only to discover it was too late…ten days too late.

When Amanda explained why she automatically assumed I had come to offer condolences she told me the reason for LaVell's unexpected demise. It seems he had gone down with flu and retaining his insistence on isolation, he refused to see a doctor or allow a doctor to come to the house. It appears he had a heart after all-a weak heart that couldn't fight a bad case of flu.

"Well, I don't know what his reasons were, but Richard transferred the title deeds for Juniper Drive over to me after Jean left. Perhaps making me the official owner was just his way of ensuring she couldn't stake a claim on the house."

So, case solved! This is the reason eleven Juniper Drive wasn't on Richard LaVell's list of assets!

"I own that house now," Amanda announced, yet gently and without the hint of a boast. "Technically speaking, Judy, I'm the one you came to see. Richard was such a precise man. He even made a final will and testament naming me as sole beneficiary. I'm sure he must have arranged a settlement for Jean and the girls because he was adamant, they would never contest the will. I argued that Jean could come back one day and demand the house. He emphatically assured me that with the steps he had taken by transferring ownership to me, that most certainly would never happen. I don't want that house, Judy. I may have wanted it once, but when Richard denied me entry to his once marital home, I vowed never to step over that threshold. I'm happy where I am."

"Then there's still a chance?" I asked excitedly, "Providing you're prepared to negotiate the sale of course."

In what to me sounded like a flat and final way Amanda said, "I'm not open to negotiation."

Those point blank and harsh words brought me down to earth with a bang and once more shattered all my hopes and dreams. Amanda Weston was after all a wealthy woman who could wait on the market to boom. Either that or she might even forsake her vow never to set foot inside the house and renovate it for herself if one day she had the desire to move closer to town.

The overwhelming disappointment at that moment was too much. It was time to tuck that dream into a corner of my heart and lock it away forever. It was over.

"Thank you anyway, Amanda. I've enjoyed an extremely pleasant afternoon," I said politely. "Even if my journey was fruitless, I feel cheered." I smiled to hide my disappointment and gallantly said, "Well, needs must, so I really should be on my way now."

"Wait, Judy, wait!" Smiling, she cupped my face in those soft, perfectly manicured hands and looked me straight in the eye. "I didn't say I wouldn't sell, only that I wasn't open to negotiation."

This was turning into one of the most mind boggling, frustrating times I had ever experienced. She sounded sincere and yet… "I don't understand," I said. It was an admission of my confusion, but what else could I do? Should I blithely tell her I understood and then just walk away without asking for an explanation?

She saw my dilemma and said, "Come back inside and we'll talk."

I followed her back into the lounge and just sat there wordless and wondering, like a child waiting to be told about the birds and the bees.

"I seem to have dunked you in a pool of doubt and uncertainty," Amanda began. "Let me put it another way. Now, please don't think I'm prying indelicately, but you've obviously allocated a certain amount of money for a deposit, so how much were you prepared to put down?"

And that was when I wholeheartedly gave my trust to this virtual stranger. "Well, leaving myself enough for the work that has to be done, I'm…I'm afraid the house has been neglected for years and it's a bit…dilapidated now." I stumbled over the words, embarrassed that Amanda might see it as my way of securing a bargain. I was wrong. She sat there with hands in her lap, quite unconcerned about all of this.

"I'm aware that—to Richard's shame I might add—the house was neglected. He refused any explanation as to why he preferred allowing it to crumble and decay rather than sell it. I finally gave up asking. Now, let's just forget about all that and in answer to my question…"

"£20.000," I told her, freely and honestly. Although for the life of me I couldn't understand why she wanted to know this if she wasn't prepared to negotiate. What's more, I couldn't understand where this trust in someone I'd just met came from. Yet here I was disclosing my financial status.

"Richard hated that house and I think it belongs to someone who loves it. Bring me a cheque for £20.000 one week today and you can have the title deeds."

"I don't understand! Although the bank has agreed to a mortgage, there's still all the paperwork to be done. I'd have to pay the £20,000 deposit into the bank once I know how much of a mortgage I need to borrow. Pardon me for being blunt, but you were a legal secretary, so you must know the drill. If you were to hand over the title deeds…"

"Then the house would be legally yours and you would be the new owner. I know exactly what I'm doing, Judy. £20.000 isn't a deposit, it's the price I'm asking you to pay for eleven Juniper Drive." Amanda's bottom lip suddenly began to tremble, and her face took on a look of such pain. "I've done little in my life to be proud of," she said. "Let me redeem myself with one selfless act. Do you agree on the price?"

I could only nod my head in agreement, speech was impossible. Amanda Weston wasn't an eccentric; she was a level-headed woman. This was all a dream, it had to be. And then her next words left me in little doubt there was no chicanery in her offer.

"Then I'll see you next Saturday! To put your mind at rest that it's all above board and legally binding, I'll ask Brian Burrell to personally hand you the deeds." She stood and regally held out her hand for me to shake on it. "Now, do we have a deal?" Her smile was no longer tinged with sadness, but bright and fulfilled.

"Yes!" I croaked hoarsely and then clumsily, awkwardly threw my arms around her neck and pressed my tear-stained cheek against hers. My enthusiasm dislodged the single comb that held her hair in place and the brown silken mane tumbled halfway down her back.

"Oh, my goodness," she laughed, "it's been a long time since anyone has shown me such affection."

It totally amazed me that this woman felt so undeserving of adoration when she was in fact the most deserving person I had ever known.

At that moment I had a sudden recollection of a time I overheard Harriet Granger, with her snooty nose stuck in the air discussing Amanda. At that time, she was simply *the other woman* or LaVell's *bit on the side*: such a common description for such an uncommon lady. Harriet had described her as a hard faced, home wrecking bitch. How pitiful that a loving, caring woman like this had been judged—or rather, misjudged—all because of her love for a man as cold and heartless as Richard LaVell.

Chapter Twenty-One

They didn't believe it, Jack, my parents, and thinking I'd had some sort of mental breakdown, my flustered mother even phoned Sophie for advice. I listened with a sort of amusement as she told Sophie I was delusional because **no one**, no sane person anyway, gave a house like that away for a measly £20.000.

Within the hour, Sophie arrived. I answered the door to find her standing there smiling cynically. "How about you and me having a one-to-one conversation?" She asked. "I don't mean to be rude, but your mother takes neuroticism to the limit."

"I bought it, Sophie! I bought number eleven."

"I gathered that much, but according to Gloria, you stole it. She seems to think you made a pact with the devil or some damned thing. I thought I'd better hear it straight from the horse's mouth because to be honest, I think she must have picked you up wrong. Either that or I've picked her up wrong." Sophie stood with narrowed eyes and hands on her hips. "Which is it?" She said, "Because you couldn't buy a scruffy little bed-sit for twenty grand."

It was a serious thing to be as good as gifted something of this magnitude. I could hardly believe it myself and here I was trying to convince everyone else to believe that I wasn't mad. It really did happen.

"LaVell's gone, dead and buried," I told Sophie coldly. "I spent the day with a woman who for years I've looked on as some sort of monster. How wrong could a person be? She turned out to be the kindest, sweetest human being I've ever met and whose only sin was falling for Richard LaVell. I was wrong in my assumption, my misguided belief that it was nothing short of common greed that motivated Amanda Weston. Nothing could be further from the truth."

"So, it is true that she sold you that house for twenty grand?"

"As true as I'm standing here, and on Saturday, it *will* be legal and binding."

"Listen to me, Judy! I don't think it's a good idea for you to go back there alone." Sophie appeared spooked. She was obviously alarmed, but she hadn't been there so how could she know? As if reading my mind, she offered an explanation. "All these years with him, you said yourself he had virtually cut her off from the outside world and it could have affected her mind. For all we know, she could be schizophrenic, an angel one day and a devil the next. I've dealt with people like this, and I know what they're capable of. With all due respect, Judy, you don't."

"Why are you all trying so hard to make me think she's playing some sort of evil practical joke on me?" My defences were down, their scepticism was rubbing off on me and now I too was beginning to doubt. Then I thought back and knew I had sensed only goodness and truth. If there was anything else, I would have felt it. No, I trusted my own instinct, not the unfounded doubts of others. "There's an easy way to find out," I said triumphantly. "Before the end of next week, I'll telephone Mr Burrell and ask him if the sale of number eleven Juniper Drive has been finalised. She would hardly have a contract drawn up if she weren't serious."

"Of course, she wouldn't." Suddenly there was understanding as well as belief and acceptance in the way Sophie said it. "I want you to promise me one thing," she asked…or was it a demand. "If it is sick joke—I'm not saying that it is mind you—but if things don't turn out the way you hoped, *don't* give her the satisfaction of seeing how hurt you are."

"Oh, ye of little faith, just wait and be surprised." I was enveloped in a warm embrace, or at least that's the sensation I felt and that's how I knew the dream I had dreamed was no longer a fantasy.

Over the next few days though, I freely admit to my quiet confidence becoming overshadowed by doubts. When all was said and done, a promise, no matter how easily and honestly made, could be rescinded just as easily. I had turned up on Amanda's doorstep when she was at her most vulnerable, having lost the love of her life so suddenly. I had eased her sorrow and she showed her gratitude with a magnanimous gesture. But with time to think, a mind could be changed and a week was a long time to think. My father in his wisdom reminded me that what seems too good to be true probably is.

I waited until Thursday of the following week and dialled Brian Burrell's direct line number. The moment of truth had arrived, and I had prepared myself mentally for the news that either Amanda had changed her mind, or she'd had it changed for her. Brian Burrell wasn't just a friend, he was Amanda Weston's solicitor and as such, he was duty bound to warn her about the folly of such a profoundly generous agreement.

He sounded quite jaunty and in answer to my query regarding the purchase of the house replied, "The documentation is prepared and all I need from you is your signature on the dotted line along with a cheque for the agreed amount." I knew he was smiling. I could tell and I had a sneaking suspicion that Brian Burrell had known all along that the house on Juniper Drive belonged to Amanda. He just wasn't free to divulge that information. All he could do was set me on the right track knowing Amanda's generosity and the possible outcome. But there was something else. The warmth and joy of lost hope found and the dying flame of love re-kindled was there in the emotional way he spoke her name.

"I've already written the cheque, Mr Burrell. It's unsigned yet though. I've deliberately left that until Amanda's there to witness my signature."

"Amanda has invited me to personally hand over the documents," Brian Burrell proudly advised me. "Of course, when that moment arrives it's only right that she has that honour. Amanda is so excited about this, Judy. She's…recovering her zest for life is the only way I can describe it. I'm so glad I took the risk of allowing you the opportunity to peek inside that folder so that you could find LaVell. Although, knowing the kind of man he was, I had to bite back the words to warn you against it. Then again, I wasn't to know his time on earth was about to be cut short."

That was the moment I told Brian that if I was in any way responsible for returning colour to her existence and the delight of just being her own self in the love of life then I was glad to have achieved this personal victory, because if anyone was worthy of a life, open and free, it was Amanda Weston.

"All that's left now, Judy, is the time for our meeting. Shall we say 1 pm at Miss Weston's residence?"

I rose very early on Saturday. Caught between belief and disbelief, I hadn't really slept that much. At quarter to one, I got in the car and set off for Benvie.

It wasn't until the title deeds were presented to me and the keys to number eleven rested in the palm of my hand that I now truly believed this wasn't a dream from which I'd awake.

There was the broadest, proudest smile on his face when Brian Burrell shook my hand and said, "Congratulations."

"And now to seal the bargain, I have a little gift for you." Amanda said and handed me a red box. Inside there was a gold key which had been especially cut. It was a presentation key to the house on Juniper Drive: my house.

I looked questioningly at Brian Burrell. His arm was around Amanda and his hand rested gently on the curve of her hip. The wide smile on his face said it all. Brian was a happy man, and the sadness was gone from his eyes.

"I take no praise and I merit no gratitude for this beautiful gesture," Brian told me. "Once you've known Amanda for a little longer, you'll understand her generosity."

I was already acquainted with her generosity when she requested my cheque be made out to the Society for Children with Cancer. And right then I knew that this woman who at one time had been branded so many cruel names would forever remain in my heart, a true friend. If she were to ask me, I would gladly walk-through fire for Amanda Weston.

Chapter Twenty-Two

How long would it take to sink in? If it ever did that is. I couldn't help taking my eyes off the road to keep sneaking glances at the three things on the passenger seat of my car. An envelope containing the title deeds to 11 Juniper Drive, a set of keys, and the red box which held that golden key. They may have seemed of little importance to others, but no. To me they were the symbol of a dream come true.

It was the sound of my mobile ringing that startled me back to awareness. *Sophie calling*, I picked up the phone and hurriedly said, "Listen, Sophie, I'm driving at the minute, but I'll call you back as soon as I get home."

"Wait, Judy, before you hang up. There's something of interest I really, really need to show you. I'm at home so could you *please* pop in before you go home? I wouldn't ask today of all days, but it is important that you should see this for yourself."

"Ok, I'll be there in five minutes." I took it for granted Sophie's main objective was to find out how things went today. She was only concerned about my well-being after all, and since she had given me so much of her time in the past I couldn't, I wouldn't deny her some of my time.

When Sophie answered the door, right there and then her flushed face and the way her trembling hand clasped her chest filled me with real concern. I gave her a friendly hug and tried to hide my fright by saying something droll. "For the love of Mike, why are you all het up when I'm the one who's just been given the keys to my kingdom?"

"You'll see in a minute," she said eagerly.

The dining table was carelessly strewn with books and papers and Sophie looked positively frantic as she searched through the clutter. There was obviously something specific she badly needed to show me, but it was difficult keeping up with her incoherent muttering amid all this rummaging.

She stopped briefly to raise a question. "You've always claimed to have an affinity with that house, right? And I remember saying it was possible that in another life you may have lived there. Of course, that isn't possible since Fairfield was built about the time you were born, so I took a hike through the archives and came across something very interesting." Once again, the papers went flying every which way and at the height of her frustration Sophie growled, "Where in Christ's name could I have put it?"

"You really should calm down, Sophie," I warned her as calmly as possible. She seemed deaf to warnings or advice amid her own confusion, and it was impossible to understand her muttered gibberish. Finally, the lost document was found and at last, she was back to the sensible Sophie I knew.

In a much calmer frame of mind she said, "We get into our cars and drive without really looking and taking stock of what's around us. That's true, isn't it, Judy?" Sophie stopped for a moment, her head nodding in a, *know what I mean*, kind of way and she looked at me as if I should automatically understand what the hell she was talking about.

Rather than question this, I nodded as if I understood and thought it best to just listen in hopeful silence. Surely, whatever had roused this eagerness in her would eventually make sense to me. But then as an afterthought I said, "Perhaps if you filled in a bit more blanks, I might be able to help." My offer went unheeded.

"Well, when was the last time you walked, not in Fairfield but around it?" She stared at me for moment or two. My lack of clarity only seemed to cause irritation rather than relief, so she carried on regardless. "I am trying to prove a point, Judy. We *should* be looking and learning about our heritage. There are so many interesting facts, links in a chain of discovery if you like. There are features and landmarks we take for granted without bothering to discover why they're there or who even put them in the places where they've stayed for possibly hundreds of years."

I listened to Sophie and began to see her logic. What she was telling me began to make perfect sense, for aren't we all just a bit blinkered and inclined to see landmarks as just being there, yet make little effort to discover the history behind them? But I still couldn't fathom her agitation or what had sparked it. I quietly sat there taking heed with only an occasional nod of the head. "You've roused my interest." That was as much as I could think of to say, then left her to do all the talking.

"I went back as far as 1812. Fairfield was arable land at that time with farms and smallholdings dotted around the area. Well, I managed to recover a map, a copy of which I'll show you when I've finished." She stopped rummaging for a moment, peered over the rim of her glasses and wagged a forefinger to stress her point. "It's very significant as you'll see. Anyway, I got copies of the factual documentation gathered from that era." Still, she carried on scrambling intently through the pile of papers.

"Can't I do something to help?" I asked, but again my words fell on deaf ears.

"Here it is," Sophie said triumphantly. And then fervently she began reciting Fairfield's early years from the chronicles of the strayed and now recovered document. "It was a hard life with little profit and a local man by the name of Arthur Bain made it known he wanted to own the entire area which is now Fairfield. Bain was reputed to be a rogue and although he was never caught and convicted, everyone knew he made his money through rustling other farmer's livestock, slaughtering the animals and selling the carcases. More to the point, Bain was becoming quite a rich man in the process."

"Let me stop you there for a minute, Sophie." I was becoming more and more confused by what appeared to be simply incoherent trivia. "True, it's a fascinating story, but what in the world does it have to do with me?"

Her tongue went tut-tut-tut and her head shook in a disgruntled fashion, "I'm coming to that," and there was more tut-tutting. "What's the use of telling the end of a story without telling the beginning?"

I humbly apologised like a disobeying schoolgirl and begged her to carry on.

"Thank you for your indulgence," she said sarcastically. "Now, where was I? Oh yes, Bain had managed to buy almost all the land, but two farmers stood in his way of gaining total possession. He *persuaded* Samuel Green, who owned one of the two remaining smallholdings, to sell his land which left only Mathew Colquhoun."

"I take it the *persuasion* Bain used had been a lot more than haggling over a price. Reading between the lines, I'd say it took a lot of threats and possibly a few beatings before the poor man reneged."

"Well, the records weren't all that specific, it was no more than inference. Now, Mathew Colquhoun, unlike Samuel Green, was a man who didn't scare so easily. He was an Irish immigrant getting on in years and riddled with rheumatism. According to historical records, Colquhoun was willing enough to sell up and go back to Ireland. He had an urge to end his days there in the country of his birth. He made it known that because of Bain's strong-arm methods, he would never let him have that last piece of land. It seems Colquhoun wasn't a man to give in to tyranny."

"So, if all this has been put on record, then it must have been common knowledge in those days that Bain used thuggish methods, possibly even murder to get what he wanted?"

"You've got to remember, Judy, the law then wasn't what it is now. People literally got away with murder. Colquhoun was a wise old man who wasn't all that oblivious to the goings on. He probably knew that he had become too frail to fight and the beast who was Bain would win in the end. Colquhoun knew his farming days were numbered."

I said, "Clearly, Bain had to have been known as a man who was more than willing to use brute force to coerce the farmers into giving up the land, he wanted…their land."

"Undoubtedly! And then along came a family of gypsies, not to be confused with tinkers, mind you. These people were genuine Romany. Well, the story goes they asked Colquhoun's permission to put their caravan and graze their horse in one of his fields. Colquhoun now saw a way to get his own back on Bain and he secretly sold a little piece of land slap bang in the centre of his field to Ramón DeBanzie for two shillings."

"Two shillings, ten pence for a piece of land, are you sure you've got that right?" I asked incredulously. This story was now starting to get better and better.

"That was the deal alright, ah, but you see Colquhoun had a wicked sense of humour. He went cap in hand to Bain and told him he was prepared to sell all the land **he** owned. Bain gladly paid the old man and believing the land, the whole jing bang was now his, Bain snatched the deeds before the old Irishman had a chance to change his mind. Then as he was leaving, Mathew Colquhoun turned to Bain and told him to look at the deeds because there just happened to be a little field of about forty square feet, right in the middle of Bain's land that now belonged to a gypsy family, Ramón DeBanzie, his wife Isabella and daughter Lucia."

"How did Bain take it, or need I ask?" By this time, I was not only intrigued but saw the whole thing as a screamingly funny farce. It was neither funny nor farcical as I was about to discover.

"Bain offered DeBanzie a reasonably fair price for the last piece of land, but the gypsy said it was his land and he was keeping it. Bain cajoled, threatened and then someone pointed out that it was in gypsy blood to travel. They were nomadic by nature. If Bain hung fire, the gypsies would soon uproot and move on. Only things didn't go to plan. Lucia was being wooed by a rather well-off young man and all in all, the family were growing quite content with their new life. They decided to put down roots in their own little acre of God's green earth…for good."

"Ah, the plot thickens."

"Oh, yes! Incensed and infuriated, Bain hatched another plot. He reported to the local constabulary that the gypsy was poaching on his land, and they'd find the proof if they searched his site. Their search turned up a rabbit and brace of pheasant hidden under the caravan. Of course, it was Bain himself who put them there for the police to find and corroborate his testimony. The events of that day have been chronicled and were at one time legendary. Sophie read again from the document. As the constabulary started to drag her father away from the bosom of his family, Lucia cried out that he was an honest man and innocent of the charges brought against him. On bended knee, Lucia begged Bain to save her father from a prison sentence."

"This is powerful stuff, Sophie, why it's almost like the script for a film. What happened next?"

"Before I come to the crunch, there's something I have to show you first. This is the old map of the area I told you about. You can see where the church and the village pub used to be, there's the well that still stands in what used to be the market square." I followed the line of Sophie's finger as she pointed out the landmarks of old Fairfield. "This was Colquhoun's land and right here," feverishly she tapped the spot on the map, "DeBanzie's field. Now, this is a more recent map of where Fairfield was built and here's the interesting thing, I wanted you to see. If I lay one map over the other, matching up all the local landmarks and then stick a pin in the exact spot where your house is you can clearly see it was built directly on the site that was DeBanzie's field. Judy, I have here a documented account of what happened that day. It's not only fascinating…it's scary."

I heard Sophie speak, listened to what she said, but like in a dream. I was at that moment filled with the stirring of mixed emotions. Feelings of fear, loathing and savage anger I couldn't account for. This had most certainly been an emotional day for me, but joyful, not anguished. Had this tale of greed and corruption really gotten to me? My mind was drifting, and I was aware of mumbling words under my breath, but in a foreign tongue that I didn't understand. Sophie was caught up in her own enthusiasm and didn't seem to notice. She was too busy quoting from the copy of that old document.

"It says here that Bain laughed cruelly at Lucia's pleading, but then he agreed to withdraw his allegation providing Ramón gave back the land and promised never to return." Sophie breathlessly tapped the sheet of paper. "This is it," she said excitedly, "this is what I wanted to show you. Legend has it that right there and then a fearful cloud cast everything into darkness, yet Lucia was surrounded by glorious light. She reached to the sky and plucked a dagger. Now the question here is, could this have been a miracle or sleight of hand? It's a fact that gypsies were known to be adept at trickery and deception, therefore, we must take that into account. The story goes that Lucia turned to Bain and said, 'Death is only a pause in time, the soul is eternal. On a day far flung from now, I will return to claim this land. Where others are blinded to truth my eyes will see many things.' I think…I'm sure she was referring to second sight. 'The souls of wronged beings I will set free.' And then she drew the dagger across the palm of her hand spilling her blood onto the spot where she stood."

I was aware of Sophie standing there, watching and listening to me with her mouth agape, and yet I had no idea why I was speaking words that to me were meaningless or where the words came from, but speak to them I did. "And this ground where I now stand, with my blood I consecrate in the name of the Lord."

"I think you've just proved what I suspected. I think it's possible you are the reincarnation of Lucia DeBanzie. How else could you have quoted exactly word for word what she is reputed to have said?" Sophie handed me the paper. "Here, look at it," she gasped excitedly, "see for your own self. Your obsession isn't with the house, Judy. It has to be with the land it's built on and that land was DeBanzie's field."

"You're telling me that you, a psychologist, an educated woman believes in reincarnation?" I found the irony rather funny, but my amusement failed to produce even the hint of a smile from Sophie.

"It's natural to question and doubt, but look beyond your scepticism, Judy. In my lifetime and in my work, I've dealt with many strange things, phenomena that no one could explain. Your case has always intrigued me. Maybe it's because we're two of a kind, or maybe it's because I know that barrier you put up in your mind hides something so scary you simply can't acknowledge it."

"So, let's just say you're right and Lucia's curse, prediction, whatever you want to call it has come true. I now own the land where my house is built and my eyes see what others don't, but what could she have meant by setting free the souls of wronged beings?" Sophie had more or less clarified all but this part.

"That's the one thing which baffles me, but if I were to hazard a guess, I'd say it's linked to whatever is locked inside your brain. Perhaps the house does hold the explanation. When all's said and done, that's where it all began. There is nothing more documented about the DeBanzie family or what became of them. I myself now think it's a strong possibility that Bain had them murdered and the fearful thing locked in your brain is connected to the past, not to the present."

"You think it's probable that the DeBanzie family were slaughtered for a little piece of land, their bodies buried somewhere in Fairfield and almost two hundred years later, Lucia has come back as me to uncover the gory deed?" I sniggered sceptically. "You think *I* might hold the key to what happened that day?"

"Oh, go ahead and laugh at my theory if it makes you feel better," Sophie said in a kind of disgust. "Whether or not you believe what I've said, it's one possibility to consider. Maybe it is just my penchant for historical facts and all the melodrama that goes with it, but you'd be surprised how many people got away with murder in days gone by."

"What became of Arthur Bain?"

"According to the records, he married a local woman, a widow with two grown-up sons. A few months after the wedding, Bain mysteriously disappeared. Common gossip had it that during a furious quarrel one, or perhaps both stepsons killed Bain, but nothing was ever proven. Mrs Bain adamantly claimed her husband just left the house one day and never returned. Listen to this. Quote, 'with gladness of heart it was strongly rumoured that Bain's stepsons had murdered the village beast who went by the name of Arthur Bain.' Poetic justice, don't you think?"

"I don't hold with murder, although this man obviously stirred so much hatred, maybe it was simply poetic justice."

"Many people thought so. Then again, these were times when a mysterious disappearance could be put down to the work of witches and witchcraft."

And then Sophie smiled and shuffled into the kitchen, returning a moment later with a bottle and two glasses. "I know you're driving, but how about one small glass of wine to toast new beginnings?"

"You must think me very ungrateful after all you've done. You are so much wiser than I am so what right do I have to show contempt for your findings?"

Sophie always had a full schedule, something that comes with being good at what you do and yet she never gave up trying to find the answer to this thing that still haunted me. She had given up her free time in an effort to trace the origin of my dilemma and to my shame, what I did basically was wantonly throw it back in her face.

"You have many, many good traits, Judy, and it has to be said, a few bad ones, but ingratitude was never one of them. When you first came to me, a troubled child with troubled thoughts, I felt your misery because I'd been there myself. It gave me great satisfaction to help you find and accept your identity so that you could come to terms with the fact you couldn't change what you were or what was inherent in you. I understood your rudeness and arrogance—oh yes you were full of yourself—but it was merely a façade that hid a frightened little girl and you, my dear Judy, were never ungrateful."

"So, what do we drink to?" I held up my glass and waited on her response.

"How about…" Sophie thought for a moment and then said, "dreams that come true."

"Or better still, an end to nightmares." I laughed at my own silly suggestion.

With one hand, I raised the glass to my mouth, clutched my keys with the other and caressed them in a miserly way. With callous selfishness, all thoughts of what I'd put my loved ones through were cast aside. I had stretched my parent's misery and Jack's patience to the limit as I strived to make possible what they saw as impossible.

"To dreams that came true," I toasted. And then proudly, I raved to Sophie that *I* was holding the world in the palm of *my* hand. I gushed that *my* dream had come true and even had the gall to suggest that *I* may have been helped by a higher power.

Sophie just sat there silently listening to my hedonistic bragging. I saw her narrowed eyes, the disapproving look; every sign was there that she was becoming increasingly angered. I chose to ignore her angry silence and class it as simply polite interest. It should have struck me as a lot more than strange.

Sophie wasn't exactly the listen quietly type when her cage was being rattled and I was doing a fair bit of rattling.

And then she let loose the displeasure which had soured her natural empathy.

Chapter Twenty-Three

My foot eased off the accelerator the instant I realised that I was way past the speed limit. My ears may have burned from the verbal slap they had just taken, but doing 60 on a 40, max road? I was all too aware that driving like a lunatic to escape from Sophie's honesty and bitter truth wasn't the way to do it. Taking flight was useless when her words still burned my ears.

I should have been a bit more observant to the angry scowl frozen on Sophie's face when I flashed the gold key and then went on to obsess in a despicable way about—not *our* home; not mine and Jack's—*my* house. I should have seen that this 'queen of the hill' attitude didn't impress her one bit. Her silence hadn't been, as I thought, polite interest. It must have been so hard for my dear, outspoken Sophie to bite back an acid reproach. How she must have fought to hold back the spout of angry, criticising words on her tongue until she could no longer fight the need to attack my egotism and express her utter disgust at the brash and self-centred arrogance I displayed.

It was true and I see it now. My behaviour had been that of a snooty, show-off schoolgirl, not the modest girl of yesterday. When time came for me to leave, I didn't as much as take time to give Sophie my usual friendly hug and kiss on the cheek. My eyes ignored the disappointment on her face and my mind blanked the wrath rising in her.

It must have been when I made a great rush for the door and yanked the handle in an even greater rush. That was the decider. That was when Sophie gave vent to the seething anger inside her at the offensive snobbery I'd displayed over *my* acquisition of *my* house. Chillingly she said, "A word in your ear before you go, *madam*. There are some unpleasant facts I need to say…and you need to hear."

Perplexity was genuine, not faked when I asked, "Why the angry face?" And then laughingly, I added, "You look like you're chewing on a wasp."

With brutal honesty, Sophie poked the finger of shame straight in my eye. "Take a warning and take a good long think about your morals," she hissed breathlessly. "You've cast aside honest to goodness decency. You are no longer the kind, thoughtful and extremely unselfish girl I knew. Now it's all *you, you, you*," she yelled harshly.

Obviously, this wasn't to be anything like a friendly homily with honeyed words showering praise. I was speechless and wide-eyed with shock. The gloves were off, but Sophie carried on punching.

"Oh yes, today you achieved an ambition and won a battle alright." She gave a slow, hand clapping applause and patronised me even more. "Well, well good for you! And now, here's one piece of advice you really should take, *lady*. If you really and truly love Jack, just remember he is more important than this achievement. He's a good man and to be brutally honest, from what I've seen in you today, you don't deserve him because you're more in love with absolute power."

Oh, how the truth of Sophie's prophetic criticising cut to the bone! I could take a mental whacking from anyone—except her.

I had always trusted in the philosophy that words spoken in anger could never be taken back. Yet I thoughtlessly hit back with heated words and bristling affront. "Yes, I feel on top of the world. Yes, I'm deliriously happy, but I'd hardly call it absolute power. Honestly, I don't know where you get some of your stupid ideas."

"Then why do I sense Jack, not by your side as an equal, but as a faceless shadow? Are you so hung up on your own importance that his role in this venture is irrelevant? Or is he excess to requirements? That's what I'm sensing right this minute, Judy. Are you aware that for the last half hour, you've twiddled those keys and talked plenty about 'it,' but never once referred to 'it' as *our house?* It's all been me, me, mine all mine. You're so self-engrossed that pushing everyone aside doesn't even tweak your conscience and it should. Keep this up and one day Jack will walk out of your life."

If anyone could make me take heed, it was Sophie. I took a good hard look at myself from her perspective, and it wasn't all that pleasant. I sort of gasped, "Perhaps, you're right."

"There's no, perhaps about it," she vehemently told me. "You are behaving like a gluttonous child. Jack is your friend, lover and partner, so include him, make him part of this momentous time in both your lives and that's all the advice I'm offering."

By the time I got into the driving seat of my car, I felt a lot more than well and truly rebuked. I felt like I'd just been whacked over the head with a very big stick and rightly so. Sophie's every word had been the caustic truth. And now, here I was ripping along the highway at top speed in a desperate effort to escape the reality of Sophie's wise but painfully truthful words. She was right. I had blatantly side-stepped Jack in an effort to grab, grab and grab in the most avaricious way. I slowed the car and cruised at a decent thirty-five in order to mull over that talking to.

I had waited a lifetime for this day, but as Sophie pointed out, it would be an insult of the highest degree to Jack and my parents if I were to ignore the fact, they too were a part of this. What right did I alone have to seize the glory when they were the ones who had to watch and suffer my vexation in silence for so long? What difference would a few more hours make anyway after a lifetime of longing for that moment when I turned the key in the front door and lived my dream? Sophie warned about heartlessly ignoring those who loved me most. I heeded her advice and made for home to right a whole catalogue of wrongs.

They would be awaiting my arrival with breathless anticipation. Dad so proud and Mum like the cat that got the cream. And Jack, well, I had shamefully wounded his manly pride by slighting him and insisting he needn't take an active part in the purchase of number eleven. Worse still, I then simply turned a blind eye to Jack's hurt feelings in the most hard-hearted way. If ever there was time to eat a big slice of humble pie, it was now. Buying their first home is something couples do together. To my shame, I had ruthlessly treated Jack like a nonentity in my scramble to grab and grasp this opportunity of a lifetime…by myself. Jack should have been in his rightful place, standing squarely by my side when the cheque and title deeds were exchanged. I was suddenly terribly ashamed of myself and so I should be.

We had no secrets-Jack and me. You could say ours was a crystal-clear relationship and if anyone was to blame for muddying the water it was me. In retrospect I should have insisted Jack came with me and, as Sophie so wisely yet vehemently put it, 'made him part of it.' Instead, I pushed him aside like, what was it Sophie called me, a gluttonous child?

Jack was at a disadvantage in the respect he was too much the gentleman to point out my selfishness when I forcefully denied him the rights and privileges he deserved, and he wasn't forceful enough to point out my egotism.

I could see now when it was too late that Amanda would have been delighted to meet Jack. She would have recognised immediately his inner goodness, kindness and gentle charm. Jack had a warm, comforting personality, the type of person people liked immediately. To my shame, I had brashly told Amanda about everything and everyone, yet so little about the man I passionately adored and who meant the world to me. And now, Sophie had forced me to see myself for this supercilious person I had become.

I loved Jack with all my heart and yet, what right did I have to brazenly ignore rather than acknowledge the important part he played in my life? How coldly grasping it must have seemed to him. Trying to convince myself that I wasn't miserly with my affections was only deceiving my own self. Intentional deceit is the cruellest act and being guilty of this only served to increase my shame tenfold.

The first thing I had to do now was make it up to Jack for his tolerance and understanding. To atone, I had to confess my selfishness to Jack and beg his forgiveness. Amanda Weston had made a generous gesture and none, but a fool would look a gift horse in the mouth, especially a gift as mammoth as this and I vowed from now on, Jack and I would share this gift and enjoy *our* home together.

They would be in the sitting-room, awaiting my return on tenterhooks for fear Amanda had changed her mind and my dream had turned to dust. Slowly I opened the door, put my hand round and jingled the keys. There was the sound of a champagne cork pop and I listened to them singing, "She's a jolly good fellow." That was when Sophie's criticism cracked like thunder in my brain, and I immediately plunged once more into that drowning pool of remorse. *She* wasn't a jolly good fellow *she* was a grasping self-centred fool.

Riddled with shame and regret, I made a solemn vow to always keep in mind Sophie's hard-hitting words and live by them. This was a day of new beginnings, so I also *must* be more open with Jack about this porthole to another time that I lived with.

When we first met, I hadn't been exactly straightforward with Jack. I liked him a lot, so much so in fact that I just couldn't gamble on him thinking I was too weird for his liking. If he knew the whole truth about the second sight thing, would it be worth taking the chance on it ending any hope of a romance between us? What if he misconstrued, thought I had a defective brain or something and ran for the hills? He didn't.

We had been sitting in a quiet corner of a little bar just talking of everyday things, and then I thought, well, this is as good a time and place as any. I twittered in a light-hearted, carefree way, "Did I ever tell you about this thing I have, like some stupid anomaly that it appears I was born with?"

"Not that I remember," Jack said without the slightest trace of worry over what or what not I had been born with.

"It's nothing serious or catching," I quickly assured him, "just a silly quirk of nature."

I don't know if he was simply being gentlemanly, but Jack didn't question it or ask me to explain. All he laughingly said was, "Isn't nature strange?" So, I left it there.

From now on, I had to include Jack in my search for the truth instead of expecting him to blindly follow me into a mysterious labyrinth of strange occurrences that he in all probability might never understand. I made another promise to myself and that was to fully explain to him my terror of the dark mist which at times shrouds me. He must be told that I had glanced briefly at some obscenity within that mist and the absolute fright had forced my brain to reject the awfulness. He had to know that a day might come when I was forced to face whatever demonic scene I had witnessed and if it did…he was the one I would turn to. The strength of his love alone could be my rescue from possible insanity if that shuttered horror were ever revealed.

But today was for celebrations. Tomorrow was for truths.

When the initial hubbub died down, it was Mum who voiced the thought that had been on my mind all week. "I wonder what it will look like after all this time," she said thoughtfully. "I only hope it isn't as bad on the inside as it is on the outside," and she made a squirming gesture with a sort of forced half laugh.

"Oh, but Jack and I appreciate that. We're aware that having lain empty for so many years it will take time and both our efforts to right the unkindness of time. We will, Jack, won't we?" Jack's pledge was in the gentle squeeze of his hand. "Trust me, Mum, it will be a labour of love for both of us. Just like Amy and Paul, remember? We are going to enjoy every exhausting day." I just knew the corners of Jack's mouth were smiling, not smugly or triumphantly, but lovingly proud. For some unknown reason, he was proud of me.

In a by-the-way manner Dad asked, "Did by any chance your benefactor and new best friend give any indication why she…did she say…"

Dad was never known to stumble over a question. He was always straight to the point. Yet here he was positively falling over his own tongue trying to ask the $64.000 dollar question.

"What I'm trying to say, Judy…was there some motive to her generosity?"

"You mean, what reason did she have for virtually giving away a valuable property like number eleven to someone she'd known for less than a day?" My mood was tolerant, and it was no hardship to make what was on Dad's mind that bit easier to put into words.

"See it from our viewpoint, Judy darling. Your mother and I talked about it, hell we were up half the night trying to fathom it out…"

That was when I quoted one of his favourite sayings. "If something seems too good to be true, then it probably is. Is that the point you're trying to put across?"

The frown on Dad's forehead deepened. "Well…yes."

"Her reason for doing what she did will more than likely remain a mystery for the rest of my life, but whatever prompted Amanda Weston to make my dearest ambition possible I accept with gratitude and bless her benevolence."

"I think I know what's worrying your dad, Judy. You don't mind if I give an open opinion, Mr Vernon?" Jack waited for Dad's nod of agreement while I waited for my darling Jack—the thinker—to tell us what he had read into it. "Well, firstly we have a lady who, by her own admission, willingly gave up everything to be with the man she loved and even accepted a reclusive existence because that was the life **he** chose."

Dad interrupted with his personal opinion. "Ah, but what you have to remember is that LaVell wasn't just any man, he was a very rich man."

"Granted, but money wasn't the incentive, even though she nevertheless did become an *extremely* wealthy woman when he died prematurely. It's my theory that guilt was the motive. If you think about it, here she was with more money than she could ever spend in a lifetime and no one to leave it to. Then along comes Judy who breaks the monotony, makes her laugh and eases her loneliness."

Mum just had to interrupt and offer her two-penny worth in this debate. "Well, excuse me for stating the obvious but enjoying the company of someone you met for the first time that day is hardly reason to write off more than

£150.000. Then again, maybe she thought of it as nothing more than giving alms to the poor. Throwing a crumb so to speak," and then she added a cheeky, "huh," for good measure.

"I'm not so sure!" Jack said. "Howard Hughes is reputed to have given away millions of dollars to a man who gave him a lift and whose company he enjoyed for a few short hours. Amanda Weston clearly liked Judy, and now this is purely speculation, but I believe she may even have seen something of herself in Judy's vitality. I don't know for sure, but I do think that whatever it was somehow gave Amanda hope. She had everything, and yet she had nothing. Perhaps she needed a reason to go on and it happened when along came Judy with all that exuberance and enthusiasm that she once had. Put it all together and doesn't it all add up to why she understood how much Judy wanted the house and that's why she made it possible for her to buy the place LaVell had allowed to go to seed? It's feasible that doing what she did was a way to ease her conscience for the wrong she'd done in breaking up LaVell's marriage and losing him his daughters." Jack looked confident that he had just solved the mystery. "Isn't that a more realistic explanation for such a supreme act of generosity?" He concluded.

Maybe there had been just a trickle of doubt or even guilt in me, now it was gone thanks to Jack's clever reasoning. "So, you really don't think I'd misled her and maybe stirred her conscience in some way? You really do believe this could simply have been Amanda's way of balancing the books and atoning for sins past?"

"Well, isn't it obvious now? This was her way of making amends."

I hadn't actually given a great deal of thought to Amanda's way of thinking…until now. But at this instant, it all made sense. The jigsaw of my thoughts was almost complete.

In an advisory capacity, Mum said, "Well, I still think it was more likely the weight of a guilty conscience."

I laid out the facts as I saw them. "Amanda honestly admitted that she really and truly did want to move into number eleven after Jean took the girls and walked out of the marriage. She also admitted how humiliated it made her feel when LaVell preferred to leave it empty rather than have her move in after the break-up."

Mum's mouth made a perfect O as she exhaled in a kind of disgust. "Well, for a man with so little morals that was a bit too moralistic," said she in a crusty, self-righteous way.

"Guess so," I agreed. "She must have felt really inferior not to even be allowed the privilege, the courtesy of being invited across the threshold of that inner sanctum he once shared with his wife and daughters."

"So, all this is really about that sad, misjudged woman giving back something of what she took? You were the pawn who made that possible." Mum fiddled nervously with her beads, the way a woman with a pricked conscience might do. "How mysterious the part we play in life's game," she mumbled.

My flighty, fun-loving mother was really a philosopher at heart and at that moment her heart went out to Amanda Weston. Not because of what she had done for me, but for the gracious, unselfish lady she had shown herself to be.

"And don't forget she gave the £20,000 to charity," I reminded them.

"Which makes *her* more of a saint than a scarlet woman," Mum said with envy that brought a flush to her cheeks.

"You'll meet Amanda one day, Mum, and I promise you'll like her. She's like you in so many ways. Kind, thoughtful, and I suspect at one time, being classed as the life and soul of the party, she was high up on everyone's guest list."

My mother smiled sadly. "There was a time when I would have been appalled had anyone likened me to her." At that moment, she had that sackcloth and ashes discomfort at having made such an error of judgement.

"I still vividly remember the whispers and titters when you, Harriet, Ruth and Emily got together, and I still remember the colourful terminology Harriet used to describe Amanda. I secretly looked them up in the dictionary, tart, trollop, whore…"

"Stop it, Judy, please. Don't you think I feel ashamed enough?"

"And so you should be," I chided, gently, but firmly. "All of you condemned that poor woman without knowing the first thing about who she really was. Her only fault was falling for an ugly brute like LaVell."

Dad stopped in the middle of replenishing our glasses and laughed wryly. "I don't know where you get some of your ideas, Judy," he said. "LaVell was brutish, no one could deny that. He was a despot who obviously scared the living daylights out of his family, but he was a handsome devil, nevertheless. All the women around here—including your mother—practically drooled when they first saw him."

"I resent that, Ralph! I have never drooled over any man." Mum pouted prudishly and then as an afterthought added, "Except you, of course."

I was aware of Mum indignantly defending herself, but her voice was echoing, far-away as if from a distance, for at that moment my puzzled mind was trying to recall LaVell's face. Why would anyone think he was handsome? Dad was handsome; George at number ten was handsome. I knew handsome when I saw it but in LaVell I saw…and then it occurred to me that what I had seen wasn't the facial features everyone else recognised as this good-looking man. I had seen his soul, cold and black as the suit he wore.

"Could we *please* change the subject?" The slightly demented shrill in mum's voice pulled me from my thoughts and back to the here and now. "Tomorrow when its daylight, we'll go into the house, Judy, and take notes of what needs doing. The sooner we start the…"

It was time to put my foot down otherwise Gloria, my forceful mother, would start her organising and before I knew it, the house would be done to her taste, not ours. I wasn't prepared to forget the promise I had made to myself that henceforth, from this time onwards every decision on the re-vamp of number eleven had to be made jointly by Jack and myself.

Boldly, firmly I said, "If you don't mind, Mum…and you too, Dad, I think you'll agree it's the prerogative of the new owners." I emphasised by pointing my index finger, first at Jack and then at myself so there was no mistaking my meaning. "That's *us*, Jack and I, and we'd like to have the honour of walking through *our* front door together for the first time…on our own." At that moment, my heart swelled with such ecstatic pride of achievement and knew Jack and I were united in this very same emotion.

My parents showed no acrimony about my wish for privacy on one of the most important days of our life. It was after all right and fitting that Jack and I should be alone that first time we stepped through the door of the home we were going to share. Making plans for a future together was a very private thing.

That night I did as I always did last thing, I sat at my bedroom window sipping Horlicks and looking out onto the street where I had grown up; only one thing was different about this particular tonight. I wasn't reminiscing about my past but looking to my future.

When Amanda took the keys from her bureau drawer, her clenched fist gripped them tightly and two lonely tears squeezed through her closed lids and dark lashes.

"She can't do it," I thought, "she's going to change her mind." I would have felt no ill-will towards her if she chose not to honour the promise made in perhaps what was a moment of folly. Of course, it didn't happen. There really was never any fear that Amanda might reverse her decision.

I picked up the set of house keys from my dressing table, fingered the medal of St Jude, and remembered the day Win attached it to this very same keyring. She had gone all the way into town on the bus specifically to buy it and when I asked her why, she told me it was because he was the patron saint of hopeless cases and she more than qualified as a cause. It would forever remain there so that I never forgot the Raffertys…as if I ever could.

I yawned and suddenly felt very weary and tired. So much had happened on this magical Saturday. It was as if the past few weeks had been gathered together and rolled into a ball that became today. All the tension, searching, hoping I still couldn't believe that after all the hopelessness and bitter despair, tomorrow, at the dawn of a new day I would throw open the windows and doors of number eleven, fill every corner of every room with sunshine, light and clean fresh air.

Tomorrow was the first day of the rest of my life. The thought was perhaps a bit clichéd, but it was how I felt.

Chapter Twenty-Four

"You do it, Jack." I handed him the keys to the door of number eleven.

"No, the honour of opening the door to *our* new home surely has to be *yours*," Jack said in a jaunty, hmm, maybe a touch tongue-in-cheek way.

It was a humbling and rather cutting reminder of my recent state of unbending arrogance and obstinacy and it certainly brought a guilty blush to my face. Touché Jack. He had every right. "Then here we go," I said meekly.

It was a bit of a struggle until the key turned stiffly in the lock. 5,000 days of both clement and inclement weather had done its worst. Cruelty of the elements, snow, sun, wind and rain: how my poor abandoned house had suffered neglect and I had been powerless to do no more than watch its deterioration and mourn as the decay took hold.

Jack, clued-up as ever said, "That lock might need a bit of oiling."

I tried not to laugh. My erudite Jack may have been a truly gifted teacher, but he was a man who didn't know one end of a screwdriver from the other. Still, at least his powers of observation stood him in good stead.

"The hinges too," I said, wincing as the door creaked loudly when I pushed it open. A load of miscellaneous junk mail which had gathered over the years spread across the floor of the hallway as we heaved the door open. Kicking a pathway through it I said, "Looks like, we'll have to sort through that lot later, Jack."

"And do you really think there'll be anything worth reading after all these years? Burn it or bin it, I say," Jack mumbled. Then he cast an astounded gaze around the space which was our new home. "Jeez, it's bigger than I thought! This is a real family house." The wink he gave was surprisingly suggestive. Then again, Jack wasn't the caveman type to sweep me into his arms and carry me upstairs. He was way too shy and self-controlled. Still, I had all the time in the world to work on that. Besides, romance among all this dust and cobwebs? I don't think so.

The walnut occasional table was still in the hall, un-budged from the spot where Amy had first put it. Only now it was covered in cobwebs and thick with dust. I blew some of the dust from the vase and pictured Amy's table gleaming once more with the rose filled vase mirrored in the gloss. As sure as the sky was blue, it would soon be crammed with flowers once more. Glorious blooms to fill the hallway with perfumed air and once more be that reminder of a man who had died too soon.

A sort of startled cry came from the lounge, and I heard Jack use language I never even knew was in his vocabulary, "For fuck's sake! Oh, Christ almighty," he cried out.

"What is it? What's wrong?" My heart pounded and my legs turned to jelly.

I froze at the sound of another terrified yell and then Jack, foregoing niceties, screamed, "The fucking place is hoatching with vermin. The bastards are everywhere." I learned another thing about Jack that day. He was so afraid of mice all control over using bad language fell by the wayside at the sight of one.

As much as I wanted to, I couldn't stop laughing. I didn't mean to make fun of him, it was just so comical to see a man like Jack, always so noble and composed, yell swearwords the likes of which only the roughest, toughest of navvies would use. He was actually shaking in his shoes at the sight of a little mouse.

By then I was doubled up with uncontrollable laughter. "They're probably more afraid of you than you are of them," I managed to say through the hysterics.

"I don't think that's possible, and I fail to see what you find so fucking funny." He was peeved and rightly so. After all, his male pride was in the process of being rather severely bruised.

"I wasn't making fun of you, honest." I bit my lip and fought to hold back a torrent of laughter, but the laughter just couldn't be controlled, and my entire body shook with the sheer effort of trying. "Oh, Jack, if you could only see yourself, standing on that chair with your trouser legs pulled up." By then tears of laughter were streaming from my eyes.

"Suppose I do look stupid," he said kind of shamefaced. "I was just taken off guard and startled to see one of those animals heading straight for me." Jack audaciously defended his actions as instinctive and perfectly normal. "It was the last thing I expected."

"I know that's all it was, darling," I said sympathetically, then couldn't resist a touch of irony, "fucking scary even."

"Oh, very funny," Jack snorted testily. "Let me also point out it was pure shock that made me leap onto this chair, not lack of masculinity."

Of course, that might have been more believable if he had actually made a move to get off the chair and back onto the floor.

"We could always buy a cat! Unless, of course, little fluffy kittens frighten you too." I covered my mouth with my hand as another fit of the giggles started. It wasn't so much derision as rib tickling humour that just couldn't be held back.

And then, Jack saw the funny side to it all. He shook with laughter, lost his balance and with nothing but thin air to grab, he was sent flying from that place of safety. In years to come this day, this time, when brought to mind would always give us cause to laugh. It was one of those events the memory of which would never dim with time. It will continue to grow funnier every time number eleven crops up in conversation. When we'd both calmed down, Jack—my hero—actually stepped over a mouse to get to the window and draw back the curtains. Light flooded the room, and I began removing dust sheets from the furniture.

"I thought it was empty?" Jack looked around in wonder. "All these beautiful and obviously very expensive furnishings just…abandoned. Now I know what it must have been like boarding the Marie Celeste. It looks like they left in such a hurry they didn't even stop to take anything with them."

"They didn't," I said, remembering the night Win Rafferty closed the door for the last time and with the hastiest of goodbyes, fled into the night with her children.

"What do we do with all this stuff? We could certainly make good use of it. Do you think Amanda Weston will want it all back?"

"She wants nothing at all to do with the house…or its contents. Everything here now belongs to us."

"Wonderful!" Jack said gleefully, and then he slapped one of the cushions, releasing a cloud of dust, "naturally, having it all cleaned professionally might be a good idea."

"Come and see the kitchen. This used to be my favourite place." I took Jack's hand and not so much led him as dragged him into the kitchen. The big pine table where Win laid out her freshly baked scones and cakes was just as I remembered it.

In my mind, I could still hear the laughter that used to echo round this very same kitchen as we hungrily relished the goodies and Win's softly lilting voice telling us, "Hey there, go easy or there's sure to be no space left in your bellies when it comes to tea-time."

"You told me it was here in this house that *it* began. How do you feel now, Judy?" Jack asked concernedly.

"Like I'd come home," I answered honestly.

"I take it that's the fountain you told me so much about. It's quite spectacular too from what I can see of it amongst the overgrowth." Jack had pulled back the now dust and grime encrusted curtain to gaze excitedly at what was once the perfectly landscaped back garden. "Give me the key, Judy, and I'll beat a path to the fountain. You can follow me out there."

"You go, Jack! I don't want to see it right now." I shivered involuntarily at the memory of the strange reflections in the pool and the mermaid's tears. "There's so much work to be done where do we begin?" My rummaging disturbed the dust and I sneezed violently.

"Bless you!" Jack said.

"I already am," I answered in utter contentment.

My Jack was like an explorer, bravely beating his way through the undergrowth to reach his goal. Aimlessly, dreamily I wandered upstairs. The bedrooms were much the same as downstairs, cobwebs and dust. Thank goodness, the furniture had been protected with dust sheets for it would make the cleaning so much easier. In the smallest bedroom, I found a little teddy bear and wondered if Daniel had missed it. Dear little Daniel. I had a sudden yearning to see him, to see all of them and hear Win's gentle voice offer me freshly made scones. What a loss that family had been from my life.

My footsteps echoed eerily on the polished hardwood floor of the upstairs landing. It was enough for one day. I was becoming quite overcome and melancholy. My feet lingered on each step as I walked slowly downstairs.

They were standing in the downstairs hall, two little girls. In the descending dimness of evening, it was too dark for me to see them properly. "Are you looking for someone?" I asked, but perhaps I'd startled them as much they had startled me, for there was no answer. It occurred to me that Jack might be their teacher and they'd seen him coming in here. "Hold on," I told them, gently so as not to alarm them further, "I'll fetch Jack…ah, Mr Wayne," I corrected myself and skipped down the last few steps. When I looked, they had gone, and I was suddenly very cold.

Jack called from the kitchen, "That back garden is going to be something else once the grass and weeds are cut back."

"Did you see two little girls?" I asked. "They were here just a moment ago."

"I didn't see anyone. What were they like?" Jack opened the front door, looked down the street then shrugged his shoulders and came back inside. "No sign of anyone."

"I don't remember seeing them around here and yet they looked familiar. It was too dark to see them clearly, but I think they could have been twins. It's possible they're not from around here, just visiting and maybe I did catch a glimpse of them at some time and that's why they were familiar to me."

"They could have shot along the pathway at the back, Judy. You know how fast kids can move."

I supposed that was the logical explanation. Besides, if they went to Fairfield High surely, I would have recognised them, even in the half light, or they would have recognised me as one of the teachers. No, in all probability they were visiting, took a wrong turning and wandered into the wrong house. "I think we should go, Jack, its cold in here. Tomorrow, I'll see about having the power restored and then we can start the serious work."

We were both in agreement with this, but if I had asked Jack to start there and then, he would have done so without question. I was satisfied for now. I had seen, savoured and remembered happy times. Anyway, this wasn't a dream from which I would wake to find it all gone. It would be the same tomorrow and all the tomorrows to come. We closed the door and left.

For a split second, I was urged in some way to turn and look back. It may have been a reflection, or the remnants of a memory, but for the merest instant, I saw a face at *our* window in *our* house or thought I did. Perhaps tiredness and excitement were making my mind play tricks on me.

I waved to Jack as he drove out of Juniper Drive. He was happy. I was contented and all in all it had been a red-letter day. Exhaustion was beginning to creep up on me though and I had a great need for a nice hot bath and then bed.

"You look all in." Mum smiled in that caring way that only a mother can do. "I remember our first house and that first day we took possession. I went from room to room, in every cupboard and corner, mentally picturing how wonderful it would be when I put my own mark on it. My signature on the finished canvas you might say. I didn't do a stroke of work on the house that first day but come evening I was just the way you are now, exhausted. You've come down from that high you've been on, Judy, that's all."

"My aim now is a hot bath and an early night. Recharge my batteries so to speak and then tomorrow…" I took my mother's hand, and in a flash, an overwhelming mantle of loneliness fell over me and I suddenly realised this was what she was feeling right at that moment-left out, excess to requirements. "This is one of those times in her life when a girl needs her mum most," I said, and hoped she didn't take it as patronising. It wasn't meant that way. I was simply a girl asking her mother for advice.

"What's it like after all this time?"

She had that look of nostalgia when memories surface and you dust off the years. The dear faces of Amy and Win came into my mind, and I knew right then Mum too was wistfully thinking of them.

"Well, first we'll need an exterminator…"

"*An exterminator?*" She almost screamed the words in that moment of panic. "Why do you need an exterminator?"

She must have envisaged all sorts of horrors that the very word exterminator conjures up. I promised her it was nothing more than a few mice and it was quite safe to go in. "It's highly unlikely the little rodents are preparing to attack," I assured her.

"If you say so, I'll take your word for it. Just don't take offence if I leave it until after *they're* gone before *I* go in." She gave a squeamish little shiver then said, "You'll need to take notes of everything that needs done. We'll browse methodically through yellow pages and list phone numbers of reputable contractors to get a few quotes—starting with the exterminator."

"The cooker and fridge, things like that are still in beautiful condition although a bit old fashioned." It was time to get off the subject of small rodents. "All that gorgeous and expensive furniture will never date though. Save us a fortune too. Finding a reputable company who can clean and renovate rugs and upholstery is a must."

"You mean that's all yours as well as the house?" Mum's jaw dropped and she looked positively green-eyed with envy. "I remember watching their furniture being taken from the van and thinking wow! That's class. I heard that everything, the furniture, rugs and curtains all came from Harrods. Must have cost an absolute fortune."

"I had a quick peek in some of the cupboards and there's even exquisite China and cutlery." I held up the teddy bear and said, "Look what else I found."

"It's Daniel's!" Mum squealed delightedly. "Maybe you should have left it there. It might have frightened the mice into leaving voluntarily," she said acidly.

We were in the midst of laughing when the yawn I had been suppressing escaped me and utter fatigue took hold. "I think I'll hit the sack, Mum. My energy levels have definitely hit rock bottom." Wearily I said, "Goodnight, Mum, when Dad comes in, tell him I said goodnight."

"Judy," there was a tremble in her voice and when I turned my mother's eyes were glassy with unshed tears. "Looking at you now, I feel as if the sun went down one day and when it rose on another you were all grown up. You know, the thing is I wasn't even aware I'd grown older."

"You didn't, and in my eyes, you never will grow old." I watched her face light up and that impish look return.

"Thank the lord you're only going to be a few doors away. What would I do without you to boost my spirits and feed my vanity?"

Gratefully, thankfully my head hit the pillow, but I think I was asleep before it did. My sleep wasn't exactly troubled. I didn't have a nightmare from which I couldn't wake. I dreamt a dream so real that upon wakening, every detail was still fresh in my mind. Those two little girls who had wandered into the house were calling my name and asking me to help them. I couldn't see their faces and my legs were leaden, which was common in dreams and then as I tried to run to them, they kept growing further and further away. Another typical dream state along with the feeling of helplessness that they were in danger of some sort and try as I may I was powerless to save them.

From now on, I would watch for those children because my inner-feelings were so strong gut instinct told me they either needed—or were going to need help. But from what? Would they come back? Of course, they would—I had no reservations on that score. They clearly needed some kind of comfort, help and advice on whatever problem was causing them grief.

I wasn't unduly worried. A little concerned perhaps since it was reasonable to assume they could be the victims of bullying at school. If this were the case, they may have made a brave decision to speak confidentially to a caring teacher, either Jack or myself. Jack and I had urged pupils to find the tenacity to unmask bullies and we made it perfectly clear bullying in any way, shape or form would not be tolerated in Fairfield High. It had to be something as simple as this.

All things considered, the weekend had been hectic in so many ways. The nervous anticipation and excitement of Saturday and then that headlong dive into total euphoria. Not to mention my crash bang wallop back to reality after an extremely precise, but in all honesty, a well-deserved earbashing from Sophie. And then glorious Sunday came and went like a grand finale to all this magic and mayhem which had been crammed into that one weekend.

Monday, this was the real start to planning and preparing for the exciting task which lay before us. The renovating of our home and the mountain of serious organising to be done. After school was out, armed with candles since the power hadn't yet been restored, Jack and I went to the house to make a list of the work. Our main agenda was planning a rota. We didn't want decorators clashing with cleaners and furniture restorers as they all tried to carry out their particular jobs all at the same time. The last thing we needed was workmen falling over each other in exasperation as one job overlapped another. The restoration needed to be executed with precision.

We finished detailing all the work and the order in which it had to be done then stood in the dust clad lounge with only the soft glow of candlelight for illumination. I was remembering how it looked before; Jack hadn't seen this house in all its glory. He only knew it as the dark and musty place which now belonged to us.

Jack's mind must have jumped two weeks ahead. Suddenly, unexpectedly he said, "Only two weeks until the Easter break."

"Couldn't have worked out better for us, what I mean is, we'll be here to see the work going on," I said. Jack made no comment, but even in the dimness of candlelight, I was aware of a strange, kind of secret smile on his face.

More in a sort of hazy awe at our achievement than anything, we stood with our arms around each other, still trying to take in and believe the wonder of it all. Jack squeezed my body closer to his and said, "What would you like for your birthday, my little Easter bunny?"

Honestly, surprised I said, "Haven't really had much time to think about my birthday, not with all that's happened."

Jack whispered in my ear, "How about a diamond or a sapphire or both if you like?"

It seemed such an illogical question I laughed and asked, "What would I do with diamonds and sapphires?"

And Jack replied, "Wear them on the third finger of your left hand and when the house is ready, I'll add a wedding ring. I'm asking you to marry me, Judy."

In that candlelit room, our room in our house, we just clung together in a loving embrace. Even amongst the dust and grime, it was the most romantic and precious moment of my life. Only an emotionless fool could refuse such a unique proposal and at that moment. I was filled with the headiest emotion. I never wanted anyone as much as I wanted Jack. Yet all I could say was, "All going well and no hiccups, the house will be ready to move into by the summer."

Jack held me closer to him and whispered, "If that's a yes, the summer it is then."

I discovered something else that night-my fiancé had a spectacularly pleasant singing voice. He suddenly began guiding me in a gentle waltz, cheek to cheek as he crooned *wonderful tonight* and Jack didn't even wince when a mouse scurried across the floor. It was all so magical if I could have captured and bottled how I felt right then…

Chapter Twenty-Five

To sit on a train and try to count trees or telephone poles as they whizz by really is an actual impossibility. Yet wasn't that the comparison to my life at that point in time? Fast as a speeding train, working like a dog and all the other euphemisms that aptly explained the frenzy of trying to be in two places at the same time.

We had trawled the yellow pages for reputable tradesmen and made so many phone calls to organise times to inspect the work we needed to be carried out for quotes on cost. On merit as well as cost we meticulously short-listed painters and decorators, joiners, landscape gardeners and of course not forgetting the most important one of all—*the terminator.* Yes, we had to rid the house of our furry four-legged friends or Jack might be forced to spend the rest of his life standing on chairs. I had become quite attached to the cheeky little mites who had taken up residence in number eleven. I just wasn't prepared to share our home with them. My mother was happy opening the door to allow tradesmen into the house but refused point blank to set foot inside as long as *those things* were still on the loose and rampantly seeking out every last crumb of the workmen's lunch.

Phase one of the work began on the first Monday morning of our Easter break. The lounge suite was taken away for industrial vacuums to remove every speck, every grain of dust before specialised cleaning agents revived the fabric to newness.

On Tuesday, a team of professional cleaners arrived to rid the house of all the dust and grime that had gathered over the years before six painters and decorators began the mightiest job of all-redecorating the entire house with fresh paint and wallpaper. It was actually quite magical seeing such a transformation take place over the next two weeks.

And then, it was time for the final step in the revamp of number eleven. Jack and I decided that having the beige carpeting cleaned might be a more economical option than the expense of replacing it with new. It was after all tasteful, top quality, extremely expensive and basically new. If it didn't work out as we hoped…And then the industrial cleaners worked their magic. All the carpeting throughout the house looked as new as the day it went down and we were delighted at the results.

We browsed furniture stores, Jack and I, and then decided that it would be stupid in the extreme to dispose of all the imported chic and stylish dark oak furniture which graced the lounge. Besides, it was exactly what we might have chosen…had the exorbitant price tag been within our means. Finally, all ornaments from the display cabinet, sideboard and mantelpiece had been carefully wrapped and crated by the cleansing and sanitising team, then stored in a large cupboard along with pictures and paintings from the walls. Jack and I now had the task of un-wrapping them and emptying the cupboard. It became something of a revelation.

"These ornaments are expensive items," Jack said in amazement as he carefully swished each one in warm soapy water. "Look at some of the markings, Judy-Royal Doulton, Royal Worcester, Lladro to name but a few. Are you aware these pictures are mostly genuine artwork, not prints?"

"I'm aware they wouldn't be cheap. Aren't we the lucky ones?"

"I know we're lucky, but that's not what I mean. The point I'm making is…Christ, there's something really scary about this, Judy."

"Why?"

"Surely, these must have meant *something* to Mrs LaVell. Ornaments are things people form attachment to, they have significance. Some of these could have been wedding gifts, maybe anniversary or birthday presents so why did she leave for good without taking at least some of them with her?"

I stood for a moment trying to put myself in that position. "If it were me, I think I'd rather forsake clothes that could be replaced and take mementos that couldn't."

"That's exactly what I mean! So why didn't she?"

"I don't know, Jack," a cold shiver ran through my body. "I really don't know."

Jack then reasoned, "Of course, because she didn't take them doesn't mean she didn't want to. Perhaps she tried and LaVell forced her to put them back."

"I suppose that's a more reasonable answer knowing the kind of man LaVell was, but guesswork, nevertheless. We'll never know the truth."

We put the ornaments and all that heavenly crystal safely back in the cupboard until we decided what to do with them. Outside, the gardens were being restored to their former glory.

The makeover, having now been completed, left only the finishing touches to be done. Together, Jack and I began hanging curtains, setting furniture and day by day, we watched the house come alive. Gone was the dust and cobwebs and to my mother's relief, no more did she have to watch in terror as an entire family of furry little creatures, without warning, darted across the floor, all as desperate to get away from her as she was to dodge them. Mother kind of over-exaggerated when she dramatically referred to them as a hoard of marauding rodents.

That magnificent bathroom, that showpiece of white, gold and peach tinted Italian marble gleamed once more and I had a vivid recollection of the night Daisy Keller gave a housewarming party. Oh, the impassioned sighing and that saturating envy as the green-eyed ladies of our street, lost for words, looked in jealous awe at the unadulterated luxury of the newly installed bathroom. Those bare breasted gold mermaids, Dr Ruth Thomson had described them with undisguised seething envy as tacky because she couldn't bring herself to say beautiful. They hadn't aged or lost their charm. Unlike Dr Ruth, they never would.

From the kitchen window, I looked out over the landscaped back garden. Gone was the tall grass and weeds. New plants with young buds edged the freshly cut lawn and the mermaid fountain, freed from the fetters of overgrowth dominated once more. It was as if I had travelled back in time to that first day when, as only a child, I gazed with reverence and wonderment at the majestic feature LaVell had built there for his daughters. It had to have held some special significance for him. Perhaps after their sudden departure, it became nothing more than a sad reminder of the family he had lost. I distinctly remember Amanda mentioning how in his fevered state before death, LaVell had begged her never to have the pond and fountain removed. Was it possible the man had been possessed of human frailties and feelings after all?

I stood alone in the darkened room with only the hall light for illumination and cried at the sheer strength of our achievement. At first, considering who had owned them, I had reservations about keeping the furnishings. I was glad now that we did. My mother said and it was true, quality never dates and that spectacularly beautiful lounge suite, in fact every stick of furniture looked brand new. Then again, not all of it was inherited with the house. Jack and I had also added our own contribution in the way of rugs, pictures that were our taste and last, but not least, one of those king-sized, four poster beds that together we had chosen to be the piece-de-resistance to our master bedroom. I also replaced most of the curtains too with my own choice. To be more specific, I had stamped my mark on our home.

I walked aimlessly from room to room, jingling the keys, fingering the medal of St Jude and running my hand over the gleaming new paintwork. After a lifetime spent fantasising and wishing, was all this truly real, or would it disappear in a puff of smoke, and I would awake to find it gone?

There was a definite connection between me and this house, a special bond. I had to question Sophie's theory that the link wasn't with the house per se, but with the ground it stood on. I was still sceptical about reincarnation but had to admit to the possibility. Not to put too fine a point on it, someone or something had steered me in all the right directions. An invisible force had turned, nudged and guided me. People who under normal circumstances would have closed the door in my face welcomed me in as though my presence had been awaited. It was my firm belief I was meant to be here for a reason and in time it would become apparent.

The last thing on my mind, especially at this late hour was to turn, and there they were again. Those two little girls were once more standing in the hallway. They were silhouetted against the light from the sitting-room and the effect was sort of ghostly. It was so cold I was sure they must have left the front door open allowing in the cold night air. I shivered and my breath formed like mist when I spoke the question, I needed them to answer.

"If you need help, please tell me what I can do. Are you afraid of something?"

In unison their hollow and what I can only describe as pain filled voices answered, "Yes, Judy," and at that precise moment, I turned as the front door opened.

"Jack," I said thankfully, "these children are definitely afraid of someone. We should do something about it."

"What children?" Jack looked questioningly at me and when I turned back to where the girls had been standing, they were gone. Once again, they had performed this frustrating vanishing act.

"The two little girls I told you about, they were here just a moment ago. Didn't you see them when you came in?" I had the weirdness feeling, a tingling which I couldn't account for. "They must have slipped past you in the dark." It was after all the most logical explanation.

Jack's brow furrowed questioningly. "No," he said, "I would have seen them pass me. Could they have run upstairs when they heard me come in?"

We searched upstairs and down. The back door was locked and bolted so they hadn't gone out that way. In a feverish panic, I began checking windows to make sure they were still locked, looking in corners, cupboards, behind furniture until Jack's arms gently restrained me. "There's something very strange going on," I told him.

"My. poor darling, you must be so tired," Jack said in a loving, but nevertheless patronising way. He might just as well have come right out with it and said I was loopy.

By then, I was in adamant mode. "They know me! They even called me Judy. I know them, just can't remember where from, but it'll come to me." Right that minute I felt my anger and resentment was justified. "They *were* here in this house and when I prove they exist, maybe then you'll stop treating me like a lunatic."

The look of pain and hurt on Jack's face at that harsh outburst was a real awakener. All he meant by it was no more than a loving and caring observation. I broke down. The river of tears I shed was more than anything an escape valve for pent up emotions. Jack rocked me in his arms repeating over and over, "It's alright, it's alright." He waited until the crying subsided then said, "I'm in this for keeps, no matter what. You saw something I didn't and that's all there is to it."

My tearful apology was genuine. "I'm so sorry. I wouldn't hurt you for the world. You know that, Jack, don't you?"

"Of course, I do, but do you know what I think? I think your mind is struggling to take it all in, Judy. You're exhausted, maybe not physically, but mentally. Look around you, this house, our home is beautiful, thanks to your organising skills."

The tension ebbed, my hands settled on my hips as I scanned what we had accomplished and sighed gratefully.

That was when Jack lightened the moment of anguish with his own droll wit. "In a matter of weeks, I'll have to carry you over that threshold, so for the sake of my poor back, no more cream buns and Mars bars for you between now and the wedding." Suddenly we were clinging together laughing, not hollow and forced, our laughter was the sound of genuine happiness.

Jack's mood was all at once serious and for him, unusually stern. "I want you to make me a promise," he said with tight lip and set jaw.

"What, a promise to give up Mars bars and cream cakes?"

"No! Just to lock the door and stay away from here for a few days at least. Please, Judy, I'm asking you to do this for my peace of mind as well as your own. All this happened within weeks and the suddenness had to be quite a shock to the system. Give your mind time to get in tune, grasp the reality of it, and adjust to all that's happened."

"If that's what you want." My reply was colder than the north wind and I deliberately omitted one of those, cross my heart, verbal promises to stay away.

We walked the short distance to where Jack's car was parked at my parent's house with not another word spoken. I bade him a meaningfully curt goodnight without as much as a peck on the cheek. I was still smarting at being put in the position of being expected to surrender to Jack's common sense by promising to spend a few days away from the house. He had to know that was one promise I couldn't keep.

Just after eleven, the phone rang. The tiff we had tonight, our first, must have tormented Jack for him to ring at this hour.

"Judy, I know it's late, but I had to talk to you." There was a cry in his voice. "You tried to tell me…to explain…I heard, but I didn't listen. I'm listening now."

"It would be like stumbling in the dark, me trying to explain what I don't understand myself. It's so…illusive, like, why do I sometimes know the answer to a question even before it's asked? Give me time to think about it because right now all I know is that a strange thing happened tonight, and the pieces don't fit…but they will. Maybe you're right and tiredness did get the better of me."

"So, we're friends again and you're not angry with me?"

"How could I be cross with you when you only have my best interests at heart?" I heard his relieved sigh and knew Jack was content that we had made up. In the gentlest, loving way I said, "Goodnight, darling. I love you and I'll see you tomorrow." The mending of Jack's slightly bruised feelings had been dealt with and I fell into a deep, dreamless sleep.

When I awoke in the morning, it was as if all my cares had vanished. Cares and worries that had simply been magnified by my tired state and now, after a restful night, I felt in top form once more.

If there was something sinister happening, I'd have known. I would have sensed it. Instead, all I felt each time I walked through the door of number eleven was a magnificent peace and serenity, like a sublime feeling of being fondly embraced. It was an overwhelming sensation that all was well.

Those two little girls were all that stood between me and total peace of mind. Who were they and why had they come to *me* for help? Their mode of dress had puzzled me somewhat. I couldn't help but notice it was a bit outdated and not what girls their age would happily wear. Perhaps that was the answer! It could be that they were being taken care of by an aunt who had frugally kept her daughter's old Fairfield High dresses, the exact same uniform I used to wear years ago. Someone of the older generation could have insisted the girls made use of the outdated and out of fashion school uniforms. Wearing them to school was unthinkable by today's standard of dress sense. I could imagine them being taunted in school and in anguish turning to a teacher for help. If that were the case they'd be back.

That morning, I walked round the playground expecting to see them, but the two strange girls weren't among the other children. In the staff room during the break, I spoke of the incident. "Two little girls walked into our house last night by mistake and I haven't a clue who they are or where they came from." I kept it matter of fact rather than mysterious. "I think I must have scared them. The poor little souls ran off before I had the chance to tell them it was alright and that they hadn't done anything wrong."

"And you've no idea who they were?" Mrs Dobson the geography teacher asked.

"That's what I'm trying to find out. I don't want them to think they're in trouble. They're about ten or eleven years old. I think they could possibly be twins who have only recently come to live in Fairfield."

I was met with blank looks. There weren't girls of this description in any of the classes. So, my sleuthing had established one thing, they were not Fairfield pupils. I was at a dead end as the mystery deepened and now something was gnawing at my brain. They were familiar to me, if only I could remember from were.

It was a brisk spring afternoon as I walked the familiar route from the school to Juniper. My feet had traversed this well-worn pathway that skirted Fairfield countless times over the years, but especially the happy times when Amy gently held my hand as we walked together along this path to school. These were cheery thoughts that brought a nostalgic smile to my face. All at once, a sensation of distress left me quaking. I suddenly had a feeling that I'd stepped back in time and was re-living that morning the LaVell twins had pleaded with their father to allow them to walk to school with me. I recalled how in that inimitably brutish Richard LaVell way, he forbade his daughters that pleasure as well as denying them the friendship of other girls their age…including myself.

I remembered that day as if it were happening right now. With it came an intense feeling of such despair for those sad, deprived children. They didn't suffer in the sense that they were denied food, clothing or an education, oh no. Their deprivation was of affection, understanding and a normal childhood. Meredith and Maxine, La Vell's great sadness had touched me then and now that old familiar feeling was with me again.

That was it! My mind suddenly cleared. The two girls were Meredith and Maxine LaVell, and I just hadn't recognised them after all this time. The mystery was solved. They must have come back from Canada and didn't know the house had been sold. But…but how could that be…? The blood rushed to my head, and I began to tremble as my legs almost gave way. They were the same age as I, so why had time passed them by? Why hadn't they aged?

I could question this till doomsday. I could make a million assumptions, but with all the will in the world, I couldn't get to grips with it. Maybe because I realised now that what I had seen were apparitions, spectres of a time gone by. It was said that houses had been known to retain remnants of another time. I chilled and the trembling increased to the point of convulsion. These so-called remnants of another time were more commonly referred to as…ghosts. If this was the case, then those two little girls, Meredith and Maxine LaVell, weren't simply figments of my imagination they…

Why did a vision of the fish pond suddenly spring into my mind? I had to phone Amanda. Perhaps, she could give me some sane answers to the insane ideas which were running wild in my brain and distorting my thoughts.

Amanda's delight was in her tone of voice. "Judy? Oh, it's so good of you to take the time to telephone. I know how busy you must be." And then excitedly she asked, "How is the house coming along?"

The moment I heard her voice, I was sure Amanda was innocent of any wrongdoing. How could she be when on every occasion we spoke all I could sense was gentleness and pureness of heart. Not once had she aroused even the slightest sensation of fear in me. Her touch had never stirred my terror of that cold and foggy place which concealed whatever blood curdling horror lay within that mysteriously dark fog.

If something terrible had happened to the LaVell girls, then Amanda Weston couldn't possibly have had a part in it. Richard LaVell on the other hand, the moment he laid his cold, cruel hand on me so long ago he momentarily opened the door to a scene so unspeakable my mind was unable to face the revulsion and because I couldn't bring myself to watch, I had simply locked it away. But the time had come when watch I must, because now I feared that somewhere in that deep black mist, I had witnessed the death of the LaVell twins. The horror and loathing I beheld could only have been their murder and it had been too much for my mind to take in.

Mentally scrutinising every detail, I was now convinced that what I had suppressed all these years was the awfulness that had befallen Jean LaVell and those poor innocent children. It was not the workings of my own vivid imagination. I never imagined what happened that first day LaVell set foot in number eleven. The cruel way he gripped my arm to wantonly exit me from the house *had* in that instant given me an insight into the evil deeds he would one day commit. Selective amnesia had simply been the lesser of two evils.

If my worst fears were realised, I also had to be doubly certain that Amanda Weston had no knowledge of the event. If at the mention of Jean and her daughters, a horrifying scene filled Amanda's thoughts then, God forbid, she had to have known. If it were so, and if I unexpectedly raised the question as to the whereabouts of Maxine and Meredith LaVell, that would open guilt's door in *her* mind. I must then be prepared to witness what *my* mind had always resisted: the slaughter of three innocents.

Casually, I said, "The other day I saw twin girls that reminded me so much of Richard's daughters, Meredith and Maxine. Tell me, Amanda, did they ever come back from Canada?" It gave me no pleasure to use her as a pawn in my search for the truth. It was even less of a pleasure to use such trickery on the woman who had shown me so much kindness and generosity. How could I tell her the truth, the awful truth that I now suspected the man she so passionately adored had done a terrible, depraved thing?

"Well, Judy, to my knowledge they've never returned to this country. Maybe it would have been too painful to come back after…" I heard the sigh in her voice, sensed her shame. "I'll let you in on a secret. Right up to the time Richard fell ill, he wrote to them every single week. He wouldn't even allow anyone to post the letters because he said it made him feel closer to his girls when he posted them himself. I used to call him an old softie at heart." This admission caused a sorrowful sob in her voice. "You know, Judy, it really saddened him that neither of his girls ever replied to at least one of those letters."

Amanda Weston's soul was as pure as the driven snow, I saw that, felt it and I now also saw the ploy LaVell used to deceive the trusting Amanda. He may have kept up the charade of writing letters, but I suspected there was only blank paper in those envelopes since he had no intention of posting them and this way, Amanda would see him as a loving father grieving for his lost children...clever.

"You mentioned the ornamental pond in the back garden, something about a plan Richard had for it, only I can't remember what you said." If fibbing was a mortal sin, then I was doomed.

"As far as I know, he didn't want anything specific done with it. Other than leaving it as it was, I suppose. The fever made Richard rather hallucinatory and at the end he became totally incoherent. For some unknown reason, his ramblings always seemed to be about that fishpond."

Amanda's sorrowful thoughts pulsated through the telephone, and I felt it like a fierce stab to my heart. I wished I'd never started this conversation.

And then in a more uninterested, couldn't care less about the fishpond way, she said, "I believe it was quite beautiful."

"It was!"

"Hmm, well, it's yours now, Judy. You're free to do whatever you wish with it. I never had a say in what happened to that house before and I don't want a say now."

There was so much bitterness and hurt in her voice and right then I understood her acrimony. Letting me have the house for a pittance wasn't just an act of generosity, it was rebellion at the hurt LaVell caused by not allowing her to take even the briefest wander from room to room. I simply happened along at the right time.

Understanding the facts brought a sort of gladness in as much as I had at times wondered if, perhaps I had been a bit mercenary. Taking advantage of a grieving woman so to speak. In fact, when all was said and done, it was I who had done Amanda a favour. I firmly believed that in a show of defiance against all those who had labelled her a gold-digger, she would eventually have razed number eleven to the ground rather than make a fortune from its sale.

I didn't cradle the phone straight after Amanda hung up. My brain was wrestling to replace consternation with logic. In the silence and seclusion of my own room, I began piecing together all the events that might be significant. Jean had received that poison pen letter and it had sparked a terrible fight, a battle that most of the street clearly heard. Then there was that anguished, blood curdling scream (again, my mother's words, not mine) and in the morning, Jean and the girls were gone.

Amanda said Richard LaVell wrote every week but insisted on posting the letters himself. Was this a red herring to make Amanda *think* his family were alive and well and living in Canada? LaVell knew his wife was an orphan and had no family, therefore he was confident no one would come looking for her.

The more I thought about it, the more convinced I became that they never left the house that night. I remembered that it was the following day builders finished the pond with concrete and mosaic tiles before placing the mermaid in the centre. The thought repulsed me but had to be faced. Was that beautiful, ornate structure actually a tomb?

When I told him about my premonitions, I know it had unnerved Jack. There was no point making a commitment to a man and not giving him the facts. Where was the truth in hiding something so important? Jack had admitted he listened but didn't hear. He must hear now and believe.

"The souls of wronged beings, I will set free." I spoke the words aloud without knowing why and then I remembered the legend of DeBanzie's field. Taking into account the documentation from that time, it had to be a lot more than simple assumption that Bain had either murdered the DeBanzie family or had one of his lackeys do it for him. Sophie was convinced that this was what Lucia had referred to, but what if that wasn't what Lucia had foreseen? What if the DeBanzie family hadn't been murdered after all? What if their nomadic nature kicked in when they'd had enough, and they simply upped sticks and moved away? What if Sophie was on the right track with the wrong people?

Did LaVell bury his family in an unmarked grave that now trapped their souls, and this was the true route of Lucia's prediction?

Chapter Twenty-Six

I stood alone by the fountain just gazing questioningly at the mermaid, my heart and my mind searching for answers. Oh, if only that sad mermaid's lips of stone could speak and tell. My reasoning may have been vague, but I just knew that this structure was undoubtedly a very important piece of a long dead puzzle. Why was I being guided by some instinct telling me the key to that puzzle was here? Maybe if I gazed long enough and concentrated hard enough the answers to everything might fall into place.

The fountain was where Jack found me. The evening was warm, but I was shivering so violently, Jack panicked, took off his jacket and threw it around my shoulders.

"Let's lock up and get you home, sweetheart," Jack said, and taking my hand he led me back to my parent's house. In the kitchen, there was the welcoming aroma of freshly brewed coffee. "We'll sit here awhile, then maybe you can tell me what happened out there tonight. You scared the hell out of me. I thought you were having a fit."

The coffee warmed me, and I found the courage to fully explain it all to Jack. Not in an abstract or unspecified way: this was to be a catharsis of my troubled mind. At the end, I said, "You see, Jack, the two little girls I keep seeing, well, they aren't real."

"So, you really believe now that it was all in your imagination?"

"No! They are *not* figments of my imagination! Listen to me, Jack. When I say they're not real, what I mean is they're not alive. Don't you understand what I have been trying to tell you? They are not *living* beings like you and me."

"Not alive?" I could almost see the questions dancing around in Jack's brain, and then the dawning of realty was there in his widening eyes, "You mean they're…ghosts?"

I explained the full meaning while Jack listened in numbed silence. "So, there it is, Jack, believe or disbelieve, the choice is yours now. I'll do nothing to influence that choice." My account of the strange happenings and the explanation as I saw it had been told in depth. Now it was concluded.

I had told him everything from my first encounter with the phenomenon more commonly referred to as second sight right up to this day and the effect it had on me as a child thinking I wasn't normal. My conclusion was nothing more than an ultimatum, for if he wasn't prepared to help me find peace of mind, then he should walk away now, forget about me because what I needed more than anything was his wholehearted support. What I didn't need was being patronised by some put-on acceptance.

My Jack, true to form wasn't in the least patronising. He said, "I can't imagine how painful this must be for you and all I ever did was contribute to that pain. You are the most remarkable person I've ever known, Judy. In my eyes, you're some kind of heroine because to be perfectly honest, all this would scare the hell out of me."

"You're wrong, Jack," I replied to this truly sincere admission of inadequacy. "I'm stuck with this, and it scares me too, but you're the real hero. You have the option to say enough is enough and walk—or rather run away, but instead, you've opted to stay, and it took guts to do that. Psychology, hypnotism, God knows they tried, but nothing could make me face this head on. Now, I can clearly see that locking horns with my fear is a necessity, a risk I have to take."

There was so much admiration on his face. Right at that moment, I would willingly have faced Old Nick himself, such was the power of Jack's love.

"What now, do you hold a séance or something to summon up the spirits?"

"Séances are for gullible people. You've been watching too many old movies." It was an inexcusably scathing answer without a thought for how cruelly sarcastic it sounded.

Jack looked at me with such scorn and contempt. "Gee, thanks a bunch. Now I feel not only foolish but totally stupid." He picked up his jacket then, clearly feeling angry and humiliated, made for the door.

I had drawn so much strength from him alone and this was all the thanks I gave. "Wait, Jack," my hand clutched his arm, "it wasn't meant to come out like that. If I made you feel stupid that wasn't my intention and I'm truly sorry."

The attempted apology was feeble and the even shabbier excuse that it was nothing more than nerves taking effect didn't wash. I had openly insinuated that Jack, a learned man, just lacked the knowledge to understand. It was the final insult.

"You obviously think me inferior, so why don't you tell it to someone who gives a damn," and furiously he pushed me away.

Jack was a highly sensitive man. He didn't like untruths and he most certainly didn't appreciate being treated like some uneducated oaf. Who could blame him? At that moment, I didn't like myself very much either.

There was a sickening feeling in the pit of my stomach. I was twenty-six years old and for almost twenty of these years, I had fought to keep my eyes and mind closed to that which I was too afraid to see.

I stood in front of Jack, both hands on his chest to stop him from leaving. "Please listen to what I have to say, Jack. I was only a nine-year-old child when my nightmares began."

"You're talking in riddles again, Judy."

"It was when LaVell grabbed my arm that started it. He murdered his family in that house, Jack, and that's what I've been running from all these years. I know he did it and their spirits want me to prove it. You probably think I'm raving like a lunatic, but it's the terror of what I have to do."

The caring, protective way Jack wrapped me in his arms and held me. This was his acceptance. With gentle persuasion he said, "Tell me what you have to do."

"It's time to…I have to bring closure and the only way is to go to the house with an open mind. I must look and see what I know will be the most horrifying sight, Jack. Walk away if that's what you want, but I'm begging you to be there within my reach because I honestly don't know what the outcome will be. I'll understand if you don't want…"

"We're in this together," he was quick to remind me. "If the best I can do is simply being there, then so be it."

The prayer I made was silent within my heart, not on my lips. "Dear God, if all else is lost, at least allow us to retain this perfect love."

The moment we stepped over the threshold into the house, I had an overpowering feeling of nostalgia. The scent of roses hung in the air although there were no flowers in the house. I felt as if all the people who had lived there, people I had come to know and love were all gathered under this one roof to surround me and let their love protect me in this, what I suspected might be the most frightening hour I would ever have to face head on.

"What do you smell?" I asked Jack.

He sniffed the air and answered, "Fresh paint, why?"

How strange it was that even if I told Jack that I smelled roses, he could never understand because his senses were basic. It was like when you visit a sick or injured friend. The first thing you ask is, "How are you?" The concern is there, but you can't feel the suffering they feel so you sympathise and only imagine. That's what it was like for Jack, he was trying to imagine how I felt.

"The entire house is shining like a new pin," Jack said proudly.

"It's exactly as I remember it that day, all newly painted and gleaming. Without waiting to be invited, I just stepped into the hall. Mrs LaVell was standing right here." I walked over and stood about two feet from the sitting-room door. "She tried to stop me from going any further, but I walked around her, straight through and into the lounge. Everything was new and I remember thinking how beautiful and elegant it was. Did I tell you most of this furniture we inherited wasn't just store bought from Harrods, it had to be imported?"

"One thing about the man, he was no tight wad."

Right then, I had the weirdest sensation of being lifted and I felt a soft breeze as if someone were gently blowing on my cheek. I was aware of Jack reaching out to me and he was talking in a kind of panicky and confused way.

As though coming from a distance, I heard Jack's alarmed question. "What is it, Judy? What's happening?"

I was being guided towards the kitchen. Without speaking, I motioned with my hand for Jack to stay away as I stepped over the threshold, into the kitchen. Without my touching it, the door closed. When I turned, they were there, as real as the last time I saw them alive-Meredith and Maxine LaVell.

My heart pumped so hard it was all I could do to breathe. Gaspingly, I asked, "What do you want of me? Why do you haunt me? Is it because you think I can help you in some way?"

Meredith and Maxine LaVell looked at each other and then together nodded their heads. "Please, Judy, open your mind, look, see."

"I can't…"

"You have to, Judy! The souls of wronged beings you must set free, this is the legacy you have to fulfil. You can and must lead us from a dark place into the light."

At last, I felt the courage to relinquish my fears. "Show me," I said. "Take me back, let me see what you saw that night," and reaching for their outstretched hands, we formed a ghostly circle.

The forces which were at work took my breath away. As farfetched as it may sound, unbelievably, I was right in the centre of a scene long past, seeing with my own eyes what *really* happened all these years ago. After all the wondering and conjecturing, was I at last about to discover the truth about the events which took place that night?

I was a ghost standing there in the room with them, an unseen bystander bearing witness to what occurred the night Jean LaVell and her daughters supposedly went back to Canada. I had penetrated the dark mist, and not only did I hear what the whole street heard that night, I was privy to Jean's screaming condemnation of her husband on discovering his affair with Amanda Weston.

"You'll pay for this, Richard; you can have your little slut, but I'll take every penny."

As in a dream, I observed a mystery unfold. I listened in shock to the malevolence in Jean LaVell's blistering verbal attack. There was so much pain and hurt on not only her face, but the faces of Meredith and Maxine. Yet I was a mist without substance or the ability to firmly touch and hold. All I was there for was to watch and listen.

"You came with nothing, and you'll leave with nothing," LaVell said menacingly.

"That's what you think! The way you've been wining, dining and bedding her, she must be a costly whore." Jean sneered at the wincing pain she was inflicting. She gloried in the way her husband visibly trembled with what she took to be fear. Only it wasn't fear. This was insane fury. Unfortunately, Jean had succeeded in touching the raw nerve which caused LaVell to snap. His disposition was no longer formal, but passionate in defence of his mistress.

"You couldn't lace Amanda's boots," he snarled. As the first blow struck, Jean LaVell reeled and clutched her reddening cheek.

Sweat dripped from my brow as finally my receptive mind took it all in and before my very eyes, I watched happen that which I had suppressed all this time- a most horrific death scene.

There was a terrible crunching sound as the heavy crystal bowl LaVell had quite casually picked up smashed Jean's skull and silenced her verbal onslaught. My heart was racing faster and faster until I was sure it couldn't possibly take any more and would surely stop. And then as Jean groaned and tried to raise her body from the floor, the second blow came with such force the bowl shattered.

"No, Daddy, no," the twins cried out in anguish, but they made no effort to run. I experienced what they must have felt right at that moment. Absolute fear of whatever punishment their father would inflict on them for naughtiness or insubordination if they dared to flee. The sensation was so strong it made my head pound and almost totally robbed me of breath.

"It's alright, it's alright! Mummy and Daddy were only playing a game." It was so against his character for LaVell to show weakness of the mind and yet, oddly he began weeping. Only the tears weren't for the horror on Meredith and Maxine's faces as they stood transfixed, looking at where their mother lay dead on the blood-soaked rug, but at what he was about to do.

He walked slowly into the hall where the girls huddled together, and I watched in wide eyed loathing as LaVell put his arms around their heads in a vice like grip and pressed their faces tightly against the black cashmere coat he still wore. The veins in his temples protruded with the effort it took to hold them. For what seemed like an eternity, their legs kicked and threshed before becoming limp. LaVell had suffocated his own daughters, those two lovely, pathetic little girls. He could never let them live to incriminate him.

Coldly, LaVell pulled on a pair of overalls and went into the back garden where the shallow pond was prepared for the concrete and tiles. He dug deeply into the dark, dank earth until the pit was as deep as he was tall and then he carried the bodies of his family outside and callously covered them with earth in that makeshift grave.

While Fairfield slept, LaVell put the suitcases Jean had packed in readiness to leave into the boot of the car and drove to an old quarry where he threw the luggage, watching as it sank into the murky depths where it would, in all probability, never be found.

The following morning, builders arrived, and unsuspecting of what they were covering up, finished the job and then placed the mermaid fountain in the centre. I now knew why she wept.

Jack, fraught with indecision, hesitantly opened the kitchen door to see what was happening. The sight that met him was me, crying and shaking, my trembling hands over my eyes to blot out the suffering I had witnessed.

"I saw it! I saw it all!" The horror of the scene that still filled my senses made my voice wail pitifully and I clung to Jack like I would never let go.

"Tell me what you saw, Judy. For God's sake, tell me and let me help you through the nightmare."

"He killed them, Jack! LaVell murdered his wife and two little girls then buried them deep under the ground where the fountain now stands." Abhorrence was now and always would be etched in my mind. "I saw it all so clearly it was as if I were there. I know now this was the terrible thing I've been running from all these years."

"You had a vision? You actually witnessed a murder that took place almost sixteen years ago?"

"The souls of wronged beings, I will set free." I spoke those same words, the prediction which more than two hundred years ago a young gypsy girl had made. It was true. This was my destiny.

Blankly, Jack asked, "What was that you just said?"

"Nothing—something—oh, I don't know, Jack. I'm so confused. There's a legend that over two hundred years ago this was predicted. I'll tell you the full story, but later." I stared in horror at the fountain. "Where do I go from here? Who do I tell first, the police or Amanda?"

"We have to tell the police."

"I can imagine the response I'll get from the police if I walk into the station and say, excuse me but a couple of ghosts told me they're buried in our back garden so could you please send someone to dig them up."

"That's not how they'll see it and besides you wouldn't put it like that."

"And what about Amanda, think how this will this affect her? It will devastate her to find out the man she adored murdered his family in cold blood. The recrimination, the pain she'll go through knowing he did it so that he could be with her."

"You do what has to be done. It's not that I doubt you, Judy, but if it's true they were murdered and buried out there…all I'm saying is, it's time they had a Christian burial and Amanda will see it that way too. It's time to draw a line under this so don't falter, Judy." Jack smiled caringly and said, "You're my heroine, remember."

When his arm limply encircled my shoulder, I could feel the mind-blowing panic that held him in its grip. It was up to me alone now. I not only had to, but I also needed to quell his turmoil.

"What a poor excuse for a heroine I am." My hollow laugh and forced attempt at light-heartedness did nothing to take that worried frown from Jack's face and I saw then that being forthright was the only way. It was Jack's way. "I have just faced the most traumatic thing anyone could imagine and yet look at the state of me. This heroine is actually turning to jelly at the thought of explaining how come I know murder was committed here *sixteen* years ago. Worse still, how do I explain to the police that the bodies are out there, buried beneath that *fucking* mermaid?"

Jack let out a great howling laugh and said, "That's it, Judy, swear like a trooper and get it all out of your system." And then, he stroked his chin and his eyes narrowed as a plan hatched in his head. "There is a way," he said.

"Like what?" I asked.

"Well, Amanda gave you her blessing to do what you wanted with the pond."

"Yes, but..."

"Telephone her and in a matter-of-fact way ask if she would be annoyed if it was moved to...say a corner of the garden? Make some excuse about how it commands too much central space and we both feel it would be so much nicer in a quiet corner. If she panics and begs you to leave it where it is then, *you'll* know *she* knows what lies beneath."

"What then?"

"Well, apart from anything else, the police will realise her innocence in as much as she'd hardly give her blessing if it meant uncovering a murder, she took part in."

"Take my word for it, Amanda Weston, had no part in it."

"Ah, yes, but would the police believe that without proof? This way she will be exonerated of any wrongdoing."

I didn't need time to deliberate over the pros and cons. Jack was right and two phone calls later it was sorted. Amanda was happy if we were happy, she said so in as many words and the builders...the same builders who as it happened put it there...agreed to come the following day to measure up and arrange a day for the work of re-siting the fishpond to begin. The ball was rolling and the plan to uncover a terrible deed had been put into motion.

Chapter Twenty-Seven

The headmaster agreed to my taking an extra few days off and on Monday morning, I watched anxiously from the kitchen window for the builder's arrival. This was the day of reckoning. This was the day not only the pond, but what lay beneath would be unearthed.

The builder, an elderly man, appeared to be baffled over something. He walked round the pool poking, prodding and scratching the bald patch on his head in a befuddled way. Carefully and methodically, he set about measuring all around the sides.

I watched the goings on for a good thirty minutes and then my heart skipped a beat. Something wasn't right. It was there in the alarmed gesturing of hands. The older man, the seasoned builder was fervently pointing something out between the original architectural specifications and the ruler he had used to measure. They hadn't even begun to dig, but something about the measurements had unnerved him. In utter panic, he walked towards the house, and I shared his panic. What if they had decided moving the structure might be in some way hazardous, an impossibility that no builder would be accountable for?

Now was the time to focus on staying cool, calm and collected. If I lost my nerve now, he might just surmise that something very wrong was going on. Then again, never in a month of Sunday's could he make a stab in the dark at what really lay beneath the fishpond. These additions *were definitely not* in the plans. "Please don't say you've hit a problem," I said in all innocence.

"I'm not sure! I did the original work and according to my specifications, the pool has sunk a good bit and that shouldn't be."

He was in a very obvious quandary, but I wasn't versed in the technology and the way building work is undertaken. I had no idea as to the kind of subsidence he was describing…or the significance. "What exactly does that mean?" I asked cagily. An overwhelming surge of nausea replaced self-assurance and the blood began to drain from my face.

Right then, Mr Builder Man gallantly defended his reputation and good name. "We are a reputable firm and don't do shoddy work," he said indignantly. "I myself prepared the plot to take the structure and I can't see why the ground would give way like that unless there was some sort of pocket or well deeper down that we couldn't possibly have known about." His scowl was indicative of hurt pride.

That was when it hit home. LaVell hadn't realised that the decomposition of his murder victims might cause considerable subsidence. This might just have been the one thing he hadn't thought of. I shivered involuntarily, yet made a conscious effort to stick hard and fast to calmly seeing this through to the bitter end.

"What can…if you can that is…what now?" My nerve had begun to give way and I fought to stem, not only my nausea, but the threatening tears. The time had come when the actual horror of it all would become apparent, and we must prepare ourselves to face the outcome.

"First we dig out the entire structure and then we go further down to make sure there are no nasty surprises underneath. If there is an old well, or worse still, an underground stream, you'll want to know about it. I hope I'm wrong, but I have a feeling we might come across something nasty."

Something nasty! Fortunately, they were unaware of what form the nasty surprise which was about to be uncovered would take. I watched nervously as the mermaid was hoisted from the place of prominence she had occupied for so long and then the pool itself was carefully hoisted from its earthen bed. I listened to the clanking of shovels as the digging began. The only thing to do now was wait, try not to imagine the unholy sight they would uncover…and wish it couldn't be.

The waiting on edge seemed an eternity and then….A shocked yell, followed by a terrified wail told me the discovery had been made. I selfishly hadn't given any thought to how cruel it was to subject that poor builder to the trauma of this macabre find.

"Get the police," ashen faced he stood at the back door shaking convulsively. "There's…there's…it's a body…buried under…"

It hit the headlines as we knew it would, but not before Jack and I drove to Benvie Farm where together we told Amanda face-to-face of the gruesome find.

Her crying was at first soft and sad, but then the full meaning crash banged into Amanda Weston's heart, soul and mind. She had forsaken youth, her chance to be a mother and her freedom in favour of the man she had loved and lived with for all these wasted years. A man who it now seemed was nothing more than a murderer and a liar. The weeping now became a furious raider of her natural composure and all we could do was to stand and watch as that good lady descended into a manic wreck.

Jack and I had taken on the responsibility of gate-crashing Amanda's sedentary world to deliver the unholy truth of LaVell's evil deed. Now we must shoulder that blame.

Like the lady she was, Amanda thanked us kindly for taking the time to come to her ourselves rather than let the police deliver the news. Apart from that, there was another possibility to consider. Under the circumstances with Amanda being cast as, *the other woman,* this could be taken as the perfect motive for murder. She might well be treated as a suspect and questioned accusingly, but her naïveté was proven in that she willingly gave her blessing to have the makeshift grave exposed and the police would see that she was above suspicion.

"Those poor little girls—and Jean of course, no matter what ill feeling there was between them, she didn't deserve to end up like that." Amanda buried her face in her hands at the onset of a fresh flow of tears. "What I can't understand is why he…why any man could do that to his own children, to those lovely little girls." All her illusions about LaVell, the man she believed to be the love of her life crumbled before my very eyes, and it was the saddest thing to watch.

In the Machiavellian pursuit of his despicable life-plan and with total indifference to moral considerations, LaVell had perpetrated lies and falsehoods he thought would never be uncovered. And now, Amanda was left to carry the burden of shame for his actions.

"Did you know Jean LaVell?" I asked as a matter of interest.

"I met her briefly, and since I had what you might call a guilt complex at being in the process of an affair with her husband, we only exchanged polite greetings. But to be honest, she seemed nothing like the shrew Richard made her out to be. Then again, as Richard pointed out, looks can be deceptive. I suppose my need to find out more about Jean was remorse more than anything. Anyway, during conversations I would ask about her, discreetly of course. It seems Jean was alone in the world. She had no living relatives and that was why she came here to work. It's the age-old story. She got the job of Richard's secretary, they had an affair, Jean fell pregnant and pressurised him into marrying her."

"He was the kind of man who would use pressure himself rather than be pressurised." It was a thoughtless inference which I immediately regretted, and I hastily corrected my blunder. "I'm sorry, Amanda, that didn't come out how it was meant. Let me rephrase it. He didn't *seem* like a man you could bully into doing something that didn't sit well. That was what I meant."

"All he wanted was to do the decent thing. That was a big mistake. Jean and he had nothing in common and according to Richard, she drank heavily and had the most appallingly violent mood swings."

Even now, Amanda couldn't see LaVell for what he really was. A cheat and a liar who used this story to make everyone think he led a tortuous life with a woman he only suffered for the sake of the children. In his calculated pursuit of sympathy and an excusable reason to release him of blame over his extra-marital affair, he branded his wife a drunk. Perhaps it was best to let Amanda retain intact her own dreams and illusions.

There were a couple of questions I would have liked an answer to. Surely, all things considered, couldn't he have divorced Jean on the grounds that she was this violent drunk he professed her to be? If LaVell was so madly in love with Amanda, why then didn't he make her his wife instead of his mistress?

Then again, for propriety's sake, some questions are best left unasked.

The police talked to all the residents of Juniper who had heard and verified that a terrible fight did take place on the fateful night Jean LaVell and her daughters disappeared.

George Granger recounted the story of how Richard LaVell had apologised profusely for the disturbance before telling him that he had driven Jean and the girls to the airport where they boarded a flight to Canada. Of course, after sixteen years, there was no way of checking whether or not they did actually get on a flight. George also told the police that LaVell wasn't his normal arrogant self, but unusually polite. "Although come to think of it, there was something unusual," George added as an afterthought. "I didn't give it much thought at the time, but he seemed somewhat distracted as if he had something on his mind."

"Oh, he did," the policeman answered with a kind of revulsion, "the murder of three innocents, his wife and daughters."

That poison pen letter written in a jealous rage had brought to light the illicit affair that sparked Jean's furious and fatal confrontation and started a murderous chain of events. There was little doubt that in a vehement fit of anger, LaVell murdered his family. Apart from the incriminating testimonies, he was the only one with access to the freshly dug pit that was to house the ornamental pond under which their bodies were buried. He was as guilty as sin, but the question now was, what came first? The plan to murder his family or the structure. Was the fishpond only built with murder in mind? The answer to that LaVell took to the grave with him.

"As a matter of interest," one policeman asked me, "what made you want to move the pool?" He watched my reaction through narrowed eyes, and I sensed a kind of uncertainty, or was it perhaps more like a hint of suspicion? He said, "Most people, including myself, would have been thrilled to have such a grand centre piece, so you see, why you would want it tucked away in a corner sort of baffles me."

"Jack—my fiancé—well, he thought it took up too much central space. It might have worked for LaVell, but we felt it would feature better in a corner of the garden. The thing is, before Richard LaVell died, it seems he had stipulated it must never be removed. Of course, we now know the reason why he specifically ordered this. Moving it would have un-earthed his secret. We asked Miss Weston if *she'd* mind us moving it to a quiet corner. She could think of no earthly reason why LaVell never wanted it moved in the first place, but he was gone, and the house was now ours, so the choice was ours."

"So, she obviously didn't know what was buried under it?"

"Well doesn't that stand to reason. If she had known what was there, wouldn't she have fought against having it moved instead of happily giving her consent?" This answer proved Amanda's innocence and gave her a clean slate. Just as we knew it would.

There could be no arrest and no trial since the prime suspect was deceased. The case was closed. After sixteen years, true to the prediction, I had set free the souls of wronged beings and Jean, Meredith and Maxine were finally laid to rest in a proper Christian burial.

There was no one, no friends or relatives to remember Jean LaVell and her daughters and yet, the little church in Fairfield was packed. Residents of Fairfield came to pay their respects, remorseful and perhaps a touch guilty in the knowledge that this ruthlessly heinous crime had happened practically right under their very noses, and no one cared enough about Jean and the girl's sudden disappearance to question it. In conversation, it was noted that if Jean and the twins had been allowed to make friends and enjoy a normal social life, things may have been different.

It was my belief that LaVell always had murder on his mind. Perhaps he had planned a fatal accident for Jean, but circumstances—namely that poison pen letter—had brought things to a head and he had been left with no alternative but to kill her that night. Unfortunately, the twins, having witnessed the murder, had to die too. The pond just happened to make the perfect grave. The real reason for LaVell's incognito existence wasn't his grief about being responsible for the marriage split, as everyone thought, and neither was it a self-imposed penance, but something a lot more sinister.

Brian Burrell offered a shoulder for Amanda to cry on as she licked her wounds and the love, she once had for him was re-kindled. I don't believe it had ever really died.

Perhaps that cruel, formidable streak in LaVell had entranced Amanda and she had mistaken fascination for love when in fact, it had only been a kind of overwhelming compulsion. He was a forceful man.

I gave it a week, just time enough to take the edge off the pain before driving out to Benvie Stables. The woman who answered the door was so different to the Amanda I first met. She wore a cornflower blue dress and gold sandals. Her hair was loose and held back with a pretty clasp. Gone was the austerely sleek and elegant style. She was almost girlish, happy, like a bird which had been set free from its cage to soar on the wind.

LaVell was gone and with him, the fetters that had bound Amanda. Loyally and sincerely, she had been chained like a suffragette of old, only not to a railing, but to a dream. When the truth of LaVell's hideous crime was uncovered, Amanda awoke from a sort of trance and for the first time was able to see him for what he really was…a heartless hypocrite who would stop at nothing to get what he wanted, and having tired of Jean, he wanted Amanda.

It was time to face the fact that if she had rebelled against the solitude, the lack of company, friends and friendship, what then? Would she have become surplus to requirements and suffered the same fate as Jean and the children? The thought repulsed her. She had shared not only her life, but her bed with this man.

The time of remorseful crying passed, and in its place, came ire and loathing at the way she had been manipulated and used. Amanda had trusted too well and believed too much. Her thoughts were deep and meaningful and in a moment of intense aggression and bitterness she cried out to Brian, "How dare he cloak me in this guilt. He did the most horribly evil thing imaginable and behaved like it was just another day at the office."

"Because, my dear Amanda, it was simply the nature of the beast. To Richard, it was nothing more than flicking away some troublesome insects," Brian answered in his own prosaic way.

"And is that how it would eventually have been with me, Brian? Only I wasn't a troublesome insect, I was a fly caught in a web. A few innocent lunches that became an affair."

"Don't, Amanda…"

"I have to say it, Brian," she said staunchly as the unchecked tears tumbled free and fast from eyes that were now all seeing. "I gave Richard LaVell the best part of twenty years of my life, and he wouldn't even allow me to have my own child. Have you any idea what it's like to wake one day and discover you've lived with a monster?"

"What he did to you *was* monstrous, an obscenity. I often wondered why, knowing your love of children, you and Richard never had a child. Now I know."

"I'll never understand where the infatuation came from. If truth be told, Richard was a habit that I couldn't break. I was never crazy in love with him like everyone thought. I only ever really loved one man, but once the bridges were burned…The regret will stay with me until my dying day for what I did to you. Now it's too late."

"It's never too late! I forgave you a long time ago. Now, it's time you forgave yourself."

In that moment, a page was turned onto a new chapter in Amanda's life. When the sun rose on a new day, Brian Burrell's car was still in her drive where he had parked it the night before.

It came as no surprise when the wedding invitation arrived. Amanda and Brian were married quietly in a civil ceremony and Amanda was able to laugh once more. She laughed at the way Brian danced her around the room and she smiled contentedly, because at last, the huge dining-room had been filled with guests, just as she had always wanted.

Chapter Twenty-Eight

"The flowers have arrived, Judy! Judy, how long are you going to lie in that bath?" My mother tapped delicately, but agitatedly on the bathroom door. "If you soak much longer, you'll look like a prune, and on your wedding day too."

She would never change. Not that I wanted her to. If my impossible mother had her way, she'd be sitting in the Chapel an hour before the priest even got there. I tried not to show my amusement when I called back, "It's alright, Mum, go and have a cup of tea or a glass of champagne or something."

"And take the chance of spilling something on my new outfit?"

I couldn't believe it! I still had to have my hair and make-up done before getting into my wedding dress and Mum was dressed and ready to go two hours before the ceremony. It was so exasperating. Why couldn't she do what other Mums did and have a glass…or three of wine to settle the nerves?

I listened at the bathroom door at Dad pragmatically saying, "Come away now, Gloria. Take off the hat and coat, kick off the shoes and you and I will relax quietly in the conservatory for an hour until Judy's ready."

"But…but, Ralph, there's only two hours, what if something goes wrong?"

"Like what, Gloria? World War Three? I promise you everything will go to plan. Trust me, I'm a doctor."

My heart swelled at the love my parents felt for each other. It was enough to bring tears to the eyes and right then, my eyes were brimming over. Dad would sit Mum down with a glass of chardonnay and gently ease her into a more composed state. She might carefully hang up her coat, take off the high heeled shoes and put on one of her neatly laundered aprons, but the hat, that exquisite and expensive creation would most certainly stay on until the last gasp.

It was time! The ivory satin cascaded around me as I slipped the wedding dress over my head, let my arms slide into the sleeves and smoothed the pearly folds as I called for my mother to come to my aid. "Could you please help me with this damned zip, Mum? I can't reach."

"Oh, let me do it." Gently, she eased the zip upwards and then carefully placed the pearl headdress and frothy tulle veil that framed my face. When she was satisfied it was just right, we stood together, looking at our reflection in the mirror: the radiantly happy bride and her supremely elegant mother.

"My beautiful, darling daughter," was all my mother could say. For the first time in her life, she was lost for words.

Charles, my big little brother, was our best man. He was even more nervy than mum, rehearsing his speech while watching for the limousine that would take him and Jack to the church.

"It's here," he called out, "our car's here, Judy. Now don't worry, if I have to physically restrain Jack personally, he'll be at the church on time," and he grabbed his speech, checked for the hundredth time that the ring was safe, then sprinted to the waiting car.

Mum was next to leave in the bridesmaid's car. She was the epitome of sophistication walking regally, nonchalantly down the path in her lavender ensemble. Dad watched her from the window, smiling fondly as she teetered slightly. He knew perfectly well when he ribbed her about it, she would insist her teetering was *not* due to the two or three glasses of wine she had to steady her nerves, but the four-inch heels on her new shoes.

"Only you and I left now, Judy," my dad said as he planted a kiss on my brow.

I felt it in that kiss, a sort of compulsion, a need to say something, so I asked, "What is it, Dad? I know you have something on your mind so tell me, spit it out."

"You've come so far and against all odds achieved so much since…You were no more than a child, too young to go through that phase of knowing so much and not knowing enough. We were no help because we didn't understand. Today, you'll leave here to branch out into your own life with your own family and I have to know…You once told us we made you feel like a freak…"

"No, Dad, I didn't mean…"

"Let me finish. I need to know if you've truly forgiven our shortcomings."

"There's nothing to forgive. You and Mum had more understanding than you'll ever know and without it I wouldn't be here today. You deserve to be blessed, not vilified."

"Thank you," my dad said gratefully, "that's all I wanted to know."

"Before we go, there's one last thing I want to say while there's still time."

"We have all the time in the world, Judy."

"I am so proud and honoured to have you and Mum as parents," and the look of sheer pride on my dad's face said it all.

The doorbell rang and Dad took my hand, just as he did when I was a little girl. "That'll be our car. Let's go, Judy, time to get you hitched."

Two weeks after our lavish wedding, we returned from our honeymoon to the house on Juniper Drive and Jack ceremoniously carried me over the threshold.

I was immediately surrounded by the familiar scent of roses, only this time, it was real. My darling, thoughtful new husband had arranged it with my mother for the vase to be filled to welcome me on my homecoming.

"I'll put the suitcases in the bedroom," Jack said, breathlessly lugging them upstairs. "We'll unpack later, but you, Mrs Wayne, can put the kettle on because I am dying for a real cup of tea."

"Of course, Mr Wayne, your wish is my command." I was giggling like a schoolgirl and as I turned to fill the kettle and they were standing there. This was to be the last time I would ever set eyes on Jean, Meredith and Maxine LaVell.

Jean stood between her daughters, holding their hands and they were smiling, not only happily, but serenely. I stood transfixed and that was how Jack found me. I told him, "They were here, Jean, Meredith and Maxine, waiting for me."

"You mean…ghosts?" Jack looked around in a sort of panic. "Are they still here?"

"They're gone, for good, I think. They only came to give me a message."

"What?"

"They said 'thank you, Judy, and welcome home'."

THE END